UNEARTHING THE PAST

"I won't lie," Fantazia remarked. "This is going to hurt like hell. And I can't guarantee what you'll be like when we're done. Are you sure you want to do it?"

You'll go insane from what they did to you, my mother had warned. I wanted to scream no, that I could just wait until the blocks broke down naturally or something else happened, but I knew in my heart that I had to go through with this.

As I couldn't find my voice, I nodded my acceptance.

Fantazia patted my head like a small child, which I guess to her I was. "It'll all be over soon, one way or the other…" She looked up at Cyrus. "Ready?"

He nodded, eyes glistening. "Oh, hell yeah."

Fantazia grinned. "Let's do it."

Other books by A. J. Menden:

PHENOMENAL GIRL 5

TEKGRRL

A. J. MENDEN

LEISURE BOOKS NEW YORK CITY

To Jeremy, for seeing what I didn't.

A LEISURE BOOK®

June 2009

Published by

Dorchester Publishing Co., Inc.
200 Madison Avenue
New York, NY 10016

ISBN 10: 0-505-52787-1
ISBN 13: 978-0-505-52787-5
E-ISBN: 978-1-4285-0682-4

Visit us on the web at www.dorchesterpub.com.

ACKNOWLEDGMENTS

Once again I'd like to thank the usual suspects—my agent Michelle Wolfson, my editor Chris Keeslar, Alissa Davis and the good people at Dorchester for all of their hard work.

A big thanks goes to my beta readers: Laura Tennant, Andrea Greynolds, Jolene Craig, and Rachel Lane and to all of the members of the OWG for their support, and to Tina Croff and Heidi Spiessl for being honorary beta readers when I needed an extra set of eyes.

Another big thanks to Susan Charman, crit partner and en-courager, as well as Sharon Ashwood, crit partner and fellow Capes and Coffins member.

I've saved the biggest thanks of all to my friends and my family for putting up with me. You're all my heroes!

TEKGRRL

PROLOGUE

At first glance they almost looked human, but the longer I studied the silent forms waiting in front of me, the more differences I noticed. Like, how their heads were just a little too big for their bodies. How their skin's golden hue was just a little too reminiscent of actual metal. How their eyes almost seemed to glow when I looked at them in a certain way. And their fingers were just too long.

"This is a once-in-a-lifetime opportunity, Mindy," my mother was saying. "Most people spend their exchange-student time in other countries; you're going to spend a year on another planet. You'll be the first human to live among the Kalybri if you take them up on their offer."

"You'll learn so much more with them than you would at any school or with any tutor we could have provided," my father promised.

My tone was soft but sliding toward petulant. "But you said I could attend *The School*." I kept my gaze locked to the floor in front of me.

My mother sighed. "That place is no more than a public school for those born with superhuman abilities, of which you have none. You'll stand out just as much there as you would if you went ahead and attended regular college at your age."

I winced at the reminder that, no matter where I went, I was a freak. "You said your contacts in the EHJ could probably get me into *The School*."

My father sighed. "They probably could. But really, Mindy, do you want to be something as pedestrian as a hero?"

"*Yes*," I said, casting hopeful eyes up at him. The world had more people with super powers than ever, but my parents had never understood my love of heroes, those colorful men and women who were devoted to Good, to helping others through acts of bravery. These were the men and women to whom everyone turned to save the world when a villain threatened to blow up the planet, or when some musty old book warned of an apocalypse. My parents didn't understand why I avidly kept newspaper clippings and paid attention to these heroes' celebrity photos, but that didn't change anything. I felt a kinship, and I wanted to believe I had a purpose in the world. I couldn't exactly pinpoint the reason. Well, not exactly.

The truth was, I had always been bored when my scientist parents dragged me from one meeting to another because they felt they were the best instructors for me, just because I was a "highly intelligent child." I'd been bored until the day they took me to meet the heroes of the Elite Hands of Justice—and one hero in particular. A hero just barely out of high school, himself.

"You're twelve, Mindy, you don't know what you want," my mother said, giving the waiting aliens an apologetic look. "A year or two with the Kalybri will give you perspective."

It was only my life, and I had no say in the matter. By her tone, it sounded like all was decided. I ground my teeth in frustration but kept silent. I had a sense of wanting to rebel, but I had no friends my age—or of any age, for that matter. If I alienated my family, I had no one.

"We are your parents, and we have a responsibility to give you the best possible education we can," my father said. "You're a child prodigy, Mindy, and the Kalybri are very interested in learning as much as they can about humans in general. But their minds are further advanced than ours. A regular human would be overwhelmed. From all our tests, you are the best suited person we know for the experience. And the Kalybri have agreed to teach you just like they would any of their children, so you will be learning about their superior technology and can bring it back to us! That is much more heroic than using your fists to fight some mentally unstable person." My father shook his head. "Plus, the Elite Hands of Justice are starting to branch out and help other worlds. An experience like this would definitely impress them . . . should you still want to be one of their number when you return."

It was one bright spot in the situation, and I snatched at it. If working with the aliens could be my parent-approved ticket into the EHJ, so be it.

The severe-looking alien who seemed to be in charge stepped forward. "We would be pleased to teach you, child," he said in the halting tones of someone unfamiliar with English.

I took a deep breath and did what my parents wanted. As always.

CHAPTER ONE

Sixteen years later

"If I ever decide to get married, I'm not having a traditional wedding with the white dress and the bridesmaids and all that garbage," I said. "Vegas is looking better and better."

"What's your problem with weddings?" my teammate and best friend Toby Latimer asked.

"Nothing like one to remind you what a loser you are," I grumbled.

"The wedding was months ago, remember? It was that ceremony we attended before kiddo here was born." Toby motioned to the infant I was bouncing on my lap. "This is the reception-slash-Wesley's birthday party celebration giving you a case of the sour grapes."

"It's not really," I said, nodding to the happy couple, two of our EHJ team members, as they greeted guests, friends, and global dignitaries with equal enthusiasm. Well, they received enthusiasm from Lainey and thinly disguised boredom from Wesley. "I'm happy for them. Honestly. If anyone deserves to be happy, it's Lainey."

"Wesley not so much?"

"He rode my case the whole time I trained with him," I grumbled.

Before any of us in the current squad became full members of the Elite Hands of Justice, we underwent two years of training with the Reincarnist, an immortal magician who didn't die but instead was reincarnated into a new man of twenty each time, usually retaining only partial memories of his past lives. It had been Robert Elliot, a reclusive and rigid forty-something, who had broken me in. How Lainey had ever fallen in love with him was beyond me, and though their relationship had been strained by his death in combat and subsequent rebirth as Wesley Charles, he was now her husband and the father of the squirming kid on my lap. She truly put the phenomenal in Phenomenal Girl five, which was her alias.

"Lainey's the sweetest person I know," I remarked. "If being with him makes her happy, I'm all for it. It's just seeing her so genuinely happy with him that . . ."

"Makes you remember how desperately alone you are?"

"Thanks, Toby."

"Hey, I was referring to myself there, too. It's been over a year since I've had a serious relationship, and at least three months since I've even had a date. The pickings, they be slim." He shook his head.

"Tell me about it."

"Don't even!" he growled. "You could have your pick of men, if only you'd get your head out of your butt and notice someone other than Luke."

I shot him a nasty look. "I date on occasion."

Toby snorted. "Yeah, guys who bear a striking resemblance to Luke."

"So I have a type, so what? You date skinny stringbean guys. You don't see me dissing you about it." I pointed out a waiter who kept walking past. "Speaking of, since that guy's too busy leering at you to do any work, you might as well ask him to dance."

"I'm not dating a waiter," Toby said.

"Now who's being picky?"

"I'm holding out for Mr. Right."

"Well, so am I."

"No, you're holding out for Mr. Harmon."

I thought about smacking Toby, but knew it wouldn't do any good. His powers made him super strong and fast—and more resistant to damage than the average human. He could take a shotgun blast at point-blank range and come away with a mere scratch. My girly punch would feel like a tickle.

Jealousy reared its ugly head, and not just at my friend Lainey's blissful happiness. I had no powers. I was a child prodigy who'd gotten her crazy intelligence boosted by aliens. I could do things with technology now that not even the smartest members of NASA could; in fact, they had gotten a lot of their patents off me when I was sixteen. But I wasn't superhuman.

Luke Harmon was more like me, a "normal" human fighting the good fight. He had an athlete's body and a photographic memory, something that came in handy while studying with many martial arts experts. That body was one of the most delicious and powerful things I'd ever seen.

"Make a deal with you," Toby was saying, interrupting my daydream.

"What?"

"I'll go ask the waiter to dance if you'll ask Luke."

"Can't," I said too quickly. "I'm on babysitting duty, remember?" Emily let out a happy gurgle and grinned as if in assist.

"Lainey will definitely not mind taking her kid back for one dance so you can make progress with Luke."

"He's probably already back in his room training or something," I said, giving a glance around.

"No, he's over there talking to one of the government agency heads." Toby stood up and pointed, causing Luke to look over at us.

"Quit it!" I said, yanking his arm down. "Be more obvious."

Toby shrugged and waved Lainey over.

"Hey, guys, how's my monster behaving?" Lainey asked, looking radiant in her ivory and gold cocktail dress. I'd helped her pick it out. I know with my magenta-streaked hair and black clothes I project a very punk image, but I have it in me to be the classy girl my parents wanted. I just fight it.

Emily acted as if God himself had walked over, the way her eyes lit up and she squealed, reaching for her mother and practically climbing over me to get to her. I sighed. I never thought I'd ever want a child until my friend had one. Now I was starting to see the appeal of a toothless baby grin.

Turning, I frowned. A couple of paparazzi had managed to work their way into our headquarters, where Lainey and Wesley had chosen to have their event. This wedding reception would make a hot news item. The photographers snapped off a couple of quick pictures and disappeared again, probably before the Reincarnist could magically transport them to some dark realm full of demons or other nasties. He was very protective of his daughter.

"Mindy's going to ask Luke to dance," Toby announced.

Lainey settled Emily on her hip and stared at me. "Really?"

"Not really. Toby's trying to get out of asking this waiter to dance by using me as an excuse. I'm babysitting Em," I said, reaching for the baby again. She immediately shrieked. Oh yeah, I'd be a stellar mom.

"She wants to see Mommy and Daddy for a while," Lainey said. "And I think Wes has used up his allotment of social grace for the day with all of these people. Some things never change." She grinned at me. "So go have fun."

"Guys, maybe I'm over Luke," I suggested—and didn't like the incredulous looks they gave me in return. "Seriously, I'm pushing thirty, and that's way too old to be harboring a crush I had when I was twelve. For God's sake, Lainey, you're only a bit younger than me and you're married with a kid! And Wesley . . . he's only twenty-one!"

"Wesley so doesn't count in this scenario. He's physically twenty-one but actually older than civilization," Lainey said with a laugh.

"You know what I mean. It's time for me to grow up," I resolved, motioning to my hair. "I mean, seriously, what am I rebelling against? I'm not a teenager anymore. Luke and I are friends, and that's all we're ever going to be. I need to have the maturity to accept that."

Lainey shot a worried glance at Toby. "We're not saying you're acting immature, Mindy, we just want you to take a chance and acknowledge your feelings. There's a chance Luke might feel the same."

I knew they meant well, but seeing Lainey in a mature, healthy relationship had only served as a reminder of how immature I was acting, regardless of what they said. I wasn't getting any younger, and if I ever wanted what she had—a husband and kids, as well as my career fighting crime and evil—I was going to have to grow up. And soon. But Lainey and Toby were right about one thing: I did need to acknowledge my feelings. So I could move on.

"Fine," I said, standing up and smoothing down my black dress. "I'll go ask my *friend* Luke to dance."

Squaring my shoulders, I walked forward to put this crush behind me once and for all.

CHAPTER TWO

He excused himself from the conversation he was having as I walked up. "What's going on, Mindy? Something wrong?" He glanced around the room, looking for trouble.

"What, Luke, I can't talk to you unless there's something wrong?" I spoke in a light tone, cursing Toby for drawing attention earlier. How was I supposed to act nonchalant now?

Luke's posture visibly relaxed. "I guess it says something about me that my first thought whenever anyone approaches is that trouble's brewing."

I shrugged. "Occupational hazard."

"I suppose."

There was an awkward silence between us as we stood there, the sounds of murmured conversation and the band's music filling the void.

"So, was there something specific you wanted to talk about, or did you just want out of babysitting?" Luke finally asked.

I spoke before I could stop myself. "Do you want to dance?"

Luke blinked. "What?"

"I'm tired of sitting around," I continued, forcing myself to study the way his forehead wrinkled with astonishment just so that my eyes wouldn't go straight to the floor. I had to at least appear like I was facing him head-on. "I want to dance."

"Oh."

"Toby's too busy trying to work up the courage to ask this waiter, Lainey said Wesley's done being social for the night, and Paul's, well . . ."

"Yeah, I wouldn't want to dance with Paul, either." Luke laughed, referring to our field leader, the man who led the team during missions, and general stick-in-the-mud. "If Kate can get him unlatched from that chemist up for the Nobel Prize, it'll be a minor miracle, anyway; they've been talking in the corner all night." He nodded to where Paul stood holding a mostly full glass of champagne and having an intense conversation with an equally stuffy-looking man.

Kate, our teammate and Paul's lover, had totally given up on him and was flirting with the bartender. He probably wouldn't hold it against her, though. Flirting was as natural as breathing to Aphrodite, the goddess of love. Yes, Kate was an actual immortal, and could control all aspects of love. Many of the gods and goddesses of myth existed; though, aside from the occasional decades-long trips to Olympus and their immortality, they were pretty much like any other person of the powered persuasion.

"So, yeah, I thought I'd ask you," I said, as if he wouldn't be my first choice. "I mean, come on. You didn't learn dancing somewhere along the way? You've compared martial arts to dancing . . ."

"Yeah, dancing that can end with bodily injury!" Luke shook his head with a smile and looked at the couples already out on the dance floor. "Though I don't think it takes much time to learn how to sway back and forth like that."

"That sounds like a yes to me," I said, holding out a

hand and willing it not to shake. I couldn't act like this was important to me and scare him off. This had to be a *friendly* dance.

He looked like he was going to say something but changed his mind. "Okay, sure," he said, and took my arm. "Just don't expect a waltz."

"Like I know how."

I winked at Lainey as Luke and I passed where she and Toby were sitting. *Your turn*, I mouthed to him, and Toby rolled his eyes but got up and went over to the waiter.

And then I no longer cared what Toby did as Luke took me into his arms. For all of my tough bad-girl talk, for all of my "I'm over him," professions, he still affected me. It was sad that someone who had never acknowledged me as anything more than a coworker, let alone a woman, could make my heart race and my stomach feel fluttery.

Even with my four-inch heels, I only came to just above his shoulder, which is where I kept my eyes as we danced. I was afraid if I looked into his gaze I would do something stupid like try to kiss him. I had come this far, after all.

"The band's pretty good," Luke remarked, filling the gap in conversation since we weren't one of those couples who could practically glue themselves together to the beat of the music.

"For this kind of thing, sure," I said.

"Not much on acoustic versions of classic rock songs?"

"I prefer the originals."

"And here I thought you'd say you prefer death metal."

"It's a common misconception," I said. "The hair throws everyone. I look like I write angsty Goth poetry in my spare time, not recalibrate my perpetual motion machine."

Luke laughed. "A reporter asked me the other day for a comment about this rapper, and acted mad that I didn't know who it was. I don't know if I was expected to know because I'm half-black, or because we're celebrities too."

"Please, I'm the one who listens to rap, not you!" I grinned. "The only thing I've heard you listen to is instrumental stuff and jazz. You like music you can meditate to, not that makes you want to fight the power."

"That's your department," he agreed, laugh lines crinkling his mouth in the way that always made my insides melt.

"I think that's the kind of thing that makes people not take me seriously," I said, sobering. "Lainey's my friend and I love her, but it's, like, since she showed up, all she's done is served as a reminder of how immature I am."

Luke frowned. "Not everyone has to get married and have kids, Mindy. I don't know if I'm the settling-down type, either."

That was like a red-hot poker in my stomach, because I *was* the settling-down type; but I went on. "It's not the married-with-kids thing. It's just . . . how she is. And how Wesley is. They're both so much more than us. A lot of us," I amended, not wanting to insult Luke. "They're like how I was when I was a kid and my parents started bringing me around the EHJ, wide-eyed and wanting to save the world. I wanted to be someone important. Not like a celebrity, but someone that mattered. Who did good. And then I joined and there were publicists and action figures, and saving the world starting taking a backseat to name recognition and patent agreements. It was all so juvenile. And then she and Wesley stood up to the Dragon and stopped the apocalypse, and what did I do?"

Luke's face was grim. "You almost died, Mindy! I was there. You were fading fast. If it hadn't been for your technology and Wesley's magic, you wouldn't still be here. And we all helped in that fight. Lainey and Wesley had a bigger part to play, but we all shed blood. Rath died, for God's sake!"

The mention of our former team leader, who had been killed in the fight against the Dragon, made things worse. I whispered, "They're the heroes. I'm just playing at being one. I'm a poser."

Luke shook his head. I realized we had stopped dancing at some point in the conversation and were standing still, his hand on my waist. It sent tingles through me. "Yes, Mindy, we lost our way somewhere. That's why I was glad to get the Reincarnist back. I really think he can help us regain our focus. The EHJ can be everything it was always supposed to be."

"I hope so."

Sighing, I turned and walked off the dance floor, heading for the nearby doors to the outside balcony. From that vista atop the Elite Hands of Justice headquarters, we could see Megolopolis in all its breathtaking glory. I hardly saw any of it as I walked outside, lost as I was in my thoughts. The sounds of the city filtered up to me.

"I know we will," Luke said, following me to lean against the rail. I felt his perusal. "And it's always good to want personal growth in your life, not just money or fame or the other misguided goals society puts in front of us."

I smiled. "That sounds like very good advice. Thank you, Sensei." That was the name by which the public knew Lucas Harmon.

He put his hand on my shoulder. "I fall just as short as you do, Mindy. I've been just as distracted by the glitter, not focusing enough on helping people," he admitted. "We could all stand to be more honest with ourselves—and with each other." He cleared his throat and looked away. "We should all make every day count."

"Now *that* is very good advice," I agreed, and felt my hands shaking against the cool balcony railing. I had to say more. He was right, I had to be honest with him if I wanted any chance of finally being a grown-up about the way I felt about him.

"Mindy—"

"Luke, I need to tell you something," I interrupted, turning to face him and not the skyline. "You know I had a crush on you when I was younger, right?"

His smile of embarrassment and the way he ran his hand through his close-cropped black hair told me all I needed to know. He cleared his throat. "Well . . ."

Fear of humiliation burned through me, and I wanted this over as quickly as possible. "Okay, so I made it obvious. We both know that. But . . . I just need to tell you that's all in the past. I feel like it's kind of kept us apart, you know?" I didn't want him to be uncomfortable around me anymore.

"It doesn't have to keep us apart." He moved closer, looking down at me with half-hooded dark brown eyes.

My soul wanted him to be staring at me with love, but my brain told me that was impossible. This was only pity I saw; kindness. I was always going to be a surrogate kid sister to him. I had to stop living in the past, in my dream world. I had to move on.

I steeled myself and said, "You're right, it doesn't. And I don't want it to any longer."

He smiled, and my heart almost hurt from how

gorgeous he was. He said, "Neither do I. I just didn't know how to approach you about it."

I shook my head, embarrassed despite my resolution of honesty. "Yeah, I made it pretty awkward between us, didn't I? I'm sorry for not saying something sooner." I touched his arm, careful to keep it sisterly. "Thank you for being so understanding about this, Luke. I'm glad we can move on now and just be friends."

He straightened, back to business as usual. How sweet of him to try to make this less awkward for me. He had probably been waiting ages for me to put this silly tension between us to rest. So many uncomfortable years, and they were all my fault. "Yeah, no problem."

"Maybe we can actually work patrols together now," I suggested. "Maybe we can schedule that, now that we've handled this. I think there's a lot I could learn from you, since we're the only two on the team who don't have any specific powers."

"Sure, that can probably be arranged," he replied. "I'd like that. Now that we're actually doing patrols again instead of publicity shots at the latest celebrity hot spots."

"I hear that." Thinking of the others, I looked inside and noticed how a lot of the guests were starting to leave. "Looks like they're packing it in. We'd better get back in there." Plus, that would end this somewhat humbling episode.

He followed my gaze, looking inscrutable. "We should. Thanks for getting me out on the dance floor."

"My pleasure."

I took the arm he held out, and we headed in to say our good-byes.

Just inside the doors, Lainey was in conversation with a glamorous woman whose flawless cocoa brown skin and dress made her look like she'd just walked off a fashion shoot. Her artfully arranged hair and simple but elegant makeup were perfection, and she had the air of someone who didn't have to work hard to pull it all off. I fought a wave of jealousy.

"Guys, this is my friend, Selena Curtis," Lainey said, motioning Luke and I over. "We went to *The School* together. Selena, these are my teammates and friends, Mindy Clark and Lucas Harmon."

"Hi," I told the Glamazon, friendly enough to be polite.

"Hello," she replied. "Tekgrrl, I presume."

"Yeah, that's me." I shrugged. "I'm afraid I don't know your alias."

"Granite," she supplied with a smile. "Any friend of Lainey's and all that."

"Uh-huh." I noticed her eyes on Luke, and my blood pressure spiked.

She held out a French-manicured hand with one tasteful ring and bracelet. "Sensei, correct?"

"That's right," Luke said, taking her hand and kissing it like a courtly gentleman from a period film. I gaped, and I know Lainey did as well. "Pleasure to meet you."

"It's all mine," she replied, giving him a dazzling smile. Even her teeth were perfect—and probably not from braces, either. How could Lainey be friends with someone like this?

She spoke up, interrupting whatever was going on between her pal and Lucas. "Selena was just telling me Paul offered to bring her in for an interview about the new position. They're going to talk tomorrow morning."

"Are you going to take it? If it's offered, I mean?" I blurted this, praying the answer was no. I couldn't imagine this woman as part of our team.

Luck was not with me. "I don't know yet," the beauty

queen answered. "Lainey knows I've turned down work-ing with the EHJ before, but with the Reincarnist back, you guys are likely to go in a new direction that I have to admit is exciting. And tempting." She gave Luke an-other dazzling smile. "Plus, work with the Fives has gotten a bit monotonous, so I'm looking for a change."

"We still haven't talked about who our team leader's going to be," Lainey said, throwing a cautious glance in Paul's direction. "Just because Wes has been directing the team since Rath died doesn't mean he's going to stay in control. There's some question . . ."

Ms. Perfect rolled her eyes. "Lainey, your man *should* be acting in that role and you know it."

"Maybe so, but it's not like he and I don't have other things to worry about." Lainey shifted her weight so that her baby could drool on her other shoulder. I could tell the poor kid was tuckered out from a long night of partying with her parents. "Raising Emily with the pos-sibility of her apocalyptic destiny is going keep us both busy." According to an ancient book, Emily was someday either going to save the world from the ultimate forces of evil or help them destroy it. The Dragon and his cro-nies wanted to make sure it was the latter and we wanted to make sure it was the former.

"Which is why you need the extra help," Selena spoke up. "And the more I think about it, the more I'm hoping whomever you all decide is team leader will think I'm the woman for the job."

Luke smiled. "I've heard about you. We could always use someone with your talent. A real powerhouse."

I shot him a look. Was he flirting with her? She did remind me of the women he had dated in the past: styl-ish and beautiful beyond the scope of the rest of us plain Janes.

Granite smiled at him. "I don't know if I'm a powerhouse, but thank you for the encouragement. I always get nervous before interviews, you know?" She raised an empty champagne glass. "I've probably drunk more of these than was a good idea. It's a good thing you offered to let me use one of the spare rooms here, Lainey."

"It seemed silly for you to come all this way tonight for the party, then turn around and have to come back in the morning," my friend replied.

"Well, I appreciate it," Selena said. "If you don't mind, I think I should probably turn in now for some much-needed beauty sleep."

"I don't know if it's much needed, but I'll be glad to show you to your room," Luke put in. "Any particular one, Lainey?"

My friend and I stared at him, openmouthed.

"Whatever's open," Lainey said, still clearly in shock.

"That'd be great, thanks," Selena enthused, as if Luke had offered to take her to Paris instead of down the hall. "I'll see you in the morning, Lainey. Lattes are on me!" She took Luke's arm. "Shall we?"

"I think I'll turn in after this, so I'll say good night, too," Luke remarked. "Mindy, Lainey, I'll see you two in the morning."

"Good night, Luke," Lainey said.

"Good night," I echoed, watching the two saunter off together.

Turning to Lainey, I muttered, "Good thing we're just friends now or I would be incredibly jealous."

"I'm so sorry! I never would have invited her if I had known she'd go for Luke like that," Lainey said. "So, what happened with you two?"

"Obviously nothing good," I grumbled, nodding to where he had walked off. "We danced, we talked, I got my stupid crush out of the way and we're going to try to be better friends. He's going to let me do patrols with him and train with him a bit. I think I can learn a lot."

"That's all?" Lainey looked more disappointed than I felt. "I thought for sure after the way he acted when you were injured in that fight with the Dragon—"

"Well, obviously you misinterpreted," I snapped. "Because as far as Luke and I go, we're friends. Friends with absolutely no benefits."

Lainey made a sympathetic wince. "I'm sorry, Mindy."

I sighed. "Don't be, it's not your fault. This is what I need to help me move on. And truthfully, I'm glad we had it out." I looked over her shoulder. "Here comes your husband."

Lainey grinned. "Husband. I'll never get tired of hearing someone say that."

Wesley put his arms around her waist in that sweet and comfortable way some couples practically ooze. "Can you tell everyone to go home now?"

Lainey bumped against him. "Could you be more antisocial if you tried?"

"Yes, I probably could. I think I've been congratulated on our wedding and for turning twenty-one again by every person in this room multiple times, and I drank enough champagne to qualify as overdoing it."

"Good thing you're legal," Lainey quipped. "Wouldn't want to arrest you for underage drinking."

Her husband laughed. "If I drink any more, you're going to have to learn how to cast hangover cure spells. But I have better things in mind." He dropped a kiss on her neck. "Since we're still in our honeymoon phase."

"Careful, you two, that's how things like *that* happen," I warned, nodding to the sleeping Emily. "But why don't you guys go ahead and take off. Paul, Kate, Toby and I can take care of shooing people out and paying the caterers."

"You don't mind?" Lainey asked. She didn't look away from her husband, and I couldn't mistake her hopeful tone of voice.

"Of course not. Just don't be late for the staff meeting in the morning or Paul's head might explode."

"As long as I don't have to get the coffee," Lainey remarked. "I should get one day off."

As the newest hire, one of her jobs since she'd arrived was to get coffee orders in the morning. Yes, we were in the business of saving people; yes, we were big-time celebrities with our pictures in the newspapers all the time; and yes, we might all be über-geniuses; but the way the EHJ was set up, one of us heroes still had to do the grunt work, and that task had fallen on Lainey. No wonder she was trying to get her old friend to come on board: She didn't want to be the gofer anymore.

"Toby or I will take care of it," I promised.

"Thanks," Lainey said, giving me a hug. "We'll be at the meeting bright and early."

"Not *too* bright or early." Wesley winked at me as the two of them walked off, his arm around her waist and their sleeping child drooling on Lainey's shoulder. I couldn't help but feel a bit jealous.

"So how did it go?" Toby asked, coming up behind me.

"It ended with Luke escorting another woman to her bedroom, so don't ask." I turned to look at him. "How'd it go with the waiter?"

"He talked about boy bands the whole time."

I burst out laughing, both at Toby's information and the expression on his face.

"I don't need to date a walking stereotype, thanks," Toby continued. He slung an arm around my shoulder. "So, we continue to be the dateless wonders of the team."

"Looks like," I agreed.

I smiled at him. I might not have a romantic relationship, but I had a kick-ass job and great friends. What more could a girl want?

CHAPTER THREE

Where was that strange hum coming from?

I blinked against the blinding light. How had I even fallen asleep with it right over my eyes, and what was that obnoxious noise? I tried to move my head so I could pinpoint from which direction it emitted, but found that I couldn't; I was held still by something cold. Metal, perhaps. I tried to reach a hand to brush away whatever it was, but discovered my arms felt heavy, weighed down by something, almost as though they had been numbed through anesthesia: I was aware they existed, but they were unresponsive. A quick test determined my legs suffered a similar fate.

Panic rose up in me, made all the worse by the blinding light and the fact that I couldn't escape. I concentrated despite the unnerving hum, and tried to move something; anything. A soft groan burned deep in my throat, and I felt pain. The more aware I became, the more my body registered that something wasn't right, and the pain soon rocketed through me like lightning. I moaned and tried to writhe, to get away from whatever tormented me, but I couldn't get far.

A hydraulic hiss filled the air and I heard footsteps, followed by heavy male voices speaking a harsh, guttural language I didn't recognize. They were arguing about something, judging from the tone of their voices. Or maybe they always sounded this pissed off?

Casting my eyes toward my feet, away from the light above, I could see large shapes moving in the darkness surrounding my bed. They inched closer, stepping near enough to become no longer sinister shadows but sinister-looking humanoids. One had skin too dark to be human, almost obsidian, and what looked like scales. Another was pale, almost bright white, and had a vaguely feline look to his eyes and nose, like those people who have gotten too much plastic surgery. A third was green, and actually had claws on the hand he used to tighten whatever was holding my head still.

As they leaned over me, my eyes widened, taking in their large, bulky bodies clad in strange attire: almost tribal-looking leathers and torn one-piece flight suits covered with grime and who knew what else, all sewn together coarsely to fit much larger forms. Their dirty and matted hair resembled dreadlocks, with bits of bone and metal twisted in. What skin showed on their bodies was pierced with hooks and bits of metal, only slightly less terrifying than the wicked-looking blades hanging from their belts. I tried to scream, but my throat caught.

The obsidian-skinned alien leaned over me and spoke in accented Kalybrian that proved it wasn't his native language, if his looks weren't clue enough. My rattled brain was still able to translate.

"Do not be afraid, little girl. It is all a bad dream."

His companions laughed with a terrible mirth, which was made all the more terrifying by the large scalpel rising above me. Any moment it would—

I awoke covered in sweat, crouched in a defensive position by my headboard. Looking around, I tried to get my bearings and take comfort in the familiar surroundings. I was in my bed, in the Elite Hands of Justice headquarters; alone, of course. I was safe, probably safer than almost anyone else on the planet, surrounded as I was by superheroes. My vision had been a simple dream, a terrible nightmare. Just like the monster said.

My head was pounding with the worst migraine I'd ever had. I was used to waking up with migraines; my teenage years had not only brought the usual female hormonal changes and suckiness like cramps and PMS, but also introduced me to accompanying headaches and intense nightmares. As I got older, these seemed to become rarer, slowing down to once a month or less. I only prayed they weren't on the rise again as I groaned at the familiar and unwelcome feeling comparable to having a scalpel jammed into my right eye.

Scalpel?

That sent me right back to that terrible dream of monsters in the dark doing God knew what to me, and the pain in my head increased. My stomach lurched, and I stumbled to my small bathroom, feeling dizzy and unable to stand upright. I just barely made it before I threw up.

Clutching the toilet like an old friend, I wiped sweaty hair away from my face and cleaned my mouth with a bit of toilet paper. My stomach was still lurching like crazy, but I figured if I didn't move for a bit I would be okay. The antiseptic smell of cleaning supplies wasn't helping any, though, and I slid down onto the floor, curling up on the bath mat with my back to the bedroom and the light streaming in.

Why were the monsters in my dream speaking Kalybrian?

I'd thought I had forgotten the language. I certainly hadn't practiced since the day I returned home. As soon as I'd come back from Kalybri, I plunged back into my life on Earth, putting the whole experience behind me.

It wasn't that it was bad; I just didn't want to remember.

My head was torn apart by another spike of pain, and I cursed.

Still feeling creepy from the dream, I forced myself to stand. Reaching into my medicine cabinet, I pulled down both migraine pills and my antianxiety medication. (Yes, I'm a hero who gets panic attacks. Sad, I know.) I took both, slurping down some water from a cup with the EHJ logo on it that I kept on the sink just for such an occasion and, pills swallowed, stripped to shower, hoping the warmth would help my head and make me feel more awake and less like I was in that horrible dream state.

Shutting myself inside the stall, curtained off from the rest of the room, gave me a thrill of terror, and I couldn't help imagining the monsters from my dream lurking outside, ready to spring in and get me. (This is why I don't watch horror movies.) I shampooed and rinsed as fast as I possibly could, skipping my scented shower gel just so I wouldn't have to stay any longer than necessary. Soon I stepped back out of the shower to towel off.

Drying my hair and running a brush through it, I caught a glimpse of myself in the mirror. I made a face, deciding at that moment that I was over my magenta streaks. It was time to join the bobbed-with-highlights crowd.

Rifling through my clothes didn't put me in any better mood. Since my revelation the night before, nothing seemed age-appropriate. I finally settled on a pair of fitted jeans and a yellow sweater I didn't remember buying, and put an updated wardrobe on my mental list of things to do. Slipping on a pair of heels, I grabbed the PDA that I had made myself out of bits of technology that wouldn't probably be on the market for another ten years, and headed to the daily staff meeting.

Toby was already setting a white Cuppacino takeout cup in front of my seat. He was the only one there. "One chocolate biscotti latte for the lady."

"Thanks, hon," I said, taking a seat and hoping the caffeine would put the final nail in the coffin of this migraine.

"You look like hell. Couldn't sleep?"

"No, I slept. Kind of wishing I hadn't right now. Had this freaky-ass dream and woke up with a migraine."

"Where's Lainey?" Paul asked, walking into the room, dressed in his usual crisp suit and tie that were stylish enough to speak of money but not trendiness. You can take the scientist out of the lab but not the lab out of the scientist. With his close-cropped dark brown hair, serious dark blue eyes and hooked nose, Paul could be cute if he wanted, but he probably would never bother. The semifashionable suit he was wearing had probably been encouraged by Kate.

"Haven't seen her yet today," Toby said, distributing the last of his coffee cups before taking a seat next to me, careful to smooth out invisible wrinkles in his expensive yet casual suit jacket and dress pants. Such a slave to fashion! "Min and I sent her and Wesley to bed early and told her we'd get everything set up for her."

Paul's narrow eyes and set mouth conveyed his displeasure. Why he was always on Lainey's case, I'll never know, but it was likely due more to Wesley than Lainey herself.

"Give them a break, Paul, they're young and in love," Kate said, gliding in like the love goddess she was. Her tall, willowy figure was clad in the latest fashions, which were clingy yet modest. Her glossy brown waves of hair looked like she had just stepped out of the salon and not the shower. It must be nice to be a never-aging immortal goddess. And Luke used to date her. Why did I have to be surrounded by staggeringly beautiful women who reminded me how inadequate I was?

"You do remember what that was like, don't you?" Kate continued, sipping her drink and flipping through the society pages of the newspaper in front of her, not bothering to look up. Her barb hit her supposed boyfriend, and he suddenly seemed interested in fiddling with buttons on the console in front of him.

Toby kicked me under the table and gave me a significant look. I nodded at his unspoken thought. *Yeah. Trouble in paradise.* It was going to happen sooner rather than later. Kate seemed to be mentally stuck back in the heyday of the gods, when relationships were a bit less monogamous. And I couldn't see by-the-book Paul being okay with that.

"Well, now I suppose we're going to spend another hour waiting on them to drag themselves away from each other to come to work," Paul complained. Judging from his grumpiness, and by Kate's comment, I wasn't the only one jealous because I wasn't getting any.

Wesley walked in just then, forgoing the business wear that everyone else here but me seemed to affect, clad in a simple red sweater and dark blue jeans and boots. He looked like a twenty-one-year-old college guy ready to take a cute coed to dinner and a movie, not a member (and possible leader) of the greatest team in the country, if not the world.

"I sent Lainey to entertain our guest while we discuss her possible hire," he said in his soft, cultured voice, taking the seat that, up until his death, had been occupied by Dr. Benjamin Rath, our previous team leader.

The subtle power play wasn't lost on Paul, who looked ready to explode—which wasn't necessarily an empty threat from a guy who controlled heat molecules. "Nice of you to finally join us," he snapped. I wondered if he should switch to decaf.

Wesley ignored Paul's ire and took a sip of his own coffee. "Who brought this?"

"I did, sir," Toby said, all Southern gentleman, as he could sometimes be.

Wesley nodded. "Thanks."

It was at that moment I realized another member of the team was missing. "Where's Luke?"

"He had a meeting scheduled with that mystic group. He couldn't get out of it," Wesley said. "I told him he could skip out."

Paul's face darkened. "Well, then, what the hell are we all doing here? You're clearly making all the decisions for us." He slammed a fist down on the table.

Toby and I were the only ones who reacted. Kate didn't look up from her paper and Wesley just looked bored. I hate the smell of theatrics in the morning.

"I thought we were here to discuss the possibility of hiring this girl, Granite," Wesley said. "That's the only reason I turned up at all. You know I think these meetings are a waste of time. We should be out there on the streets, helping people, not sitting around discussing it."

"It's not all discussions of strategy. There are other reasons to meet. Even though senior members make the decisions on whether or not to hire someone, we like to consider the opinions of the others on this team—and that includes Luke, whom you've excused," Paul growled. I could tell by his gritted teeth that he was seething.

"He already told me he agreed with my recommendation: to hire her," Wesley said. "He spent some time with her last night and thought she'd be an asset."

An *asset*. I inwardly winced.

"Well, we still need to discuss it," Paul said. "I think there are some points that we need to take into consideration."

"I'm for hiring her," Kate spoke up, flipping a page of her newspaper. "Wesley's for it, and he's a senior member. Toby?"

Toby recognized he was in the middle of something he didn't want to be, but he admitted the truth, anyway. "Well, I approved her way back when we offered her the job the first time around . . ."

"So that's a yes." Kate glanced at me. "Sorry, Mindy, you're not a senior member, so you don't get a vote, same as Lainey. So, that's majority. We hire her. End of story."

I began to worry Paul was going to have a heart attack, the way he was sputtering. "B-but . . . b-but . . ."

"Excellent, I'll tell Lainey to give her the good news," Wesley said. "I suggest she team up with one of the senior members for our nightly patrols. As a matter of fact, it's probably a good idea for us all to continue to pair up for the meantime." After years of the EHJ only showing up when summoned, the Reincarnist had us all back on the streets for patrol. It had met with a mixed response from the gang. "Now, if there are no other pressing matters, I've got to go wake up Emily and make her breakfast."

"There's talk the government's looking into starting a committee related to the hero teams," Paul blurted, clearly not controlling the meeting and hating it. "They're sending over some aide today to get our input."

"Our input? 'No. It's a bad idea.'" Wesley stood. "If you'll excuse me." He exited the room, coffee in hand.

"I'll meet with him if you want, Paul," Toby said, always the peacemaker.

"Yes, thank you, Toby," the shell-shocked Paul responded. I noted that he truly thought it was important yet pawned the responsibility off on someone else. Figured.

"I've got a lunch with the editor of *Fashionista*," Kate said, rising. "I'm up for best-dressed celebrity again this year. Extend my congratulations to Selena." She exited the room, leaving me and Toby alone with a fuming Paul.

I had no responsibilities for the day, but wasn't going to admit that—not with Paul looking the way he did. Tapping the screen of my PDA and getting a growl in response (darn sentient technology) I said in a possibly too bright voice, "Oh, look, I've got that thing with those scientists today. I'd better go get ready."

"Do you need help carrying stuff to your car?" Toby asked.

"Yes, please," I said, and we stood and beat a hasty retreat.

We booked it down the hall as fast as we could, leaving Paul alone, fuming. "I don't know what I'm doing today, but it's something that keeps me out of this building," I said.

"No doubt," Toby agreed. "You could have cut that tension with a knife. Now I'll be spending the day with some stuffed shirt."

"Keep your hands on your wallet at all times. Politicians are made up of equal parts trickery and greed."

At that moment, Lainey walked in the front door of

the building. She was carrying a takeout cup of coffee, and the glamorous bane of my existence sashayed in her wake.

"Hey, guys!" Lainey looked between Toby and me, and she quickly read the stress on our faces. "Uh-oh. What did I miss?"

CHAPTER FOUR

"You sure you want to do this?" Lainey's eyes were wide in disbelief.

"I don't back down from anything."

"You'll never be the same afterward."

"I know. I've made my peace with it."

"Are we dyeing or not, ladies?" The stylist was not amused.

I nodded. "Take me back to my natural color."

"Honey, are you sure you even remember what that was?" The stylist poked around my roots, tsking. "Besides, it doesn't need to be *your* natural color, just *a* natural color. Maybe some highlights, some lowlights in red, maybe a bit of blonde around the face. Just nothing that looks like it came out of the spray can of some graffiti artist."

"Whatever you want, I'm in your capable hands."

The way his eyes lit up, you would think the stylist had won the lottery. "And if anyone asks where you got your hair done, you'll mention me?"

"I'll practically take out a billboard." With my wild punk look, I was easily recognizable as Tekgrrl on the street. Lainey could more easily blend in, and with her daughter in tow could have been any of the posh mommies that could afford to have their hair done here. Soon though, I too could start walking down the street incognito.

Lainey gently pushed the stroller next to her back and forth as a sleeping Emily threatened to stir. "So, how bad was he?"

"Who?"

"Wes. I knew I should have gone to that meeting, but he practically insisted I occupy Selena so she wouldn't have to sit there and feel on the spot as we all talked about her. I should have known he'd take the moment to wind Paul up."

"It's not like he did it on purpose."

Lainey gave me a look. She knew her husband better, I guess.

"It's just that Paul is so easily wound up right now," I said. "He's been like that since Rath died. Rath gave Paul the job as field leader after he stopped that terrorist from killing all of those children back when I was a teenager. And Paul might be a pain a lot of the time, but he's always been good at his job. He wants to step into the position of overall team leader . . . only I don't know if he thinks he's ready, judging by how tense he is. And it seems everyone else has unanimously decided on Wesley."

"They're going to have to work this out on their own. It's getting ridiculous," Lainey said. "Wesley has no patience for meetings and group dynamics and all of that, but he's just going to have to get over it and deal. I don't care if he is old and stuck in his ways."

I smirked at her phrasing, considering his supposed twenty-one years of age. "Paul's going to have to relinquish some control that he never had in the first place. Yes, he's good at making command decisions on a mission, but that doesn't mean he immediately gets the promotion to team leader. Maybe we just all need to sit him down and tell him we want Wesley to be the new boss. I think right now they're both operating on the assumptions they've made, right or wrong, and maybe the team needs to sit down and tell them what's what."

Lainey shook her head. "Men. If we weren't on the team, they'd probably end up beating the hell out of each other over something stupid, never bothering to sit down and talk about it. But I'll tell Wesley to try to be a bit more diplomatic."

"Maybe we can have Kate say something to Paul."

"Yeah, but if they're not getting along . . ."

"What's up with that? Pretty bad when our own goddess of love can't hold on. She's the one who always ends up complaining that the relationship is boring and leaves. I bet she's never actually been in love."

"That's actually kind of sad, really." Lainey was such a softy. "To have lived as long as she has and to have never really loved anyone . . ."

"Why's it so sad for her?" I groused. "I've been so wrapped up in work and . . . other things that I've never given any of the guys I've dated a chance to turn what we had into a relationship."

We both knew that the unspoken "other things" were my unrequited feelings for Luke, but Lainey wisely left that well enough alone.

"Now that you're giving the new hair and clothes thing a try, I think your dating life should be a fresh start, too. Who do we know that's single? Heroes, of course."

"On other teams?" I thought about it. "I don't know. Desmond's kind of cute."

"Desmond the Comet?" At my nod, she frowned. "Isn't he dating that Brazilian supermodel?"

"Like they all don't date supermodels at some point." The guys in our set were nothing if not predictable, either dating the drop-dead gorgeous female heroes whose uniforms looked like lingerie, or dating the women that actually modeled lingerie.

"What about the Illusionist?"

"We hooked up once when the EHJ and the Justice-bringers had to team up to stop that villain who was poisoning everyone with mind-control spores. He maintained the illusion that he was a decent guy until the next week, when he kept dodging my calls through his secretary."

"Well, what about someone who's not a hero?" Lainey resolved.

"What, like a villain? Interesting thought."

She laughed. "No, like why don't *you* date a hot underwear model? Or a quirky movie actor? Heaven knows you've attended enough social gatherings with celebrities."

"They don't like smart women."

"What about a scientist then? You're always helping them out."

"They don't like women smarter than them." I sighed. "There really aren't any quality single men in this town."

The stylist shot me a glare. "What am I, chopped liver?"

"No quality, single, *straight* men," I amended.

"With this new look, they'll be flocking to you. You won't have to hunt them down." The stylist took my drape off with a flourish and turned me toward the mirror. "Ta-da!"

I hardly recognized my reflection. I had been transformed from someone trying to rebel into someone, well, glamorous. Nowhere near as glamorous as Kate or Selena, but someone less hard and more feminine. My wavy hair was now a dark chocolate brown with red highlights dancing among the waves, and the light blonde around my face somehow made my eyes bluer.

Lainey was grinning. "I love it! Do you love it, Min?" She looked nervous.

I was still staring at the stranger in the mirror. "Wow. I'm . . . pretty."

"Never knew you had it in you, huh?" The stylist grinned. "Make sure you sing my praises now."

After practically promising the stylist to skywrite his name, and paying roughly the same amount as that would cost, Lainey and I headed out onto the street, pushing Emily in her stroller while managing my shopping bags and browsing stores I hadn't already visited. The pursuit of my new, more stylish look had resulted in the dropping of vast amounts of cash.

I pointed out a lingerie shop. "You should go buy something."

"You know I'm never wearing *that as a uniform*," Lainey replied.

We both cracked up. "No, I meant for Wesley."

"But then it won't be on long." She winked, and we started laughing again.

And that's when the jewelry store across from us exploded in a shower of shattered glass and smoke. Alarms were going off everywhere; people were screaming and staggering away. A man in blue armor came clunking out of the hole in the window, arms laden with jewels. His armor might be protecting him from any damage he might incur should the cops get there in time, but it also slowed him down. A lot. Dummy.

"Who's that?" Lainey asked, checking to make sure Emily was all right.

"No one I've ever seen. Must be a new one." The EHJ

kept a database of criminals and heroes alike, and it usually kept us in the know. "It's almost cute when some random slob gets delusions of grandeur."

"Can't we even enjoy a simple afternoon off?" Lainey complained, but her eyes shone and I could tell she loved it. She didn't get out heroing much since becoming a mom, and, well, if I were honest, even before that, since Paul first instituted rules about the newest person always sticking around home base. "Fire spells and that kind of thing aren't going to work on him. What have you got?"

I dropped my bags and patted my pockets. "I don't think I brought much. I wasn't expecting armed robbery by a guy in a robot outfit." My fingers found a small round button in my pocket, which I pulled out. "Oh. I brought a disabler."

"What does that do?" Lainey glanced over to where Robot Man was making his very slow getaway. Cop cars roared up at the end of the street.

"To a human, it's a bit like a Tazer: shocks them so they can't move. Don't know what it will do to his suit. Might short-circuit it temporarily so he can't move."

"He can barely move as it is." We turned back just in time to see the cops open fire, but their bullets ricocheted off his plates. The man in the suit retaliated by blowing up one of the cop cars. "It'll have to do," I said.

"Hit him with it, I'll see if I can't pry the armor apart." Lainey tagged a woman with two small kids who was backing into one of the stores. "Hi, can you watch her for just a moment? I'll be right back, thanks." She pushed Emily's stroller inside, along with the shell-shocked woman and her kids, and shut the door behind her. With a few quick mumbled words in Italian that I barely caught, she locked the door with magic. "The protective ward will hold, but not for long. I'm still learning. How close do you have to get to hit him with the disabler?"

"A few feet away."

"We'll have to fly, then." Lainey grabbed me by the arms and lifted me up. We were soon flying into the war zone where bullets flew.

"*Schermo*," Lainey said, and several bullets hit an invisible wall around us.

"You're going to have to set me down and get away before I shoot this thing off; it'll hit anyone within radius," I said.

"No problem," Lainey replied. She reached down and touched the disabler. "*Spinta di potere*."

"What did you just do?" I asked.

"Gave it a bit more kick. Good luck." She dropped me down behind Robo-Dope.

I pushed the button before he could turn around, and a shock wave burst out from me, pushing me back with its power. Lainey wasn't kidding when she said she gave it a power boost! I was barely able to retain my footing.

It hit the criminal's armor square in the back, visibly weakening the seams. Making a strange creaking noise, the guy did a face-plant onto the ground. Looked like he was decommissioned.

Lainey landed next to me. "Shall we see what's inside?" She rolled the guy over on his back and, using her overly strong fingers, she pried the helmet off, revealing a very sweaty and very geeky-looking teenager.

Lainey looked up at me. "It's a kid?"

"I'm impressed. Did you make this yourself?" I asked. It was bit comic-book, but not bad.

"It's my dad's," the kid admitted. "He's an engineer. I thought it would be fun to try it on, like in a video game."

"What kind of video games do you play, kid? Street Villain Seven?"

Lainey sighed. "This is what I have to look forward

to. Or worse, this is who'll want to date my daughter."
She reached down and pried the hands of the armor
open, taking back the goods that had been stolen.

"My dad's going to be so pissed," the kid whined.

"Gee, ya think?" I might have become a rebellious
teen, but at least I never stole my parents' inventions to
go on a joyride-and-robbery spree. They should thank
their lucky stars. This kid even blew up a cop car!

Several officers had swarmed into the jewelry store
and returned, and a few others now surrounded us.

"Gentlemen, I believe this is what you want," Lainey
said, holding the kid up by his arms as he squirmed and
tried to get away. "Go easy on him if no one was hurt.
He's young and not too bright."

The police told us they'd just lost a cruiser, and then
they handcuffed the kid, who was crying about being
grounded for life. He would be lucky if that's all he got.

"Wow, that was fun," Lainey said, grinning.

"Hon," I replied, "we need to get you out more."

"Tell me about it." She walked back to where she had
stashed Emily with her impromptu babysitter, and broke
the ward while I gathered up my bags. Surprisingly, I
hadn't lost a single one.

I heard unmistakable sounds behind me, and I turned
to look. Sure enough, some paparazzi had shown up.
Well, we *were* in the celebrity district; they may have
been stalking other prey and gotten sidetracked. They'd
managed to beat any regular reporters to the scene.

Lainey appeared carrying Emily in one arm and pushing the stroller with her other hand. "Uh-oh."

The photographers immediately started clicking. "It's
Phenomenal Girl Five!"

"Was this a new villain?"

"Have you fought him before?"

"All in a day's work," Lainey said, clutching Emily a bit closer. The baby didn't seem to like the flashes.

"Just a mixed-up young kid we turned over to the authorities," I said, edging closer so we could escape the swarm together.

The photographers looked at me. "Who are you?"

I frowned. "Tekgrrl!"

"No way, you're way hotter," one of them said.

I tried not to be insulted but was flattered at the same time.

"Okay, take your picture and then back off before I start swinging this thing," Lainey warned, motioning at them with the stroller.

Yep. All in a day's work. We grinned and posed for the photographers.

CHAPTER FIVE

"Can't leave you two alone for a moment," Toby teased as soon as we walked in the door at EHJ headquarters.

"You're kidding me. It's on the news already?" I dumped my packages off in the hallway.

"News travels fast in this town," Lainey said. Emily gave a gurgle of agreement—or it might just have been her way of saying the shoulder of Lainey's shirt, which was now wadded up in her tiny fist and covered with drool, didn't taste good.

I noticed Toby looking me over. "What?"

"Your hair."

"Yeah, I had it done. That's where Lainey and I were before the chaos broke."

"I don't think I've seen it any natural color since you were a scrawny twelve-year-old with big blue eyes behind pop-bottle glasses."

"Nice insult hidden in a compliment, Tobe," I retorted, frowning. "Don't make me go looking for the photos of you rocking the acid-washed jeans and feathered hair." Sometimes it was easy to forget that Toby was in his forties, since he looked around twenty-five. Must be nice to be related to the Reincarnist and age slower than normal.

"I was meaning you look nice. Grown-up. Mature. A new Mindy." He stuck his hands in his pockets. "That was the look you were going for, right?"

"Leave her alone," Lainey said. "We've all gone through phases we'd rather forget."

"Sometimes whole lifetimes," Wesley joked, walking into the room and kissing Lainey hello. Ah, young love. It was enough to make me green—with envy or nausea, I wasn't sure. "I just heard the word 'forget.' What are we talking about?"

"Mindy's new look." Lainey nodded to me.

Wesley turned from making a goofy face at Emily to give me a once-over. "Looks nice."

"Thanks. It's just a new hair color and cut." I explained, starting to feel a bit self-conscious.

"And I saw you had a bit of excitement," Wesley pointed out, taking Emily from Lainey, who absently wiped at the drool-covered shoulder of her shirt and then gave up. "You two did well containing the situation so quickly."

"Thanks."

"Yeah, good job, team," Toby said with a wink.

"The police seem to have the matter in hand, but was it anything we need to investigate further?" Wesley asked.

Lainey shook her head. "Just a dumb kid out for a joyride in his dad's body armor. We had more trouble with the paparazzi than him, honestly."

Wesley frowned. "Yeah, I saw that. I thought we discussed how we didn't want Emily's picture in the news."

Lainey matched his frown. "Yeah, well, there's not much I can do when they mob us in the street. I thought it was best to let them get their one picture in and then come out swinging if they didn't back off."

"You could have flown away."

"Wes, we're in the public eye. The more we try to hide her away, the more they're going to try to get pictures of her. They'll start talking about her not being real, or like she's an alien or something—like that actor and actress the tabloids are always claiming have abnormally big heads that hide a third eye . . ."

"That's because they *are* aliens," I put in. "And they do have a third eye."

Wesley and Lainey's attention turned to me.

I shrugged. "The Swiftes. We had to work security at one of their functions because they had a bunch of 'out-of-towners.'"

Toby started laughing. "I remember that! Simon got smashed and hit on that woman with four arms."

"That wasn't all she had," I remarked. Simon Leasure, before he was fired from the EHJ when his craving for publicity had him making unwise deals with villains, had been a bit of an unrepentant ladies man.

Wesley ran a hand through his hair. "I know we can't hide Emily forever, but I want to do it as long as possible. We don't even know if we got rid of all of the Dragon cultists."

"We'll be careful," Lainey soothed.

The door whispered open and Luke walked in. "We all holding a meeting in the hallway or something?" he asked, looking around at the four of us.

"No, Lainey and Mindy were just telling us about their girl-time that turned into a police action."

"Some kid hijacked a mech suit," I told him. "It was on the news."

"Sorry I missed it," Luke said, moving closer. "Nice hair."

I touched it. "Thanks."

He nodded. "Are we on for patrol tonight?"

"You bet." I was a bit surprised he had remembered us discussing it, after being distracted all night by Selena, but I wasn't going to pass up the opportunity to spend some time with Luke. My friend.

But speak of the glamorous devil. Selena swished up in a crisp white shirt and black pencil skirt and heels. With her hair up, she looked like a stereotypical secretary. As if to illustrate the point, she carried a personal organizer, stylus poised and ready to jot something down. She flashed us all a bright smile, and it might not have been my imagination that she focused on Luke just a bit longer than the rest of us. "Excuse me, guys, but, Toby, the secretary from downstairs just called up and your three o'clock is here."

Security had tightened since the Reincarnist showed up. We used to be a bit more lax and show multiple tour groups around; random civilians were in the museums downstairs at all hours. Not only had our fight with the Dragon changed things, but having a possibly world-ending kid in the mix meant we had to watch who was in our building.

Toby nodded and straightened his jacket. "It's that politician. If you'll excuse me." He turned to go back to our private elevator.

Selena gave me a friendly smile. "Your hair looks very nice, Mindy."

Why did she have to be nice? It made it harder for me to hate her.

"Lainey, hon, you're going to have to show me again how to work this computer system," Selena said.

"As long as I'm not taking back secretarial duties, sure," Lainey replied, following her down the hall.

"Good. Mindy, since you have some free time, I thought we might go over the security network," Wesley was saying to me, ignoring the drool leaking from his small child. How do parents just brush that off like it's not happening?

"Great," I said in what I hoped was a cheery tone. An afternoon of tinkering around with the Reincarnist, who would likely be critical of everything I did. I was having flashbacks to my training years.

At least he was eye candy this time around.

By the point I finished going over new security system ideas with Wesley, who seemed to delight in picking apart anything I did no matter what body his soul was in, my head felt like I had an ice pick jammed into my right eye. My migraine had returned with a vengeance. I retrieved my bags from the hallway where I'd left them, feeling like my head was going to literally explode. I bumped into Kate coming out of the kitchen carrying a green bottle of water.

"Hi, Mindy," she said, sounding distracted.

"Hey, Kate." I barely glanced up, but what I saw forced my gaze back to her face. "Are you okay?" Her usually flawless eye makeup looked smudged, and underneath looked a bit red and puffy.

She gave me a false smile. "Sure, why wouldn't I be?"

I called her bluff. "Because you look like you've been crying."

"Oh, it's just allergies," she said, waving a hand dismissively and taking a sip from her bottle. But I noticed her hand shaking. She might fake a cool demeanor, but I could tell she was upset.

Kate and I had never exactly been close. Her beauty and powers of attraction and love meant that men flocked to her, so she wasn't exactly popular with any ladies, and she did nothing to mend that fence. In fact, she seemed to almost delight in her gift, like she was a queen and we were nothing but her ladies-in-waiting. But seeing her upset and trying to hide it, well, that put her back on the ground with the rest of us mortals. And with how she and Paul were acting earlier, clearly nothing was right with them.

I could have been mean and dug further, but I decided to let it go. Frankly, my head hurt too much to cope. "They can be bad this time of the year."

"Yeah," she said in a quiet tone. Then: "Your hair really looks nice, Mindy. Very sophisticated."

"Thanks. Everyone seems to like it. I hope you feel better." I hoisted my packages and started to go.

"Thank you," she echoed quietly, and disappeared down the hall.

Part of me wondered about her situation, but my pounding head was telling me that my teammates' drama would have to wait until a time when every sound didn't seem extra loud and when Kate's perfume didn't make me nauseated. I made it to my room, dumped my packages down—the poor clothes would be wrinkled forever—and went into my bathroom. As I removed my makeup I could smell Kate's scent on me, and it was making my headache worse. I gulped down a migraine pill and some water and hit my bed without even bothering to take my clothes off. Pulling the sheet up over me, I soon fell into a fitful sleep.

I was back on Kalybri, in a small but well-lit room that was almost too bright for my eyes. I was dressed in a white linen wide-sleeved unisex shirt and pants, the requisite uniform of every other student. The golden color of the other students' skin made the uniform look almost ethereal on them; I looked like a ghost. But I was used to not fitting in.

I stared at the holo-pad in front of me, mentally translating the Kalybrian script into English, the swooping curls and symbols into letters and numbers. This was history class, and if Earth students think learning native history is boring, they should try learning a whole other race and planet's.

I wasn't the only student whose mind was wandering. Kalybrian students sat in holo-pad chairs, all lined up in a row, facing the teacher. They were supposed to sit up straight, but I could see the delicate slump in the shoulders of the student in front of me and hear the subtle shift in the chair of the one behind. I was sitting next to the open window, and the exotic and spicy scents wafting on the breeze practically begged me to fly outdoors and explore the alien flora and fauna.

"Man-dei." The teacher spoke my name in her odd accent that turned it so foreign. "Do you know the answer?" Once again, she spoke in Kalybrian, but my mind translated the words into my native tongue as easily as Spanish or French, the two other languages I'd been fluent in since I was ten.

"That was in stardate twenty-three, one-hundred-eighty-nine, madam," I responded.

She nodded. "Thank you, Man-dei."

Satisfied that I wasn't going to be called on again for a while—generally everyone in the class got called once per topic—I sneaked a glance to the outdoors. What I saw made me gasp.

The bright light of the warm day was gradually disappearing, as if a giant shadow was covering all. Like the sun was being taken away. A harsh wind replaced the previous delicate one, whipping the trees into a violent frenzy. A distant rumble could be heard, like thunder, but the sound was almost metallic. A rotten smell of death and decay blew in through the open window, causing me to gag. I rose to my feet with a cry.

The rest of the class continued as if nothing was happening: The teacher called on students and they recited back to her random dates. Outside of the window, wrenching screams of torment and agony could be heard, like they were gushing up from the bowels of hell, and yet no one in the class paid them any mind.

Shaking, I started to move to the door, to look for escape, when my arms were seized from behind and I was forced back into my seat. I looked up to see my teacher standing over me, clamping my arms down into shackles that hadn't been there before.

"It's time for your treatment, Man-dei," she said in her heavily accented English, and held up a large drill.

I screamed, thrashing against the restraints, feeling them bite into my hands even as the drill came closer and closer to my temple, and then there was the blinding white pain as it entered my flesh and skull—

I sat up in bed, gasping for air and holding my head with both hands, feeling the ghost of the bit at my temple. I shuddered. *A dream, it was just a dream.*

I heard a knock on my door. "*Gamji,*" I responded automatically, feeling a metallic taste in my mouth. Had I bitten my tongue and drawn blood?

Luke peered in from the hall as the door slid open. "Pardon me?"

"I said come in!" I responded, touching my tongue to my fingertips. Sure enough, I found blood.

"I don't know what you said, but it wasn't 'come in' in any language I know," Luke said, a teasing lilt to his voice.

"Yes, I did. I said . . ." I trailed off, realizing that what I had in fact said was *gamji,* which was "come in" in Kalybrian. I was speaking Kalybrian again, a language I hadn't given a thought in so many years. But I was dreaming in it again.

"Were you asleep?"

"Yeah. Bad dream." I was still shell-shocked. Why was Kalybri haunting me now? I had put it behind me, out of my mind, the minute my foot returned to Earth's soil.

"Must have been. You said you wanted to go on patrol with me tonight. It's about time to get out there."

"Okay." I nodded, numb. "Give me a minute to get dressed."

"All right." He looked me over again. "You sure you're okay?"

"Yeah. Just having migraines today. And nightmares."

"You sure you're up to patrol?"

"I'm fine!" I snapped. Seeing him visibly recoil, I softened my tone. "I'm fine. Just give me a few minutes to get ready and I'll meet you outside."

"Okay." He laid a hand on my shoulder. "I'll see you out there." Turning, he walked out of the room.

I lay a hand on my shoulder, where his had been, seeking comfort from that simple touch to remind me that I was in the present, not the past. I was safe here with my friends. I was not back in the grip of the people who had run experiments on me like I was a lab rat. Or the people who had given me over to them in the first place.

CHAPTER SIX

It was dark by the time Luke and I were ready to go on patrol. Standing on the rooftop of our building, looking out into the city, I found the night had a surreal quality, like a monster: The buzz of traffic and people below were almost like its snores, the lights of cars and buildings like its many half-lidded eyes, the smells of exhaust, smoke and cooking food like its breath.

Or maybe it was dream residue giving me a healthy dose of creep factor.

I shivered, some from the cold and some from the memory of a drill bit in the temple, and rearranged the small weapons and random technology I kept attached to my belt. Lainey had made a joke earlier about how many female superheroes dressed like they were wearing lingerie, and my uniform was hardly an exception—though I knew I didn't pull it off as well as some. Created by a noted fashion designer right when I joined the team, my suit seemed to serve hardly any function except showing off as much of my body as possible. Made of a midnight blue fabric that was supposed to keep you warm or cold depending on environment, the one-piece outfit clung like a second skin on my slim frame and almost nonexistent curves. The suit rose out from my waist in a literal X, crossing my breasts and finally turning into long sleeves. A large portion of my midriff was exposed, and my neckline too. I always had the vague feeling that, whenever I bent over, people looking got a show.

Luke got one just then if that was the case, as he glanced over and said, "Maybe you should see a doctor."

"Excuse me?" I was lost in thought about why I hated my uniform, especially in comparison to his fully concealing, samurai-looking black shirt and pants.

"You said you were having migraines again. Maybe you should go see a neurologist, make sure it isn't anything serious."

I frowned. "I've had enough doctors in one lifetime, thanks."

"At least talk to Paul about it."

"No more doctors!" I snapped. "I've had practically every MD and PhD in this country ready to slice and dice me—and that was after I came back from having the exact same thing done to me off-planet. My parents let them run test after test to make sure I was safe for other people to be around. But no more. Just. No. More." I turned away, feeling again how real the experimentations had been. The further I got away from those times, the less I'd thought about it.

Until today.

Luke was studying me, looking strained. "I'm sorry, Mindy. I didn't mean to bring all of that up."

"It's not you, it's these dreams I've been having," I said. "Of Kalybri."

"Is that what language you spoke tonight?"

I nodded. "I thought I'd forgot all about it. Now it seems I remember. More than I want." I gave a halfhearted and inappropriate laugh. "Forget about it. I know I want to. Let's concentrate on patrol."

Luke looked like he wanted to say more but instead changed his mind. "We're supposed to cover Sector Nine."

We'd lucked out. Instead of getting the drug alleys and the crack houses, we had pulled the cushy straw: the theater and nightclub district, where the posh went to party, to see and be seen.

I held up my left wrist, which contained a small teleportation device that I had designed for each of our team members. Dialing coordinates, I motioned for Luke to do the same. "Let's try to keep our teleportations at a minimum. The area isn't that big, and it's taxing to both the machines and us." Having my atoms scattered and put back together after I already felt like hell did not sound like fun.

Luke nodded. "I prefer the on-foot approach myself."

A cool, tingly feeling washed over me as the teleport took effect, with only the mildest uncomfortable sensation, almost like a rug burn, and then we were standing atop the roof of a building clear across town. I flexed my hands to make sure everything was still in its proper place, as I'd seen the results of a faulty teleport once. That's why the government still doesn't use them.

Luke motioned to a ladder. "We can get down here and then follow the backstreets and the alleys. If there's going to be any action to be had, it will likely be back there."

I followed him, skimming down the ladder easily and dropping to the dirty ground. Yuck. The pungent odor of trash filled my nostrils. Letting him take the lead, I next followed him down several side streets. Our footsteps echoed softly around us.

Wanting to break that silence and yet not tip off any criminal element, I spoke softly. "So, what do you think of the new girl?" Why I chose that topic, I don't know; I must be a glutton for punishment.

"Selena?"

"Unless there's another new girl that I'm not aware of."

"She seems like she'll be an asset to the team. We can always use another heavy hitter."

"Uh-huh." I skirted a puddle, not wanting to walk in soggy boots for the rest of the night.

Luke smiled. "You don't like her."

"Is it that obvious?"

"Only to those who know you well," he said. "You should really give her a chance. You weren't like this with Lainey."

I shrugged. "Lainey's different."

"Why is Lainey different?"

Lainey never had her sights on you, I thought. Though I was all right with letting Luke go, I wasn't all right with letting him go to a Glamazon. At least, not yet.

"She just is."

"Is it because Selena's Lainey's friend and you're Lainey's friend?"

"No, it's nothing like friend-envy," I growled. Frankly, Lainey was too busy being a newly married mom and hero to spend any time hanging out. Sad, it was still a fact of life. And, to be honest, I hadn't known Lainey long enough to miss her. Our friendship roles could still adapt.

"Let's just drop it." I continued down a side road.

"Is it because you think she's prettier than you?"

I whirled. "Oh, and now she's prettier than me, too? Thanks. Any other insults you want to hurl in my direction, Luke? Does this outfit make my ass look big? Do I look like I've gained weight? Do I have a zit you want to point out? What's next?"

A movement caught my eye, and I turned to see two shadowy forms disappear down the alley ahead of us. Luke put a hand upon my arm in warning, and I could tell he had seen them too. A finger to his lips, he motioned for me to move forward. He'd go down another side street to catch and hem them in.

I crept toward the alley. One of the figures attempted to break away, heading back toward me, but I still couldn't see either clearly for the darkness. The other figure followed, grabbing the first by the arm and shoving her roughly against a brick wall, eliciting a shallow feminine cry. "Please," I heard, and then the unmistakable sound of cloth tearing.

That sent me into motion. I wasn't going to stand there and witness a rape and do nothing. I charged forward, paying no mind to my loud footsteps. The two figures didn't pay them any heed either, and as I neared I heard feminine whimpers mixed with male grunting.

I pulled a small Shocker out of my pocket, enough to temporarily stun an adult male, and put it to the back of the rapist's neck. Just at that moment the man said, "You like that, don't you?" Ew.

"I like *this*," I replied. "Let go of her. Now."

The rapist paused. "What the hell?"

I jammed the Shocker farther into his neck. "Move away from her, right now."

He moved back from the woman, not bothering to hitch up his pants, which were around his ankles. "Listen, bitch . . ." He started to turn to face me, but that's when Luke came out of the shadows and grabbed him, locking up the arm he'd swung in a punch I hadn't seen coming, driving the guy to the ground in pain.

The woman screamed. "Stop it! Leave him alone!"

I turned to face her. "Listen, I know you're in shock, but it's going to be okay. You're safe now."

"Safe? What are you talking about, safe? I'll give you whatever you want, just leave my boyfriend alone!"

Boyfriend? I felt a sinking feeling in the pit of my stomach. "You mean, he's not attacking you?"

"Attacking me? Of course he's not attacking me! The only people attacking us are you two. Just take some money and go."

"We're not trying to rob you, we're heroes," Luke said. "We're trying to help!"

The woman snorted and pointed at me with a manicured finger. "So you people get off by dressing up in crazy outfits and 'helping' people. Others like to have sex in public places. That's not a crime, is it?"

"N-no," I stuttered.

"Indecent exposure maybe," Luke suggested, still holding the boyfriend.

"In a dark alley where only freaks like you hang out?" The woman clutched her ripped blouse shut. "Let go of my boyfriend right now, before I sue your ass."

Luke let go of the guy, who quickly went for his pants. He rebuttoned them, pink-cheeked, and turned to his girlfriend. "Let's just go, Lucy."

Lucy took her boyfriend's arm. "Are you okay, Barry? Maybe I should take you to a hospital."

"I'm fine!"

"You said the same thing when you fell off the bed and hit your head on the nightstand table. That time you ended up having a concussion."

"I said I'm fine!" He'd turned bright red. "Let's go!" He tugged her along, away from us.

"You two need to get laid once in a while!" Lucy called back at us as he dragged her away.

Luke and I stood a moment in awkward silence, eyeing each other. Then I saw the corners of his mouth twitch. I gave him a small smile. We both burst out laughing.

"For what it's worth, I thought we made a good team there. If not an entirely bright one," Luke remarked.

"You can add 'stupid' to your list of insults, I suppose," I joked after a moment. "Possibly lonely."

"I'm no better, I thought he was attacking her too," Luke said, still laughing.

"So, I guess you've never done anything adventurous like that, either?" I said—then realized too late what I had just said. And to whom.

"I guess my adventurous nature is more suited to saving people and not the bedroom. Or *outside* of the bedroom." He smiled wryly. "Or maybe I just haven't met the right woman yet."

I ignored the tingle of attraction that surged through me. "Well, I think you'd have to be pretty desperate to decide to move things out here in order to spice things up in the bedroom." I gestured around. "It's, well . . . unhygienic. And cold."

"I suppose I should be grateful," Luke said, sobering. "If that whole thing wasn't an icebreaker, I don't know what is."

"Sorry I yelled at you like that," I said. "And maybe it is frivolous female jealousy that's getting to me. She *is* gorgeous."

"See, that's one of the things I don't understand about women. So she's pretty, so what? You're pretty. You never see men not be friendly with someone because he's more attractive."

"We are mysterious creatures," I agreed, taking delight that I'd gotten a compliment out of him. I'd only had to be insulted and embarrassed beforehand, but hey, a compliment is a compliment. "But I will try to rise above petty insecurities and be nice and friendly from now on."

"Insecurities? You can rewire shuttles to take people into space, and you're insecure . . ." He shook his head, as if amazed. I fought back even more pride. "We're still going to work out together tomorrow, right?"

"Right," I said. Oh, no. What was I doing? I'd implied I was going to start training more with him, but that had been the champagne talking. I avoided working out like the plague. Luke acted like it was a form of religion.

"I'll invite her to join us. It'll give you two a chance to get to know each other."

"Well," I decided, "no one is glamorous while sweating."

"Exactly." He gave me a wink.

I knew I had to play nice. "All right, it sounds like a plan," I agreed.

He started off down the alley, back toward the main street. "Let's wrap this patrol up. I have a feeling there isn't much villainous activity happening in our quarter tonight, and it's best we don't mess up any more . . . intimate encounters." He laughed. "Tomorrow I think we'll start off with a nice long jog, bright and early. Good way to get the blood pumping."

"I thought that's why God invented caffeine," I replied, joking weakly.

A jog at the butt-crack of dawn with the Glamazon? What had I gotten myself into?

CHAPTER SEVEN

I groaned and sat up in bed, fumbling for my alarm. It was still dark out, so why had it gone off?

Everything came back to me: Luke and I on patrol. The kinky couple in the alleyway. My promise to go jogging with Luke and Selena, so we could all be one big happy dysfunctional hero team. It was too early for this without coffee.

Throwing on an EHJ T-shirt and a pair of yoga pants that I'd bought when Toby and I optimistically promised each other we'd do yoga every morning (we actually only did it once), I found my sneakers in the back of my closet and tied my newly dyed hair back in a ponytail. Then I headed downstairs in the early morning darkness.

Stepping out of the elevator and into the quiet and empty lobby was a bit disconcerting. While we owned the building and our personal accommodations were on the top floor, the downstairs held a gift shop, a coffee house, and a crime-fighting museum focused mainly on the history of the EHJ. The floors between were offices for our corporation—we were a brand, after all, with lawyers and publicists. Paul and I both had full-floor laboratories for our work, though I liked to do a lot in my room. What can I say? I constantly tinker.

My tennis shoes squeaked on the newly waxed floors, and as I walked through the double-glass doors I could see Luke and Selena standing right outside in the cool, foggy morning air. Selena was laughing about something he'd said, and she touched his arm in a flirty and intimate gesture.

Seeing me, Luke flashed me a smile. "Mindy! Good morning."

"Morning," I mumbled, never the picture of grace or sweetness in the a.m., especially not until after I've had my caffeine fix.

"Good morning," Selena added, cheery. "All set?" She was dressed in one of those expensive matching zip-up sweatshirts and pants that are cropped to be like a second skin. They usually have some sort of phrase written on the butt, but I didn't want to stare at her perfect ass to find out what hers said.

"Ready as I'll ever be."

She laughed. "I hear that."

"So do I," Luke said. "You both volunteered to do this."

"I like to keep in shape," Selena said, giving him a dazzling smile. I grunted something affirmative.

"Best to keep up an even pace," Luke instructed us. "I'm assuming you already did some warm-up stretches, Mindy?"

"Oh yeah, of course," I lied, like I hadn't just rolled out of bed. Was *stretching* what they called what they'd been doing?

"All right, let's go," Luke said. "If we get separated, we'll meet back here." And we began our slow descent into hell, aka our morning jog.

It wasn't so bad at first. I kept a decent pace, managing to stay even with Luke, the crazy fitness nut, and Selena, who didn't look winded or break a sweat. By the time we had gone a few blocks, however, I was starting to feel sweaty and my calves stung, and Luke was ahead of me. (At least that made the view nice. Here was an ass I didn't mind staring at.) Selena was just a bit behind him, safely between us. I didn't bother to feel jealous.

We went a few more blocks, and I began getting a pain in my side. My calves felt like they were on fire and I felt like I couldn't breathe. And Luke? He was out of sight.

Cursing my out-of-shape body, I slowed to a walk, breathing hard and holding my side. I hadn't gone too far at this new pace when I ran into Selena, who was leaning against the side of a wall, hands on her knees, staring at the sidewalk. I guess being super strong didn't always translate into having super stamina.

Hearing my approach, she looked up and smiled. "Boy's got stamina, huh?"

I nodded. "You could say that."

She brushed back a few strands of sweaty hair from her face, which somehow made her look artfully mussed, whereas I probably looked like a wet mop. "The things we do for hot guys, huh?"

I shrugged. "I need to get into shape. Obviously." I motioned to my sweaty clothes.

"Lainey told me that you had a thing for Luke."

Nice. How kind of Lainey to blab about my pathetic crush to this woman who probably had men flocking to her by the droves, and who now had Luke in particular wrapped around her little finger. "Had. As in, past tense. We're just friends," I said.

She studied me. "I don't want to get in the way of anything."

In the way? I wondered if nothing had happened between them yet. That seemed unlikely. "Trust me, Selena, there's nothing for you to get in the way of."

There was a bit of regret in my voice, and she must

have noticed. She said, "That was the best thing about my last team, The Fives: It was all women, so there were no strained relationships or competitions over guys."

I snorted. "I'm no competition to you."

"Please, Miss Smarter than the Whole Planet, I'd love to have just an eighth of your brains. Ask Lainey. She had to tutor me all through school. I was a total brick—which isn't just a remark about my powers."

"Like guys care if a woman is smart or not," I grumbled.

She frowned. "What kind of guys have you been dating, girl? Do you know how many times I've been made to feel like the pretty, dumb girl who should just stand in the back of the room and shut up because I don't completely understand what a black hole is or know the exact trajectory of the sun? Both of which I'm sure you could explain in your sleep."

I tried to allow myself to feel a bit better.

"Look, Mindy, I asked Luke if I could tag along with you guys this morning," she said, standing straight.

"You did?"

"Yeah, I asked him to ask you last night, to make it sound like his idea. It's not what you're thinking, that I wanted to horn in on your time with your friend. I really wanted to get to know you a bit better."

"Me? Why?"

"You all seem to be a tight-knit group, and that's nice. I'd like to be a part of it. Lainey's my friend from way back, and she knows I didn't exactly have a large number of friends in school. Something about me just puts people off."

"Maybe because you're perfect?" The words slipped out before I could do anything to stop them.

Selena looked startled. "Perfect? Me?" She let out a sharp laugh. "Please. Everyone expects me to be, but I'm not. Much to my dad's chagrin." Then, as if she'd said too much, she shook her head. "Never mind, no one wants to hear my parent issues, especially when I'm too old to still be holding on to them."

"That might be the one thing we have in common, other than Lainey," I argued, mentally adding: *and Luke*.

"Oh? You too?"

I nodded. "Scientists hailed by everyone, including the government, for their contributions to humanity. But they didn't really know what to do with a super-smart kid."

"My mother's a former model turned district attorney. Dad's a geneticist. I was cared for by the nanny."

"I had tutors, so they could drag me everywhere they went."

"I went to boarding schools, and they would only come and get me for Christmases and summers, though I either stayed with the nanny or was shipped off to some camp."

"I was never allowed to play with toys that weren't educational, or to read kids' books because they were 'beneath my intellect,' whatever that means."

Selena laughed, clearly enjoying this game of one-upmanship, too. "I was never allowed to eat junk food because my mother wanted me to be a model and was worried I'd gain weight."

"I was never allowed to eat junk food because my parents knew all of the side effects from processed food."

"I was never allowed to wear shorts or pants as a child, only dresses that I couldn't get dirty."

"My parents gave me long, complicated, after-the-fact explanations of the consequences of my actions, instead of saying, 'Don't put that fork in the light socket.'"

Selena shook her head, surprised. "When I found out

about my powers, my parents started sending out applications for me to join teams, and they said I'd join whichever was the most prestigious."

"My parents sent me to live with aliens who experimented on my brain."

Selena stared at me, openmouthed. "I can't top that. Seriously, that's what happened?"

I shrugged. "They didn't know exactly what was going to happen."

"But still."

I nodded. "But still."

She nudged me. "This kind of shared pain deserves a mocha."

I smiled and agreed, "A venti, at least."

"And extra whipped cream."

"With chocolate shavings and a drizzle on top."

"Girl, you read my mind!" she said, giving a look around. "Think Luke will notice if we skip the rest of the run?"

"He said if we get separated to meet him back at home. We'll meet him there. In the café."

"I like the sound of that," Selena laughed, and we turned around, chatting all the way home.

I couldn't hate Selena anymore. She was a decent person. Drat.

Back at the EHJ building, we skipped the line in front of the barista—owning the place has its perks—and, after collecting our coffees to the accompaniment of clicking camera phones taking pictures I so didn't want to see on Page Twelve, we found a seat in the small café. A television was tuned to one of the all-day news channels, and a few corporate types were sitting nearby, probably waiting to check the stock report.

After taking a sip of my mocha, I steeled myself to do what I knew I had to do. To be a grown-up.

"Selena," I said, taking a deep breath. "I think you should ask Luke out. If you haven't already."

She lifted her eyebrows in surprise. "You do?"

I nodded. "He hasn't dated in I don't know how long, and he needs to again, to get out there and stop being all about his job."

"But, what about you?" she asked, toying with her coffee. "I mean, I know you like him . . ."

"He's my friend. I want him to be happy." I realized that was true. "And you seem like a nice person, and you two seem to have a connection. So, why not?"

"I don't know, Mindy."

"You're the type of person he should be dating; not a model or a starlet." *Nor me*, I silently added. "You're the type of woman he should be with."

Selena took a sip of her coffee. "If you're sure . . . ?"

I wasn't, but I knew I had to be. "I am."

She looked over at me, smiling. "Then, I will. I'm not going to lie; he just about took my breath away when I met him at Lainey's reception the other night. And I thought there might be some chemistry there . . ."

"Great," I said, my voice a bit weak. I guess they hadn't actually hooked up. But I supposed it was only a matter of time.

As I glanced out the window, I saw Luke approaching the building. "Speak of the devil."

He pushed open the door and looked around, saw us. Moving with purpose, his long, heavily muscled body glistening with sweat, he approached. Selena and I stared, trying not to drool.

"What happened to you guys?" he asked.

"We met you back here, just like you said," I replied.

"Yeah, but I was ahead of you. There's no way you made it all the way around and back before me!"

"Maybe it's our new powers," I teased.

"Maybe you two chickened out," Luke argued, crossing his arms and giving us a hard look.

I maintained innocence. "No way!"

"We cut down some side streets," Selena said. She stood and stretched, showing off her own gorgeous and lean body. This time, Luke was the one staring. "Want a green tea? I'm buying."

As she took his arm and led him to the barista, I felt a gnawing in the pit of my stomach. She was going to ask him out now. I had done it; I had practically gift wrapped him for her. Not that she needed it, but I had helped her. Why, I'm not certain. Being a mature person sucked.

I glanced over at the television screen and saw a familiar face. Doing a double take, I looked again. Was that . . . ?

I got up and walked to the screen, edging past a businessman who gave me a sharp look that I ignored. Sure enough, there he was: Simon Leasure. My former teammate. The last time I saw him, he'd been saving me from being devoured by a creature that looked like it was spawned at the gates of hell, and almost dying in the process. That wasn't something I forgot easily.

Nor were other circumstances we'd shared. The second to last time I saw him, Simon was being dragged off by Luke to explain to the authorities just why he had betrayed the Elite Hands of Justice to get some extra publicity for himself.

Decked out now in the best suit money could buy, in a serious but calming tie that matched his dark blue eyes, he looked less like a movie star and more like a politician. His face was sober as he spoke, and I edged forward and hit the volume button.

". . . will do the job to the best of my ability. I think my previous experiences will give me the understanding needed to act in this capacity," he was saying. "Thank you, ladies and gentlemen of the press."

Simon stood behind the podium and kept his hands folded in front of him as reporters shouted out questions and flashbulbs popped. Was it my imagination, or did I see a hint of a smirk on his face?

"That was Simon Leasure, the son of Senator Jackson Leasure," the announcer was saying, "and the new Presidential Secretary of Heroes . . ."

CHAPTER EIGHT

"What the hell?" Paul spat, looking around the table at us. "There's a Presidential Secretary of Heroes now? And it's none other than that asshole Simon Leasure?"

We were all in shock.

"What does that mean, exactly, Presidential Secretary of Heroes?" Lainey asked. "He's going to do what, act as a liaison between us and the government?"

"Or monitor and police us," Wesley grumbled, fingers steepled in front of his mouth.

"It doesn't mean that necessarily," Luke said.

"Oh, who the hell knows," Paul blustered. "Of all the people in the world, it would have to be that self-righteous little prick."

We all stared, surprised by the language he was using. And then I remembered why Paul might have a problem: Simon was one of Kate's former flings.

"Toby, didn't you meet with someone about a committee yesterday?" Kate asked, unruffled by Paul's unnatural behavior.

"Yes. Forrest Ward," Toby said, ruffling his hair with his hands. "He's the liaison assigned to the Elite Hands of Justice. But he said the committee was being formed in an effort to improve communications between the hero teams and the government, kind of like Homeland Security. In the event of a natural disaster, the government will communicate with us through the liaisons."

"What, it was too easy just calling us on the phone?" Kate laughed.

"Bureaucrats love reorganizing things to make them think they're doing something important," Paul remarked, shaking his head. "Toby, why don't see if you can contact this Forrest, have him straighten this out for us."

Toby nodded. "I'll give him a call." He whipped out his cell and punched in a number, stepping out to make the call, I suppose to hear better without us in the background. It was just like him to have already programmed the liaison's number into his phone, in order not to lose it. Good thing, too. I couldn't count the number of times he'd misplaced his security card and I'd had to give him a new clearance.

"I have a bad feeling about this," Wesley said. "Whenever the government steps in, that usually leads to trouble."

We all felt the weight of his words and experience.

"We don't know enough yet to have a bad feeling about anything," Paul spoke up.

"We know that Simon Leasure's in charge, which ought to tell you something," Wesley said.

Kate gave a soft laugh. "It's going to be poorly run and highly publicized?"

"It can't be trusted," Wesley corrected.

"Simon wasn't all bad," I put in, feeling like I should defend him. "He did save my life."

"Mindy's right," Luke spoke up. "Let's not judge someone by one mistake they made."

Wesley snorted. "One?"

"Let's just wait until we know more about the situation before jumping to conclusions," Paul said. "Though I do have to agree that if Simon's in charge, I worry."

I glanced at Lainey, who gave me a knowing look. If

Paul was agreeing with Wesley, this was the apocalypse.

Toby walked back into the room. "He's in an executive meeting right now, probably with Simon, but his secretary said he could be available to speak with us right after."

"Great, set it up," Paul said, and Toby nodded and spoke into his cell phone again, walking back out of the room. "We'll reconvene later."

"Are all of your meetings like this?" Selena asked as she, Lainey and I exited the room.

"Well, sometimes we *know* things," I joked.

"And sometimes we actually have criminals to fight," Lainey added.

Having time to kill before the next meeting, I decided to do the one thing that would make me happy: go work in my lab. Grabbing a bottle of water out of the kitchen and downing another migraine pill—my head was better but still not 100 percent—I headed for the elevator and scanned my ID badge into the reader that would allow me access. In a moment, the elevator dinged, and I entered my lab, donning a clean lab coat as I walked, my boot heels clicking in the silence.

To say my laboratory was state of the art is an understatement. I had things in there that would make the top technology specialists in the country weep with joy at just being able to touch them. Things that my own hands had created, things that followed me back from my off-planet travels, both as a child and again with the EHJ, were littered everywhere.

I stepped up to the gray table in the center of the room that held my latest project, a transporter that would hopefully work like a gun: point and shoot. Instead of ending up dead, a criminal would end up in a cell in a maximum-security prison, unharmed. At least, it would if calibrated right. I had been testing it on plants, trying to transport them from one side of the room to the other, but something was making the transporter go wonky, and the plants were ending up on the other side of the room with their planters shattered and their buds ripped off. Not exactly unharmed.

I sighed as I got a similar result—the poor geranium—and got out some tools to work on the gun.

Before my first space travel (which I don't like to dwell on, as you know) I was a precocious child, maybe even a prodigy, but I wasn't *this* smart. I might have grown up to be a scientist like my parents and worked with a team to create something like this after months of planning and testing; but after my time with the aliens, suddenly I could just dream it up and start building on any Saturday night when nothing was on television and I was dateless. It happened all the time.

Something changes when I start working, however. It's like I go into a trance: My fingers and hands seem to move of their own accord, and my mind processes things of which not even I am aware. Hours will pass without me realizing, I'll skip meals and forget about bathroom breaks until whatever I'm working on is done. I always come to with an aching bladder, a rumbling stomach, and the realization that it's now night.

A similar experience came over me as I started work on my transporter. Tweaking this, recalibrating that, I worked furiously, in my own little world, my aching head eventually forgotten. The air conditioner turned off and on without me really realizing, and the tick and hum of the machinery around me was nothing but a background. I was alone.

I see you.

The voice sounded right behind my shoulder, as if someone was leaning in and whispering. I whirled to look, and a loud clatter sounded as several of my tools appeared out of nowhere and landed on the metal table.

Heart racing, I looked around, seeing nothing out of the ordinary and no one. "Who's there?" I called, then winced, realizing how much that sounded like a horror movie cliché. "Hello?" I put a bit more edge to my voice. "You're so funny, Toby. Knock it off."

There was no response. Shivering a bit, I reached for the stunner I kept in my pocket. I edged toward the door, my nerves jangling and my skin prickling. "I'm going to knock your ass out for messing with me, I hope you realize."

No one replied. My eyes landed on my "gun," its guts sprawled across the lab table. It seemed to vibrate, clattering against the table, and then, as if an unseen hand took the weapon up, the barrel whirled to point in my direction.

"So not cool," I said.

"Mindy? Who are you talking to?"

I jumped again, before turning to see Luke standing in the doorway near the elevator, a quizzical look on his face.

"I thought there was someone here," I said, motioning into the room. "I was by myself, working, and I thought I heard someone whisper at me."

"You thought you heard someone? You, the same woman who doesn't hear people calling her while she's working unless they set off a nuclear explosion?" Luke gave me a teasing grin.

I grimaced. "Yeah, that's what made it so freaky! And then my project moved." I pointed back to where it was sitting, barrel pointed away from us.

I blinked. "What the . . . ?"

"What?"

"I swear it was moved." I walked over and laid a hesitant hand on the device. "It's cold."

"It's metal."

"It's extra cold."

"What, you think it was a ghost?" Luke asked.

I shook my head. "There's no such thing."

"Says the coolheaded scientist who was scared out of her mind from talking to herself."

"Ha-ha." I made a face at him. "And I wasn't scared out of my mind."

"You looked pretty panicked."

I sighed and rubbed my aching head. "Did you come down here for a reason, or just to torment me?"

"A reason. The liaison is here to meet with us, and Paul wants everyone there pronto."

"Did he say pronto?"

"He said pronto."

"All right, I'm coming."

I shrugged out of my lab coat and hung it next to the hook on the door. Absently, I reached for the switch to turn off the lights. They went dark a split second before my finger flipped the switch.

I moved my hand away fast but didn't say anything to Luke. I just knew I didn't want to be in this room for a while.

Our new liaison was lean and well-dressed in the manner of many politicians, in a way that was polished and studiedly nonthreatening. He had close-cropped sandy brown hair that looked as if it would curl if he let it, though that would probably ruin his image. A goatee was his only rebellion against an overwhelmingly conservative appearance. He also looked a little nervous to be addressing a room full of heroes.

"Everyone, this is Forrest Ward, whom I met yesterday," Toby was saying as we all took our seats around the large table in our war room. "Forrest, this is White Heat, Aphrodite, Sensei, Tekgrrl, Phenomenal Girl Five, the Reincarnist, and our newest member, Granite."

Forrest nodded. "Nice to meet you all, and thank you for agreeing to see me." As if it had been his idea and not ours. Such a politician. "Well, as I told Toby—um, the Magnificent—yesterday, the president decided better communication with the leaders of our country's hero teams was needed in case of national emergency, and he decided to set up the committee that I am now a part of. I'm the lucky guy assigned to work with you all." There was no sarcasm evident in his tone. "Now, who is the leader of this team?"

"I am," Paul and Wesley said at the exact same time. They shot nasty glares at each other.

"When did you decide you were taking my job?" Paul snapped.

"When Benjamin died," Wesley replied. "*He* was the leader of this team, not you, Paul."

"And what makes you think you can just step in? After years of telling us we were all popularity-obsessed fools that you wanted no part of, now you want in?"

"I formed this team."

"*You* didn't form this team, *you* have only been around a year or so, *Wesley*," Paul reminded him. "It's been many lives since you led anyone anywhere, considering Robert wanted nothing more than to stay locked away in his mansion and only come out when necessary, though he was happy to pass judgment on us all for not being up to his standards. I've been field leader for years now, and I've been leading this team during combat situations while you've been living the life of a hermit."

Forrest looked around awkwardly. "It's not important

to know who's leader now, I suppose. I just need to know whenever you decide."

"They both are," Kate spoke up, and we all swung around to look at her. "Right, Toby? Luke?" She was asking the more senior members if they could go along with that suggestion.

"Wait a minute," Paul said. "I—"

"That's right," Luke overrode him. "Shared responsibility, just like back with Rath."

Toby nodded. "Sounds good to me." When Kate gave him a sharp look he said, "I mean, yes."

"Why is it any of the government's business who our leader is?" Wesley asked, characteristically suspicious. "We're glad to help out whenever needed, just like always, but we've never had problems with communication."

"And why is there a Presidential Secretary of Heroes?" Paul shook his head. "Why is that position even needed?"

"Are you setting up a system to monitor us?" Wesley demanded.

"Are you suggesting that we need policing? After all we've done? After so many of us have died trying to keep the world safe, you're going to put some government crony on our tails?" Paul asked.

The coleaders had found their unifier: distrust of Simon Leasure and the government.

"N-no, nothing of the sort." Forrest looked a bit surprised. "Our purpose is to simply improve communications between other teams and yourselves, and between the government and yourselves, especially in case of a threat to national security."

"So, what's Simon's role in all of this?" Paul asked.

"He's overseeing the committee, and reporting directly to the president."

Meaningful glances were exchanged all around.

"So, it's like I told you, it's similar to Homeland Security," Toby remarked, trying to ease the tension.

Paul eased up. Turning to Forrest he said, "Well, with the exception of Simon running this program—probably to a spectacular failure—we will continue to help our government and our country whenever needed. We look forward to working with you."

"Yes, I'll be in contact," Forrest said, nodding.

"See that Selena has all of the pertinent contact information," Wesley directed in obvious dismissal.

The liaison took the hint. "Then I'll just be returning to my office. If you should have any further questions, please don't hesitate to call."

"I'll see him out," Toby remarked, motioning for Forrest to follow.

We were all silent as the two left.

"I still don't like this," Wesley said.

I chewed my lower lip. I hated to say so, but something about the whole situation bothered me, too. Maybe it was because it had come out of nowhere.

"Well, I don't like Simon being in charge, but otherwise it seems like just another way for the government to waste money," Paul put in. "Another impotent flexing of muscles by the president."

"Just another way for the man on top to make himself feel big and important, eh?" Kate remarked, shooting a dark glance at her lover that he ignored. I was beginning to wonder if Kate and Paul had broken up.

Selena spoke up, efficient as expected. "I'll coordinate with Mr. Ward to set up any future meetings. Once we're out of this meeting I'll test all my contact numbers."

"So, nothing's going to change," Luke said. "We'll just do what we normally do, help out when needed."

To me it seemed like everything was changing, but I didn't voice that fear. Instead, I joined everyone as they stood up. Luke walked over to Paul and said something in a low voice. Paul nodded, keeping his eyes on the table. I wondered what they were discussing.

"I hate politics," Lainey whispered to me, which I wholeheartedly affirmed with a vigorous nod of my head. Whether or not we here at the EHJ thought things were changing, the future was dependent upon whether Simon had changed.

CHAPTER NINE

"So, I asked Luke out last night."

"Ow, that's hot!" I yelped, concealing my surprised choke by pretending to burn my lip on my coffee. I gingerly pried my lid off the cup and blew over the rim, eyeing Selena as I did. We had run a couple of blocks with the object of our mutual affection as our morning "workout," then again hightailed it back home for coffee and biscotti.

"Are you okay?" Selena asked, sounding genuinely concerned. I wasn't sure if it was because of my faux burn or the fact that she'd had to deliver this news.

"Fine, fine." I waved her concern away like a cloud of gnats. "Go on. So, you asked Luke out last night?" Again, I was a bit surprised they hadn't moved faster.

"He was a bit surprised. He said he was usually the one doing the asking." Selena dunked her biscotti in her latte and gave me a smile. "I told him I'm progressive."

Huh. Luke was a bit old-fashioned. He believed in chivalry and opening doors for ladies, them being the weaker sex and all. Which was sweet, if a bit sexist, but I was willing to forgive that. Of course, now that I considered, I could only imagine what his reaction would have been last night. "So, what did he say to that?"

"He said he was okay with being asked out, as long as I let him pay." Selena grinned. "The last couple of guys who asked *me* out wanted to go Dutch, so I wasn't turning that down, you know?"

"Uh-huh," I said, forcing a weak smile in return. "So, where are you guys going?"

"To L'Orange for lunch today," she answered. "Have you been?"

I nodded. "It's nice." Toby had taken me there one year for my birthday. It had a nice, cozy atmosphere. But . . . Luke and Selena were having a *lunch* date? You generally didn't take to lunch a woman you were trying to get into bed; you took your mom or your sister or your business acquaintance. Dinner, with the option of breakfast to follow, was more standard operational procedure.

"Cooled off?" Selena asked.

"Uh-huh." I sat back in my chair, perplexed. "So have you got your date outfit all picked out?"

"I try not to stress too much about that kind of thing," Selena said, looking down at her running clothes. "The moment I start agonizing if this looks too slutty or that looks too matronly is the moment I'm trying too hard— and I'll look like it. I'll probably just dress like it's a usual day at the office, since we *are* going on our lunch hour. I've put in for the time."

"Makes sense. I guess you don't want to walk around all day in a little black dress," I conceded. And she would probably look fabulous anyway. Life was so unfair. "Wait. Paul still makes you schedule a lunch hour?"

"Yeah, usually between noon and one, so I won't miss any calls. Generally the whole world takes off noon to one, or so he'd have me believe."

I shook my head. "Wow. He hasn't changed at all since I started here."

"Eh, you know how these superscientific types work.

They fear change and stick to routines and scheduling, don't have an impulsive bone in their bodies." She winced. "Sorry, Mindy. I forget you're one of them because you seem so opposite of that."

"Thank God!" I said. "Though I think my attitude comes from defiance of my parents. They make Paul look laid-back and mellow."

"Well, may you not end up like them when you hit fifty," she remarked.

I laughed. "Poor Paul's only forty."

Selena giggled. "Don't tell the boss man I aged him."

"It's an understandable mistake," I decided. "When I was a kid and my parents brought me here for a visit, he scared the hell out of me, always going around barking orders. And that was when he was in his midtwenties! I think some people are just born uptight. Really, if you think Paul's tough, Wesley's old self was just as bad. He's a lot more laid-back now."

"Explains Lainey's attraction to him," Selena mused. "She's always liked the serious, reserved guys."

Luke was serious and reserved, just in a different way. Maybe Selena's and his relationship would crash and burn before lunch ended. Not that I was hoping. I truly wanted both of them to be happy.

Luke suddenly entered the coffee shop, his body glistening with sweat. Selena and I were silent as he approached.

"So, ladies, this is the second time you've beat me back," he remarked.

"Got to be fast, so I can get to work early," Selena replied. "Just in case I want to take a two-hour lunch break."

"Paul's not going to say anything if you're with me," Luke assured her. Their eyes met and held.

All of this flirting was making me queasy. "Well, I've

got to go shower and get ready to do some work myself," I said, standing up and tossing what was left of my coffee in the nearby trash. "Have fun at L'Orange."

"Thanks, Mindy," Selena said, giving me a small wave.

"Are you going back to your lab?" Luke asked. Was it my imagination, or was there a flicker of concern in his eyes?

"Probably. But don't worry. I'll be on the lookout for ghosts," I joked, trying to ignore the way my stomach felt about yesterday's weirdness.

He frowned. "Is your head still hurting?"

"I'm fine. Really, Luke, don't be worried about me."

"Well, if you need anything, you can always come to me," he said, clapping a hand on my shoulder. "I'm never too busy for a friend."

I managed another weak smile. "I appreciate it. Have fun on your date." Then I turned and walked to the elevator before I lost my composure.

After a quick shower, so I wouldn't smell stinky—unlike Selena, I actually sweat during a jog—I felt a bit better. Determined not to let their developing relationship get to me, I wrapped my towel around my body and set about getting dressed and on with my day.

My PDA was blinking like crazy, letting me know I had messages. I had taken bits of alien technology and cobbled together an even more advanced version of the iPhone years before its invention, thank you very much. And mine still had a spark of life.

"Messages," I said as I walked to my closet, seeking another of my brand-new-Mindy outfits.

"Report," it replied, crackling in its odd voice. "You have two new messages."

The first was from a defense contact, wanting to

know how it was going with my prisoner-teleporter gun. The military was always so impatient.

"Tell him I'm almost ready to do field testing and I'll call him with results ASAP," I told the phone, slipping on a pink and black cap-sleeved shirt that had a high neckline but a V-back, and some nice black trousers. Lainey had assured me the pieces were corporate but stylish, and just right for a nearing-thirty-something.

I fielded another question, this one from a reporter wanting a quick quote about new DVD technology—"I believe direct downloads are the way of the future"— while hunting for my black pumps. I located them near my bed, and thus dressed and, with no other pressing matters, I did my daily ritual of chugging down water and migraine pills before heading for the elevator.

I didn't feel anything as I stepped into the elevator; only as it dinged to signal my laboratory floor and I got out did I feel a sense of dread. Was I too scared to go back in there?

This is stupid, I reminded myself. There were no such things as ghosts. I was a cold-blooded scientist and knew that most unnatural phenomenon could be explained by science. The rest could be explained by magic and, after living with magic users over the years and now with two under my roof, that was another ho-hum fact of life.

Maybe Lainey or Wesley were practicing telepathic spells, or maybe there had been a different telepath in the building, an outsider taking a tour, which would explain the strange voice. If I mentioned it to Wesley, he'd probably want to beef up security so much that it hurt, and I didn't want that headache added on to my daily migraine. Especially not when it was possible I had imagined the whole thing. I hadn't been sleeping well of late, and I had to take that into account.

Somewhat settled, I shook my head and put my hand out to open the door. And . . . froze. I really didn't want to go in there.

It took a bit more time than I liked convincing myself that I was being silly. *It was brought on by migraines and exhaustion,* I reminded myself, but I spent a full fifteen minutes outside the door before finally psyching myself up enough to turn the handle and go inside.

No evil spirits attacked, and I immediately had to admit that I was terrifying myself for no good reason. I walked over to where my project lay, still with tools scattered around it, and sighed, trying not remember how they had crashed down around me. I slipped my lab coat on and tossed my hair up into a ponytail so it wouldn't get in my way, then got to work so I could make good my promise to our defense contact.

I'm not sure how much time passed as I ran tests and adjusted settings, but suddenly in the back of my mind I registered the sound of the elevator stopping on my floor, then the handle turning on the door to my lab.

"May I come in?" I heard.

I looked up. "Sure. Did you miss a floor, your lab's upstairs," I joked as Paul walked in wearing a lab coat over his usual suit pants and shirt.

"No, I came to see you, actually." He looked around, grimaced. "Do you always keep your lab such a mess?"

I tensed and gave a quick glance around. Aside from the tools and pieces I had scattered about the table, nothing was out of place.

"I was working," I reminded him. "I'll clean up before I leave tonight."

"See that you do. You should always treat your tools with respect."

"Yes, sir, I'll get right on that," I said with dripping

sarcasm. Really, could he be more obnoxious? "Was there something you wanted, other than to nag me?"

"Yes, actually, I wanted to see you because Luke is concerned."

"Concerned about me?" I ignored the weird flutter in my stomach. "What about?"

"He said you've been having nightmares and popping migraine pills like candy."

My hackles went up. "I'm fine." Paul was here in a medical capacity, and I wasn't having it.

"Then he mentioned something about you hearing voices and seeing things when you were working down here." He glanced around. "You thought there were ghosts?" His tone made it evident how ridiculous he thought that was.

"I'm fine. I was just tired."

"Maybe, but I think his concerns are valid."

"I've had nightmares and migraines since I was a teenager," I grumbled. "It's an old condition."

"But why are they intensifying?"

I shrugged. "I don't know. Stress, hormone levels?"

"And you hearing and seeing things?"

"Exhaustion, probably. It could be anything." I crossed my arms over my chest. "I'm not crazy."

"I'm not saying you are. I'm just saying we need to check you out. You're right, Mindy, it could be anything. It could even be a brain tumor."

"It's not a tumor," I growled.

"Or," he continued, ignoring me, "it could be something having to do with your time with the Kalybrians."

My mouth narrowed to a hard line. "It has absolutely nothing to do with that."

"Luke said you were talking in an alien language the other day."

"I'm not discussing that." I turned my back on him.

Paul sighed. "Really, you're still going to be like this? Even when it's *Luke* who's concerned about you?"

"What's that supposed to mean?" I picked up a pair of pliers and tried to concentrate on work, but Paul slipped up behind me.

"Coming from anyone else I know you'd ignore it, but when Luke says something, I'd think for sure you'd act like it's advice from on high."

I slammed down the pliers and turned to face him. "What the hell is that supposed to mean?"

"Oh, come off it, Mindy." Paul crossed his arms over his chest and looked down at me like an angry parent. "You follow Luke around all starry eyed, just waiting for him to throw you some scrap of attention. You get your hair dyed and start dressing differently, all in the hope of being what you think he wants. Selena."

"That is so not true!"

He continued as if I hadn't interrupted. "For that reason, I thought you'd leap at the chance to have me run some tests on you—because our own Sensei suggested it."

"You know nothing about me, Paul, so stop acting like you do," I snapped. "I'm over Luke. I did the hair and clothes thing for myself."

"Uh-huh. Keep telling yourself that, Mindy. Delude yourself however you want, just let me run the tests." He turned to go.

I wasn't having it. "Delude myself like you do with Kate?"

He froze. I continued.

"Like, how you delude yourself into thinking she actually loves you. Even when we all know she's cheated on you. Even the tabloids know that."

It was a low blow and I knew it. I could see his shoulders slump and his body bow like I had physically struck him. I shouldn't have done it, but I was so angry and defensive that I'd lashed out with everything I had. Why was he pestering me, anyway? I hadn't asked for his help.

His response was through gritted teeth, and he didn't turn around. "Tell me about the Kalybrians, Mindy."

"No."

"Tell me what daily life with them was like."

"I'm not going there."

He turned, stared me down. "Tell me what they had for dinner. Tell me about their holidays and their religious practices. Tell me everything."

My head was pounding. I hadn't realized he'd spent much time thinking about my past, no more than to once consider what I'd told him in my entrance interview, and I didn't want to believe it was particularly relevant now. "I don't like to think about that, Paul. You know that!"

His dark blue eyes glittered. "Tell me about the night before they took you away. Tell me what you were doing the second before they dragged you down to that cold medical facility and opened up your brain so they could have a poke around."

"I don't like to think about that!" I was shaking and crying now, and my head hurt so badly that I grabbed the table for support. I was going to pass out.

"The truth is, you *can't* think about what they did to you, Mindy," he said, taking me by the arms and holding me up so that I wouldn't fall. His eyes drilled into me, and I could see there was no malice in what he said; just concern. "You can't access those memories at all, can you? I'm sure you wouldn't *want* to remember, but you physically can't, can you?"

I was shaking so hard that I held him for support. "What are you talking about?"

He shook his head. "You need to talk to your parents

about this, Mindy. Tell them about the headaches. Tell them about the dreams. Tell them about the large hole in your memory that you and I both know is there." He steadied me on my feet. "And do it today or I'll have to sideline you."

He turned and walked to the elevator without another word. I stumbled over to the trash can and immediately threw up breakfast. My head hurt so badly I couldn't see straight. Sliding down to lay on the floor, I stared up at the ceiling, willing my stomach to stop flipping and my head to stop pounding. I decided to try to think of something else, like how much I hated Paul at that moment. But he was right, damn it. I needed to talk to someone.

"PDA, call a driver," I croaked from my position on the floor. I was answered by a resounding beep. "I need a car as soon as possible."

I was going to see my parents.

CHAPTER TEN

"Miss, we're here."

I was jolted to attention by the driver's voice and looked around, noticing we'd pulled up in front of a slick steel and glass skyscraper that housed one of the many think tanks in Megolopolis. Sliding my sunglasses on, I flipped up the collar of my trench coat like I was a spy meeting a source or something, and stepped out of the protection of the darkened car and into the bright sunlight.

Wincing at the heat of the sun on my still-pounding head, I moved toward the door held open for me without a second glance by a suited doorman, and stepped into the cool air-conditioned building. A man behind a counter inside was saying into a phone, "Thank you for calling Clark Towers, how may I direct your call? One moment please."

"I'm here to see the Drs. Clark," I said, interrupting his rhythm.

"Do you have an appointment?" He didn't even bother to look up, continuing to answer phones.

"No, but they'll see me."

"The Drs. Clark are booked solid and cannot take any unscheduled meetings," he replied, picking up another call and immediately placing them on hold.

"They will see me," I repeated.

He finally looked up, exasperated. "I don't think so, Miss."

I lowered my sunglasses. "Clark. Mindy Clark. The Drs. Clark's daughter. Tell my parents I'm here to see them. Right now."

He studied me as if in disbelief—okay so the new hair probably threw him—then blanched, finally recognizing me from my many newspaper photos. "Of course, Miss Clark! Right away, Miss Clark!" He picked up the phone and dialed a number, hands shaking, and then quickly hung up the receiver. "Only . . ."

"Yes?"

"Your father is out of town on business. And I'm not sure if your mother is in the building."

"Well, can you check please?" I asked, trying to remember my manners. It wasn't this guy's fault that I'd only visited the building a handful of times, and my parents not much more than that since my return to Earth. "And can I please wait somewhere a bit more comfortable?" I motioned around at the chairless and empty lobby.

"Yes, of course, Miss Clark." He dialed the phone again and, after a few terse words, handed me a security badge. "Take the elevator up to the thirtieth floor and someone will be waiting to take you to your mother."

"Thank you," I said, accepting the badge. "Have a nice day."

"Thank you, miss. You, too," the man said, and went back to answering phones, though obviously shaken.

Stepping into the elevator and holding up my security badge in front of the reader, suddenly I was on my way to see my mother for the first time in years.

I'm as much to blame as they are, I reminded myself on the trip up. Neither of my parents had ever been the nurturing type, and when I came back from Kalybri a little harder to handle—whether because of what happened to me or natural teenage hormones—it was decided by everyone that I needed a change of scenery. This led to my attending college at the ripe old age of thirteen, followed by graduate school at seventeen, making service trips to help third-world countries with my professors during breaks. I'd subsequently joined the Elite Hands of Justice and trained with the Reincarnist, so there just hadn't been much opportunity to go home. Not that I was ever invited.

The elevator doors dinged open, interrupting my thoughts, and a woman strode out purposefully.

"Miss Clark?" the woman asked, and I nodded in affirmation. "Great, if you'll just follow me, your mother has a window of ten minutes in which to see you."

"Nice of her to make time," I responded.

"Yes, she had to rearrange a few things," the secretary agreed, obviously not getting my sarcasm as she led me through a silent corridor and a set of double doors. She handled several security clearances while I waited silently.

We finally entered a large lab where a woman with graying brown hair and wearing a plain black suit and white lab coat was having an earnest conversation with a man similarly dressed. She looked up as we approached, pushed her wide glasses up on the bridge of her nose.

"Yes?" she asked, as if she had no clue who I was or why I was there. Although how she could not recognize me I didn't know; I was her mirror image, give or take a few decades and wearing more stylish clothes.

I stepped forward. "Hi, Mom. Thanks for taking time out of your busy schedule."

Sarcasm is lost on scientific types. "Of course, Mindy. It's good to see you." She moved forward to embrace me. "You are looking very nice. I'm glad you finally decided to change your hair back to normal and dress a bit more appropriately."

"Yeah, well . . ." I didn't want to do this in front of her staff. "Is there somewhere we can go to have a discussion? In private?"

My mother blinked, like it hadn't occurred to her until now that other people were around, and that I might not want to discuss my mental issues in front of them. "Oh. Yes. Why don't we take this into my office? Isla, bring me a mineral water. Mindy?"

I waved her off. "Nothing, thanks."

"One mineral water," my mother said, motioning for me to follow. "It's not that I'm not happy to see you, Mindy, but you've caught me off guard and I simply don't have a lot of time to spare these days."

"So what else is new?"

She frowned and opened the door to her plush office. "Now, Mindy, don't take that tone. You know things are always crazy around Nobel season."

"I know, Mom. I'm not trying to pick a fight," I said, taking the plush, buttery leather seat to which she motioned. "I just meant that you're always busy. That's nothing new."

"Now, what's wrong that you needed to see me immediately?" she asked, taking the chair opposite and behind her desk. It was unquestionably the position of power.

I took a deep breath. "My migraines are getting worse."

"Well, you've suffered from them from such a young age. Maybe it's time to discuss changing medications."

"And I've been having terrible nightmares again, too."

She nodded. "I'm the side of the family you get that

from, Mindy, remember? It's always worse around *that* time—your menstrual cycle is a big part of the problem. You might want to discuss with your gynecologist getting on birth control pills that limit your cycle."

I shook my head. "Mom, the dreams are about my time on Kalybri. And I'm hearing voices and experiencing . . . well, weird things."

My mother's face went white. "What are you dreaming about Kalybri, Mindy?"

"These . . . monsters are operating on me." I shuddered. "They're speaking Kalybrian. I'm speaking Kalybrian after I wake up, and I thought I'd forgotten the language." I set my hands on the edge of her desk. "Mom, I know that I was experimented on when I was away. I know that." My voice dropped to a whisper. "But I don't remember anything else."

"You don't want to remember, Mindy," my mother said in a quiet voice.

I smacked my palms on the top of her desk. "No, Mom, that's not it. Paul's right, I *can't* remember. There's a huge gap in my memory from the day you put me on the ship with the Kalybrians to the day when I woke up back here." I took a deep breath, feeling my head pound and nausea burn in my throat. "The day I woke up back here in considerable pain and thousands of times smarter."

My mother's eyes actually filled with tears, the second time I ever remember seeing her cry. The first was the very time I was mentioning.

"Mindy," she said.

"You told me that I was experimented on, that they weren't trying to hurt me, they were trying to help in their own way by making me better, smarter. That the best thing for me to do was to try not to remember." I felt a tear slide down my cheek. "Did you know that I couldn't, Mom?"

She paused, then nodded. "I'm sorry, Mindy. They told us it was for the best."

"Who did?"

"The Kalybrians. They told us about what had happened to you, and said that from all of the trauma associated . . . well, it would be better if you didn't remember. They were worried you'd go mad. So they put up memory blocks."

I frowned. "So, let me get this straight. While they were opening up my brain and rearranging things to make me smarter, these aliens also decided to block all my memories of my time there."

My mother nodded. "It was for the best, Mindy." She cleared her throat. "You didn't see yourself when you came back."

"I was in a coma!"

She shook her head. "No, you weren't. Not when you first arrived. You were wide awake. And you were screaming." She shuddered. "I still hear your screams when I'm trying to fall asleep. Lord, it was terrible. You scratched and clawed anyone who tried to come near you, even me and your father. The Kalybrians said that the blocks would help."

"Wait, you *let* them put blocks up? After what else they did to me?" I got to my feet in horror.

She tried to touch me, and I dodged her hand like it was poisoned. "Mindy, you don't understand. You can't understand." She wiped her eyes with a handkerchief. "The Kalybri were horrified about what happened . . ."

"They should be!"

"And so was I. I had done this to you, I had unwillingly put you into the hands of monsters, and I wanted to make things right."

"By doing it again?"

"They said it would make you better. And it did."

"Why didn't you say anything to me about it?" I asked, crossing my arms on my chest. "Why did you lie to me? Did you know that anytime someone even brings up Kalybri I get a headache?"

"If you knew, you'd just make it worse by trying to think about what happened. They told us with the blocks would come a side effect."

"What about the dreams? And the voices?"

She shook her head. "I don't know. After it first happened, you had dreams for a while—until we figured out that hormone fluctuations would for some reason work against the blocks, your subconscious working its way around them."

"Well, my headaches are all the time, not just when I try to think of Kalybri." Even I had a feeling I knew what that meant. "I think the blocks are beginning to fail, Mom."

My mother was turning pale. "Oh God, Mindy, I'm so sorry. I never should have let you go there. We thought it would be the best thing for your future, we never dreamed . . . The decision has haunted me every day since."

"Is that why you've avoided me since I came back?"

"I never!" she blustered, until I fixed her with a glare. "I might have buried myself a bit in my work, but I never avoided you. No more than you've avoided me."

A knock sounded on the door behind me, and we both turned to see the secretary peek in. "Excuse me, Dr. Clark, but your next appointment is here."

"Of course, Isla," my mother said, taking the bottle of mineral water her minion held out. "We're just finishing up here."

I wasn't finished, but she was obviously finished with me. "Did Paul know you did this to me?"

My mother hesitated, and then nodded. "He suspected after your interview. I explained what had happened and cautioned him not to say anything. I didn't want to cause you any more unnecessary pain."

"Well, these blocks are hurting me now. I'm taking them down in whatever way I can."

My mother dropped her bottle of water and it crashed to the floor, shattered. Ignoring the mess, she stepped over it and reached out to take my arm. Her grip was viselike. "Don't do it, Mindy, I'm begging you."

"What?" I looked at her, trying to shake her off. "You want me to get a brain aneurysm or have a stroke? Whatever's waiting on the other side of those memories has to be better than this."

She tightened her grip impossibly. "You had to be restrained to keep from hurting yourself or others, Mindy. For the love of God and your sanity, please don't take the blocks down. Have your scientist friends monitor your brain patterns and see if there's any way a telepath or a magic user can help, but whatever you do, please don't take those blocks down." She was shaking. "You . . . you won't be able to handle it."

Her secretary reappeared with another stuffed-shirt scientist, who took one look at the mess on the floor and then asked my mother hesitantly, "Is everything all right?"

My mother straightened, dropping my arm and returning to a cool and composed demeanor. I rubbed at the bruises she'd left on my arm. "Everything's fine. My daughter was just leaving."

I nodded. "Good-bye, Mom. Give Dad my love." I turned and followed the secretary down the hall and to the elevator, went down and tossed my clearance badge on the desk of the shell-shocked receptionist.

It wasn't until I'd reached the comfort and safety of the car, with the shade up between me and the driver, that I let myself burst into tears, but then I sobbed all the way home. What in the hell had happened to me? My mother couldn't deal with what she had unknowingly done, and I couldn't handle not knowing. But if what lay on the other side of my memories might drive me insane, was staying in the dark a better option?

By the time I arrived home and went upstairs, my eyes were dry and I knew what I had to do.

Paul didn't mention my red-rimmed eyes, if he noticed them. "Yes?" he asked, looking up from his computer screen as I appeared in front of him.

"Run whatever tests you want."

CHAPTER ELEVEN

What seemed like hours later, I was still a guinea pig. Paul was running what seemed like every possible test on me. I had been poked and prodded, scanned and monitored, and I was more than a little sick of it. It took me back to my first days returned to Earth, or at least the ones I remembered, where I'd lain in a hospital bed while machines beeped and doctors buzzed around me.

"Are you cold?" Paul asked, and I realized that I was shaking.

"A little," I admitted, running my hands up my arms, trying to soothe the goose bumps popping up with my memories. "These hospital gowns are a little thin."

"Well, we're almost done," he said, fixing an electrode to my head and double-checking the reading.

Our animosity hadn't changed, as we hadn't really addressed what was said previously. We'd had to travel to an actual hospital, because the EHJ didn't have all of the necessary equipment. My mind started buzzing with the possibility of building it for us, but that would take a bit of work. And I didn't have a medical background like Paul, so I'd probably need his help. He'd stand there and tell me I was doing everything wrong, like the know-it-all he was. Big, smug jerk.

"What was that?" Paul asked, holding up the printout and showing me the spike. "What were you just thinking about?"

"How much I hate you," I growled.

He frowned. "That's not funny."

I shrugged.

He tore the printout off and clipped it to his clip-board. "We're done. Get dressed and I'll meet you outside." He got up and walked away.

Thankful to finally be done, I yanked the electrodes off my body and got dressed, not wanting to spend any more time here than absolutely necessary. When I stepped out into the hospital hall, Paul leaned against a nurses' station, talking in low tones to a white-coated doctor. Seeing me, he straightened and they both fell silent.

"You'd better not be talking about me," I said. "Doctor-patient confidentiality and all that."

"You're not my patient, you're my coworker," Paul replied. "And get over yourself, Mindy. Not everything and every discussion is about you." He picked up his clipboard. "The car's waiting downstairs; they moved it to the lower-level parking garage to get away from the paparazzi."

"The press found out we're here? How?"

"Some orderly probably tipped them off." He led me through the maze of hospital corridors to the elevator, and we rode down in silence, staring straight ahead. Paul seemed to think he was above small talk, and that was fine with me.

As soon as the elevator door opened we were met by popping flashbulbs in the face. I growled and held up a hand to try to ward them off. Paul grabbed my arm and yanked me toward the car.

"Tekgrrl, White Heat, why are you here?"

"No comment," Paul said. "Move, please."

"Tekgrrl, is it true you have a drug problem?"

"What? No!" I said indignantly, and mentally cursed Paul for getting me into this. He continued to pull me along.

"White Heat, who's leading the Elite Hands of Justice? And would you like to make a comment on your former teammate, Simon Leasure, and his new government position?"

"Absolutely not," Paul said. "Now you really need to move."

My head was back to pounding again, probably from the stress, and I just wanted everyone to get out of the way so I could get into the car and get out of there.

Abruptly, all of the photographers moved backward, as if in response to my wishes. Paul seized the moment to shove me into the car and get in, too.

"Go," he ordered the driver as the paparazzi swarmed forward.

The driver did as he was told, and we careened out of the garage, leaving the press in our wake. We'd probably have a few jump into their cars to follow, but we were free for the moment.

"Thank God they moved," I said. "I didn't think we were going to get out of there."

"Glad they listened to reason," Paul said. "They're usually not so cooperative." He sounded thoughtful.

"So, do I get a clean bill of health?" I asked, interrupting whatever reverie he was in.

"Hmm?" He snapped back to attention. "Well, these mental blocks are going to be hard to detect medically, but everything else looks okay. No abnormalities, other than what they did to you."

"What's *that* supposed to mean?" I was worried.

"Well, you know they increased your intelligence when they experimented on you." At my nod, he continued: "Your brain's lit up with more neural connections than most people's. It's like a circus in there." He tapped my forehead with a finger.

I swiped it away. "So what else is new?"

"Most people don't have the capacity to learn and retain all of that information. Whatever genetic tinkering they did, they upped your retention factor by huge gains." He held an X-ray up to the light and frowned. "If we compared a scan of your brain and the Reincarnist's, I have a feeling they would be somewhat similar."

"He forgets things all the time. Every lifetime," I reminded Paul.

"Yes, because there is only so much room. He still doesn't lose what the rest of us do. What I'm saying is . . . you two have similar capacities, and that's a lot more than the rest of humanity."

"So I'm supersmart, that's nothing new."

"No," he said, sighing. "I suppose not. So . . . your brain is healthy, if crowded with information, which is good news. But a memory block won't show up unless it's associated with head trauma. The best we can do is monitor your brain waves and patterns every so often to make sure they aren't hurting you."

"They're giving me headaches," I pointed out.

"Hurting you more than the average migraine," he amended. "And . . . I'm not sure what the best course of action will be if they're truly failing: to try to fix them or to let them fail."

"My mother said I needed to get them fixed," I said, shivering at the reminder of her warnings.

"Well, I'm going to talk to some of my contacts to see what they think. Until then, you need to let me know if any more symptoms present."

"All right," I said.

I suddenly realized I shouldn't be so hard on Paul. He was just trying to help. It wasn't his fault that I was so traumatized by what had happened on Kalybri that I freaked out whenever a doctor came near. And he might be a stuffed shirt full of antipersonality, but how many of those had I known throughout my life? That's just how truly brilliant scientists were, and he was trying in his own way to help out a teammate. I had to make nice.

"Thanks for making sure I was okay, Paul. I know I'm a pain when it comes to doctors," I said. My voice was quiet.

"We're only trying to do what's best for you," he said. He seemed similarly subdued.

Our car detoured and pulled into our hidden garage; the paparazzi must have been lying in wait outside our building and I hadn't noticed. Paul got out and held the car door open. "Keep a record of how often your headaches come, how intense they are, and what you're thinking about before they happen. Also keep a record of how often the dreams are coming, and if they coincide with the headaches."

"I will be nothing if not meticulous," I promised.

"I'll let you know as soon as I find out anything," he said. "And if any further tests have to be run, I'll try to make sure I'm the one who does them. That way, it's someone you know and not a complete stranger."

"I appreciate it," I said.

"So, what were you working on?" he asked, walking over to the elevator and pushing the button.

"Huh?"

"When I interrupted you, what were you working on? It looked interesting."

"Oh, it's going to be a gun-transporter. Instead of shooting a criminal with a bullet, I'll shoot them with a pulse that will transport them to preset coordinates— like, to a jail cell."

"Interesting." He nodded as the elevator door swished open and we got in. "How are your trials on it going?"

"So-so. I think I fixed something, but that's what I was getting ready to check before you interrupted."

"Well, let me know how it goes. Did you discuss patent rights yet?"

"Military commissioned it."

"Have our lawyers look everything over," he directed.

The elevator dinged and we were met by Luke. He looked a bit worried.

"Great, you're back," he said. My heart leapt. "You were gone for quite a while."

"Paul wanted a lab rat," I joked, by my heart wasn't in it.

Luke eyed me. "Is everything okay?"

"Mindy's fine," Paul said, as if we'd all been overreacting. "We just need to keep an eye on things. Let me know if you experience anything else out of the norm," he said to me.

I nodded like a good little employee. "Yes, sir."

"So, she can go out on patrol tonight?"

Paul studied me, then nodded. "I think she's fine for duty."

"Well, let's go, girl," Luke said to me with a grin. "It's past patrol time."

I didn't realize it had gotten so late. "I'll go change and we'll head out. So long as we can pick up takeout. I'm starving!"

Paul looked alarmed. "No eating while in uniform! It looks tacky."

"Yeah, who wants to promote the stereotype that women eat? Even heroes," I retorted.

"Not while in uniform! Eat on your own time," Paul griped. "Next thing you know, people will think we're endorsing Taco Hut because Tekgrrl was seen eating there."

"I eat there in my off time!"

"And you're not Tekgrrl then, you're Mindy Clark."

I barely saw the distinction, though I understood it. But I was still hungry.

"We won't eat, sir," Luke said, but as soon as his back was turned, he mouthed to me the opposite.

That's why I love him.

CHAPTER TWELVE

"Mmm, these are the best tacos ever," I said, fishing one out of the take-out bag and taking a big bite, dripping sour cream and nacho cheese everywhere. This was probably why Paul didn't want us to eat in uniform: He didn't want us fighting crime in a suit covered in food stains.

Luke dropped down onto the rooftop ledge next to me. "I only got one drink, so we'll have to share."

"That's fine." Not exactly how I wanted to swap spit with Luke, but I was cool with it. "Did anyone recognize you?"

"The kid that I paid ten bucks to walk into Taco Hut and get the order did. I had to sign a napkin." Luke gave me a wry grin.

I laughed. "Well, I appreciate the trouble you went through to get it. Don't know if my thighs will thank you tomorrow, but . . ." I cringed. Why did I go and mention my big thighs to Luke?

"Well, I figured I owed you for Paul. Siccing him on you, I mean." He made a face as he reached for a taco and began unwrapping it.

"Yes, you do," I said, giving him a frown.

"I know how you feel about doctors, but I was really worried, Mindy. And I thought you'd feel more comfortable if it was Paul checking you rather than some strange doctor."

"Does anyone ever feel comfortable around Paul?"

Luke about choked on his taco. "True. Did he at least find out what's wrong with you?"

I shrugged. "Did you know I had memory blocks?"

"What?" His shock told me all I needed to know.

"Guess not. Paul apparently figured it out when I first came to work for the EHJ." I went on to explain the whole terrible story, complete with my mother's dire warnings. By the time I finished, Luke was shaking his head and looked pained.

"I'm so sorry, Mindy. I can't believe that happened to you."

"Neither can I, really. Even knowing it happened, it still seems surreal. And apparently, if I think about it too hard, I'm going to get a really bad headache."

"So what are you going to do? Are you going to get the blocks fixed or chance them falling? Or go ahead and take them off completely?"

"Paul says we just have to keep an eye on the headaches, the dreams, make sure they don't get worse or anything unusual happens. He's going to talk to some contacts he has, and then hopes to figure out the best course of action."

"Well, what do *you* want to do?"

"Honestly, I don't know. I'm just getting used to the idea that someone messed with my memory in order to protect my sanity."

"Damn, that's tough. I'm almost sorry I said something."

"No!" I touched his hand. "I'm touched by your concern, Luke. I'm glad that you care enough to try to help me—even if it was by ratting me out to Paul."

He patted my hand but looked awkward doing it. "You're my teammate, Mindy, and I've known you since you were a kid. Of course I care."

I winced and moved my hand. He didn't have to remind me of the fact that I was forever a younger sister in his eyes. "Thanks."

"I'm sorry this had to happen with you. As if things weren't bad enough as it is," Luke continued.

"Tell me about it," I grumbled, taking a sip of our drink and tossing my empty taco wrapper into the bag. "You can practically cut the tension between Paul and Wesley with a knife. It does *not* make for a comfortable work environment."

Luke seemed happy to change the subject. "I thought I was the only one feeling it."

I laughed incredulously. "Definitely not. And, God, what is going on with Paul and Kate? If that situation gets any more tense, it's going to spontaneously combust."

"Apparently he gave Kate an ultimatum: Either she chooses him and only him or they're through."

"Who'd you hear that from?"

"Kate."

"Why'd she tell you?" Then, too late I remembered their past. "Oh. Yeah."

"No, it's not like that," Luke said. "That's ancient history. But we're still friends, and she felt like she could turn to me to be her sounding board."

"Of course." Because she alienated everyone around her except ex-lovers. "So, which option did she choose?"

"She told me she cares for him and wants to make it work, but it's not exactly in her nature to be faithful."

"Huh." No wonder Paul was cranky. It was about time he did something, though. I shouldn't have hit him with that low blow earlier. "So, what'd she tell him?"

"She'd have to think about it."

Ouch. I *really* shouldn't have low-blowed him earlier. "You think she'll be able to do it if she chooses him?"

"Honestly?" Luke shook his head. "I think if she says she's going to be faithful to him, she'll try her best, but ultimately she'll give in to temptation. It seems like the gods all act like spoiled children, wanting what they want and not thinking about how it will affect the people around them." He shrugged. "With that much power, it's bound to happen. We're just lucky most of them stay in Olympus and the few who mix with us are like Kate and try to work on the side of good. It's not like Paul didn't know the way she was before they got involved."

"Still, no one likes to be cheated on or become a laughingstock," I said. "Everyone knows Kate has an impulse-control problem when it comes to gorgeous men wanting to be with her . . ."

"That's why it was never serious between me and her," Luke admitted. "I wasn't stupid enough to think I could change her, and Paul was."

While I agreed with Luke that Paul *was* pretty stupid to think he could change Kate, I couldn't help but consider his point of view. He was a scientist, like me; and geeky, brainy types like us didn't usually attract the drop-dead gorgeous types. For Kate to have shown the least bit of interest in him probably made him feel like he'd won the lottery, and he was willing to overlook a few things, like infidelity. At least, he had been for a little while. Again, the situation made me feel a bit bad for him.

"So they're still trying to work through all of that," Luke said, cutting into my thoughts. "Add in the stress of the team still adjusting to the Reincarnist and Paul's shared leadership, and whatever is going on with the government, and I'm waiting for"—he made a little motion with his hands—"*boom.*"

"I think it's going to get better, teamwise. At least between Paul and Wesley," I said. "They seemed a bit more cooperative at the end of dealing with that government official. It'll just take some time for adjustment."

"Selena said every team she's ever been on has had leader dynamic problems."

Of course he'd had to bring her up. "So, how was L'Orange?"

"Good. Really nice." He looked like he didn't want to discuss it with me. "Selena's a great person."

"Uh-huh." That was kind of a lukewarm reaction. Had it not gone so well? "So, come on, make with the details."

"That's a little weird, isn't it?" Luke said.

"What, because I used to have a thing for you? I thought we were past all that. Besides, you talked about your ex-lover's current relationship; you can't talk to me about your date?"

He seemed to consider.

"Pretend I'm Toby or something. You know he'll want all the details. And you've got to know Selena's making with all of them to Lainey as we speak."

He grinned. "Okay, okay . . . It was really great."

I ignored the way my stomach plummeted. "Such detail, Luke."

"Well, I don't know what to say!" He looked embarrassed. "It was a great lunch. She's led a really interesting life. And, she's very outgoing and personable. We got along really well."

"Did you kiss her?"

"Mindy!" He looked embarrassed, which surprised me. "I don't kiss and tell."

"So that's a yes. Otherwise you would have said no." I kept my tone light and friendly, but inside my stomach was forming a cold pit. God, it was truly over, wasn't it? He liked her and she liked him. Friendship was really all I'd ever have.

Which, I reminded myself, was all I wanted. Hadn't I started working toward it?

"We're going out for dinner and dancing tomorrow," Luke continued. "Salsa dancing, if you can believe it. Can you see me salsa dancing?"

"No," I replied. I was still shell-shocked. Dinner and dancing, with the option of breakfast the next morning?

"You know what, Mindy, you've not had a serious boyfriend since I've known you, and you haven't dated much lately," Luke was saying. "You're so pretty, you must have guys lined up around the block. So, why aren't you pursuing that?"

"Work's been busy," I said.

"You don't want to become a lonely workaholic like Paul," Luke remarked. "You know, maybe a romantic relationship is just the distraction you need right now, to keep you from thinking too much about blocked memories and the aliens."

"Yeah, Luke," I said halfheartedly. "Lainey was just saying something similar the other day . . ."

"That just proves I'm right! Let's see, who do I know who's single?"

The last thing that I wanted was to be fixed up by Luke. As luck would have it, I was saved from having to come up with a reason to turn down a blind date by the sirens that came blaring up from below.

"Sounds like they're playing our song," I said. "We'll have to discuss my love life later." Or never.

"Let's go," Luke agreed, snapping into focus and gathering up our trash. We ran down the fire escapes of the building we were perched on, probably waking the tenants with our clanging as we passed. Luke paused by a dumpster to get rid of our garbage, and caught up with me at the mouth of the alley.

"Which way?" he asked.

I listened to the sirens. "Towards midtown, I think."

"You have good coordinates up there?"

"Probably the high school's safe." I punched in numbers on the pad around my arm, then shared them with Luke.

"Got 'em." He glanced at me. "Are you ready?"

I nodded. "Ready."

We both clicked our transporters at the same time. After a moment's cool tingle of sensation, we were on the edge of the high school roof. Below, it seemed like every patrol car in the city had surrounded the building.

"What the hell?" I heard from below. I looked down at the cops, who had their guns drawn and pointed at us.

"I think we just accidentally transported directly into the scene of the crime," Luke remarked.

"There's more of them!" someone below shouted, and Luke and I spun to see who was talking.

"No, wait," I called.

"Isn't that Sensei?" someone asked a little too close to the police bullhorn. "Who's the girl with him?"

"Is it Tekgrrl?"

"No way, she's too pretty. Tekgrrl's the one with that purple shit in her hair."

Before I could retort, Luke took control of the situation. "We're here to help," he called down. "If someone could tell us what's going on . . ."

"We said no heroes, or the kiddies in the dance buy it!" a voice shrilled behind me, a split second before I got cracked on the head.

I went down hard, but in my haze I could see the culprits: a group of five villains who looked like they had stepped out of an old movie version of what the future would be, with shiny silver suits and goggles.

Though my head was ringing, I managed to reach

down to grab my energy whip. My assailant had swooped in from above with a jet pack. (A jet pack? Seriously? How pathetically twentieth century could you get?) As he leaned over me, I seized the opportunity and cracked my energy whip. The quick movement wrapped the cord around his neck. His hands went to his throat to try to free himself, but I hit the power button. A jolt of electricity thrummed through the whip's fibers, and the villain went down like a felled ox.

One down, four to go.

I stood up and leaned over the side of the roof to yell down, "Hey, can you get up here to cuff these guys?" The cops could cart the bad guys away; we had to focus on stopping them.

I saw Luke, who had been dodging swooping attacks from another of the villains, finally outmaneuver his foe. He took a flying leap, tackling the guy, but the jet pack continued over the side of the roof and the two men's combined weight was too much; they vanished downward.

I gasped in horror, dropping my whip and running for the edge of the building. It was at that moment that I was grabbed from behind and lifted off my feet. I wriggled in the grasp of whoever held me and managed to head-butt them with the back of my head.

"Hey, you want to fall?" my captor growled. "Keep wiggling, bitch, and I'll drop you."

We climbed higher and higher into the sky, and I was afraid that was his intention, anyway: to take me up high and then drop me. I had to put a stop to him. "Why are you messing with a high school dance, anyway?" I asked, trying to keep him talking as I fumbled for the scrambler on my utility belt. "You angry because no girl asked you?"

I heard him sneer. "Ransom, of course. No one wants to see a kid get blown to pieces, so imagine how much money we'll get if we threaten a school full of 'em?"

"I bet you were the head of your class," I said before I twisted the dial on the scrambler and slapped it onto his jet pack. My fingers slipped and missed the activation button.

Nonetheless, the scrambler turned on with an audible hum. I didn't have time to think about it; instantly the jet pack stopped working and we started to plummet. The villain shrieked like a girl and let go. I tried to reach for him, but it was in vain and I missed. The ground was coming up fast, so I hit the teleport button and prayed for the best. It was still locked onto my former coordinates, and I zapped back to the roof of the high school, landing hard enough to knock the wind out of me but not break anything. My ex-captor was nowhere in sight.

I lay for a moment, curled up in a ball, gasping for air, until I finally got it together.

"You all right?" one of the cops now on the school roof asked.

I gave him a subdued thumbs up and stood. "Where are the rest of the gang?"

"We've got two: this one, and the one your partner delivered. He went after a third."

"What about the guy that dropped me? Did you see what happened to him?"

"They're calling for an ambulance right now."

It sounded like he was still alive, though that could change. God, I hoped not. We in the EHJ didn't make a habit of killing villains, and I hadn't meant to hurt the guy. Paul would be superpissed if he died. Wesley would probably be more forgiving. Having two leaders of opposing minds was like being the kid of divorced parents; you learned how to work both. Still, I hoped I wouldn't have to spin the villain's death.

"How are the kids?" I asked the cop.

"We're evacuating them right now. Apparently the villain who was watching them hightailed it when he heard the ruckus."

"I'm glad the kids are okay," I remarked, wincing at a pain in my wrist. I might have fractured it in the fall.

"Are you really Tekgrrl?" one of the other cops asked, helping the first villain to his feet. The villain looked particularly uncomfortable, still groggy from the power whip.

"That's me," I said.

"You look different."

I rolled my eyes. "It's the hair."

One of the cops held up a cell phone. "Do you mind if I take a picture? My kid will never believe that I met you."

I shrugged and acquiesced. It's one of the easier parts of being a hero.

Pictures taken, I teleported down to ground level, still careful of my wrist, and was met by Luke, who also looked a little worse for wear.

"Are you okay?" I asked.

"I think I may have broken a few ribs, but I'm okay. Got one, the other got away. How about you?"

"Might have broken my wrist. I got two, but one's in pretty bad shape. He had a hold of me with a jet pack, and when I dropped us with a scrambler he fell before I could grab him."

"We'll have to tell Paul and the authorities." Luke was nothing if not a stickler for protocol.

I nodded, sighing. "Of course."

"Don't look so worried, you were just doing your job. I'm sure you didn't use excessive force. And we both sustained injuries, ourselves." He gave my shoulder a squeeze. "It'll be okay. Come on, I'll pop for a cab ride to the hospital. We should get our injuries checked out before we go home, and the trip will give us time to decompress that just teleporting won't."

I smiled. "Tacos and cab rides. Selena's a lucky woman."

If only it didn't hurt so much to say that.

CHAPTER THIRTEEN

Because of my injured wrist and my continued head-aches, I had gotten a pass on patrol for a bit. I grumbled a bit, but it did give me more time in the lab. Weeks later, it was business as usual.

"All right, Goth Boy, put the nice man down."

The young villain put down the homeless man from whom he had been draining energy and frowned. "Count Cranium! My name is Count Cranium!"

I burst out laughing. I couldn't help it. "Like that's any better."

Luke appeared out of the shadows. "Whatever your name is, step away from the civilian."

Seeing Luke, the psychic vampire edged toward the mouth of the alley.

I frowned. Just a teenager, and already a criminal with a bizarre moniker. What was the world coming to? "Don't you dare run."

No sooner did the words leave my mouth than Goth Boy tossed the bum at me. I collided with a mound of alcohol-scented flesh and went down. Luke stopped to help me up, and I got a glimpse of the edge of a cape disappearing around the corner. Goth Boy's outfit proved he took the vampiric portion of his powers a little too seriously.

"I'm all right, just go!" I waved Luke off as I tried to push the weakened and obviously intoxicated bum off me and got groped for my trouble. "Looks like I'm going to get my cardio for the day."

Luke grinned. "Bet you're wishing now you spent more time actually jogging in the mornings."

It was true that, after a few weeks of morning runs with Luke that turned into coffee breaks with Selena, I wasn't any closer to either him or losing those five pounds I'd being meaning to shed. Darn the lattes!

Luke took off after our villain. The homeless man gave me a gummy smile. "You're pretty."

I sighed and followed Luke.

Breathing hard, I stopped for a moment, watching Luke chase our Goth bandit down a hill through midtown, dodging pedestrian traffic and getting looks and curses along the way. From my vantage, I saw Luke was going to lose him in the crush, so I quickly dialed in some coordinates to an alley I knew ahead and hit the button. Luke didn't like to use his transporter unless necessary, but I wasn't above using my inventions to make life easier.

A queasy feeling hit as I was transported, and when I reappeared in a new location, it was with the added bonus of a pounding headache. Trying to shake it off, I stumbled out of the alley and got the pleasure of seeing I'd calculated correctly. The villain's eyes widened. He tried to skid to a stop to avoid me.

"I told you not to run," I snarled, holding up my prison-cell transport gun. "If your molecules get scrambled, don't blame me." I had run enough tests to know they wouldn't scramble, but a dose of healthy fear in a villain isn't a bad thing.

I pulled the trigger, and the beam blasted toward the villain's chest. I waited to see him vanish into nothingness, hopefully transported to a maximum security prison cell across town. The beam sizzled into nothingness.

I stared at the gun and then back at Count Cranium in confusion. "What?"

The villain held up a pentagram amulet that I'd thought was just a weird homage to Dracula. "Personal defense shield," he crowed. "My girlfriend's a magic user."

"She's got bad taste in men," I retorted.

"I'll bet heroes are better to drain than regular humans," he said, suddenly edging toward me with a strange smile. "And I'll bet you're particularly tasty."

I held up my Shocker. "Come near me and you're going to jail unconscious," I warned.

He laughed. "Your little sci-fi shit won't work on me."

"Let's find out," I said, and pushed the button.

The shock that would normally take out a full-grown adult fizzled without any obvious effect. I cursed magic in general. I needed a weapon that would circumvent it. Maybe Lainey or Wesley could help, and if I threw together some neural-transmitter transducers . . .

This is so not the time to focus on wish lists, I reminded myself. The villain had decided he had the edge, and was running toward me. I stumbled back.

He made a grab for me and I dodged, managing to land a kick as I did. He doubled over as the wind was knocked out of him. Apparently physical blows could penetrate his shield. Ha, take that, magic!

"Tekgrrl?"

I looked over to see Luke approaching. "It's okay," I said—but then the vampire grabbed me by the hair and yanked me close. It was the second time in recent history that I had been grabbed from behind, and I made a silent promise to myself to never ever turn my back on a villain again.

"I'll drain her, Sensei," Goth Boy snarled. "Step back."

Luke took a few steps back, hands in the air. "Let's all stay cool."

"Don't use your patronizing negotiator tactics on me," Count Cranium said. "Now, you two heroes are going to do what I say."

The very fact that I was going to get munched by a psychic vampire pissed me off. And how humiliating, being taken out by a minor villain in front of the guy I was trying to get over. My headache was back with a vengeance, and I was again feeling like someone shoved an ice pick into my brain.

I focused the pain and humiliation into rage at the villain yanking my hair. I hated Count Cranium, and hated his stupid name and stupid vampire getup, and most importantly, I hated his stupid medallion. I wanted to rip that stupid medallion off of his neck and throw it on the ground and stomp on it until it was nothing but itty-bitty pieces. And then I'd smash *him* into itty-bitty pieces.

Something round and metallic came flying over my shoulder and skidded across the sidewalk. The villain released his hold on my hair. "What the hell? How'd you do that?" I turned to see he no longer wore his medallion.

Without knowing what I was doing, I threw all of my remaining rage at him. The villain flew off his feet and slammed into the mailbox behind him, making a huge dent in it, and he crumpled to the ground, moaning. Luke leapt forward and rendered him unconscious with a nerve-pinch maneuver he had perfected.

I immediately whirled and threw up in the gutter. I felt light-headed, like I might pass out. Stumbling to my hands and knees I breathed deep, trying to focus on staying conscious. The blinding pain in my head slowly receded until it was only a dull throb.

"What was that, Mindy?" Luke's quiet voice brought

my attention back, and I found I was able to stand up again.

"I-I don't know," I said, shaking but managing to walk over to where the medallion now lay, shattered to nothing but itty-bitty pieces.

"Was it someone else? Is there some other hero around?" he called out. He was gazing to his right and left, looking nervous.

I shook my head. "I don't think so." I remembered the ghost in my lab. The instruments floating in the air, the light switch shutting off a split second before I wanted. The scrambler turning on when I couldn't reach. "Is it possible to develop powers late in life?"

Luke shrugged. "You're the scientist, you tell me." His eyes widened. "You think you're developing powers?"

"It was, like, something psychic." I looked down at the unconscious villain. "I was just so mad at him and the situation, and I kept thinking that I wanted to rip that stupid magic medallion off his neck and beat the tar out of him."

"And you did." Was it my imagination, or did Luke look scared?

I bit my lip. "I don't know. I was certainly focusing my rage on him. Like a telekinetic or telepath would."

"And you've never displayed any sort of telekinesis before?"

I shook my head. "No, I was tested when I was young. I'm just smart; that's all. No powers."

Luke stared off into the distance for a moment. Then, clearly not relishing his words, he asked, "Do you think this has something to do with your aliens?"

I cringed. "I hope not." But in the back of my mind I believed he was right. Even though the tests Paul had run detected nothing, I was beginning to wonder if those aliens hadn't blocked something else in me besides memories, and those blocks were now failing.

"You need to go tell Paul right now. I'll take care of this guy, but you need to make sure everything's all right," Luke was saying.

"Everything doesn't have to be about the aliens, you know," I growled, my nerves jangling. "Maybe I'm just developing powers late in life. It could happen!"

Luke looked as if he didn't believe that any more than I did. "You need to go see Paul," he repeated.

"No, I don't! Paul said I could stay on roster as long as nothing unusual happened. If I tell him about this, not only will he do a bunch more tests, he'll take me off the team!" I had just gotten back on the streets, I didn't want to be taken off again.

Luke's mouth was a thin line. "Maybe he needs to, Mindy."

I stared at him in shock. His words hurt me more than I could say. I couldn't believe he would suggest I wasn't fit for duty.

A sound like a teleporter buzzed behind me, a split second before I heard, "Hey, guys!"

Luke's face immediately brightened. "What are you doing out on patrol, baby?"

"Making sure you're not getting into trouble, sugar," Selena replied. Their relationship had barely started, and they already had pet names? Gag me.

"We just took care of this guy," Luke said, motioning to the unconscious villain. "I was just about to take him in and Mindy was heading home to talk to Paul." His eyes narrowed on me.

Selena gave me a questioning look. "Is everything okay?"

"Everything's fine," I said, in a fake bright tone. I didn't want to go into the whole thing with Selena, who was nice but not a superclose friend. I didn't even know if I wanted to talk to my best friends about my condition.

I gave Luke an equally sharp look. "I'm fine."

"Well, do you mind if I tag along while you escort this man to jail?" Selena asked.

Luke grinned. "I wouldn't mind the company." He turned back to me. "Go on home and talk to Paul, Mindy. I'll see you later." He and Selena typed coordinates into their transporters and soon shimmered out of sight, taking the unconscious villain with them.

I frowned. I couldn't believe Luke thought it might be better for me to be off the team. Weird new powers and blinding headaches and nightmares aside, there wasn't anything interfering with my work. The new powers certainly weren't a deterrent to fighting crime. And really, why did Luke think he could just boss me around? He wasn't my father or my husband or even our team leader. He had no right to tell me what to do!

On the other hand, maybe it wasn't just bossiness. While I had to admit I was prickly where my "condition" was concerned, I was also rational enough to know that there was some truth in what he had to say. Weird new powers didn't just occur in people past puberty unless there was some sort of outside intervention. Powers were a genetic condition that usually showed up when a person's hormones did. The very fact that they were coming out of nowhere with me was a bit troubling.

My cell phone rang, jarring me out of my worries. I pulled my cell phone from its holster on my belt. "Hello?"

"Hey, girl, where are you?" It was Toby, and by his boisterous voice and the background noise he was in a bar and likely on his third mojito.

"Just finished putting a villain to bed," I said.

"So, you're off duty?"

"For the foreseeable future," I replied.

"What?"

"Nothing."

"Well get your cute little butt on over to Cozumel's."

Okay, maybe he was on his fourth mojito.

"I don't know, Toby," I hedged. "I'm still in uniform and I don't really feel like partying tonight." Despite my words, I starting to walk in that direction.

"Honey, I've seen women wearing crazier getups than yours already in here, and they're trying to make a fashion statement, not rid the world of crime. Their fashion sense *is* the crime."

"Tobe, exactly how much have you had to drink? You're really starting to sound like a stereotype."

"Come on, quit sassing me and get your butt over here!"

I had to smile. "All right. I'm on my way."

Paul and my possible suspension could wait.

CHAPTER FOURTEEN

Cozumel's was packed, as promised by Toby, with women wearing much stranger clothing than my uniform. By the time I passed a woman wearing a silver dress that looked like chain mail and barely covered the essentials, I was no longer the least bit concerned that I would stick out. In fact, I was beginning to wonder how Toby looked in the suit he likely wore.

The club was one of those former warehouses seemingly converted into a hot spot overnight. Tables and couches where glamorous men and women lounged sipping brightly colored drinks were scattered randomly near the bar, leaving a rather large space open as the dance floor where half of the club patrons were packed, sweating and writhing to the music the DJ was playing.

I fought my way to the bar to flag down the bartender, and received my own electric neon drink served in an oversized martini glass. Sipping it, I looked around, trying to find Toby in this madhouse.

I did a double take when I finally picked him out of the crowd. He was slow-dancing with a lean man with close-cropped sandy brown hair, but that wasn't the shocking part. I would have been more shocked if he hadn't picked up some young hottie already; no, the shocking part was my normally conservative friend wearing black leather pants and a tight black long-sleeve shirt.

I wove through the crowd. Tapping on Toby's shoulder, I interrupted with, "Raiding Lainey's wardrobe?"

Toby turned and saw me. "Hey, you made it!" He eased away from his dance partner to lean down and kiss me on the cheek.

I kissed him back with a wry smile. "Yeah, I made it all the way to the alternate universe where you wear leather."

He turned red. "Shut up."

"Are you going through a midlife crisis or something?"

He frowned. "It's not like my work clothes are any tighter or more ridiculous than this."

He had a point, but I couldn't resist teasing him. "Toby, sweetie, I think once you hit forty there's a law against you wearing leather pants unless you're a biker or a rock star. And if you start wearing them, Paul might start wearing them, and then I'm going to be psychologically scarred for life."

"Please. Paul couldn't pull off this look. And by all means, please keep mentioning my advanced age in front of my boyfriend."

"Boyfriend?" I looked back at the guy he'd been dancing with, who had been standing by in silence all this time. I did another double take. "Forrest?"

The EHJ's political liaison smiled at me. "Hello, Mindy."

Toby gave me a sheepish look. "We've been seeing each other since he came down for the big meeting."

I shook my head. "Wow. Keep a secret much?"

"That's why I wanted you to meet us here. I thought it was time my best friend knew."

I looked at Forrest. "As the best friend, I am required by law to remind you that if you hurt him, I'll hurt you."

Forrest nodded. "Of course."

"Always good to get that out of the way." I smiled. "Well, then, I'm happy for you guys."

Toby hugged me. "Thanks, Min."

"Like you needed my blessing anyway." I hugged him back. "You do realize that I'm mad at you now, right? I am officially the only single person left on this team."

Toby made a face. "I'm sorry. I think that calls for a drink."

"I'll get it," Forrest interjected. "Mindy?"

"Something nonradioactive," I said, passing him the bizarre drink I'd initially been served.

"Get me a mineral water, darlin'. I think I've had enough tonight," Toby said.

"Got it. One mineral water and one nonradioactive drink." Forrest leaned up to give Toby a brief kiss. "Grab us a table." He headed off to fight his way through the mob.

I sighed. "Ah, young love."

"Shut up." Toby gave me a goofy smile. He was definitely smitten.

We fought our way through the crowd to find an empty table. I made a dive just as another guy went for it at the same time. I perched on the chair and gave him a defiant look. He looked like he was going to say something, but then noticed Toby glowering at him and decided against it.

"And once again, your bad-boy looks save the day," I joked. "Forrest is one lucky politician."

Toby took the seat opposite me. "I knew you were going to say something about that."

"I'm just teasing. I never would have thought you'd date anyone in politics."

"Neither did I, actually. My family has a long history of disliking politics."

"This'll be harder to explain than the coming out," I

said. "Your mom's going to ask why you can't date some nice Southern businessman."

"Tell me about it."

"Paul or Wesley could possibly have a meltdown about you sleeping with the enemy."

"Forrest isn't the enemy!"

"No, but neither Paul nor Wesley is exactly thrilled by this committee thing. Especially since Simon's heading it. It might be guilt by association."

"I'll just remind them Forrest's the one looking out for our best interests. We need every friend in Washington we can get."

"Every friend-with-benefits, you mean." I winked. "But you know I'm thrilled for you. He's really cute."

"I know. I have excellent taste in men."

I rolled my eyes. "I have to admit I'd much rather watch you two make out and make goo-goo eyes at each other than Luke and Selena."

Toby made a face. "Luke took off on you to go out with her tonight?"

I nodded. "After we bagged the bad guy."

"Well . . . I thought you were over Luke."

I shrugged. "I'm trying to be."

Forrest reappeared with new drinks. "A G&T and a mineral water." He sat them down in front of us.

"Thanks," I said, taking a sip. Much better.

"Like the table?" Toby said, gesturing. "I had to use my powers of intimidation to get it."

"Sexy." Forrest took the chair next to him. "So, what was going on tonight?"

I shrugged. "Had to fight a psychic vampire. I ended up kicking him in the stomach, and Luke had to nerve-pinch him to knock him out." I conveniently left out the part where I psychically lashed out.

Forrest nudged Toby. "See what you miss when you play hooky?"

This was new. "Paul doesn't know you took the night off?"

Toby shook his head. "And don't you dare tell him, either."

I sat back in my chair and took a sip of my drink. "What'll you give me?"

Forrest laughed. "You two sound like teenagers sneaking out of the house. Daddy's waiting!"

"What it feels like sometimes." If they only knew what I was hiding tonight. My head started pounding again in remembrance.

"It's got to be hard to hold a team together, especially one as powerful and important as the Elite Hands of Justice," Forrest was saying. "That's a lot of responsibility, even when it is divided up between two people."

Toby patted Forrest's leg. "He's used to men in power acting like dictators and treating their underlings like children."

"You're not going to go off on the corruption of power again, are you?" Forrest replied.

They were all ready bickering good-naturedly like an old married couple. I had a feeling this was a relationship that was going to last. Good for Toby. Bad for me. I no longer had anyone to commiserate with about my old-maid status. I glanced around the club, checking out the men who didn't have a woman attached. I hadn't dated anyone, serious or not, in months. Maybe that's why those nightmares were coming back. At least with a man in my bed, I had enough distraction to chase the bad dreams away, if only temporarily.

A sharp pain spiked through me so hard I couldn't

see straight. I groaned and grasped my head in both hands, as if that would help.

As if from far away, I heard Toby say, "Whoa, Mindy, are you all right?"

Another spike went through me, drowning out all of the background noise in a weird sort of hum, almost like white noise on a television, a hissing that started out soft and grew to a roar with every surge.

I see you.

It came through so loud and clear, like I had turned all other sound off in the room. I jumped up and actually looked for the speaker.

No one will defend you.

The pain was intensifying as I looked around, searching out the voice. I was dimly aware of Toby trying to grab me but I shook him off. I had to know—

No one will protect you.

—who was talking to me—

You're all alone.

—and how.

Laughter seemed to boom in my head, blocking out everything else, all of reality, until I wanted to push, hit, and do anything to get it out of my head and away from me.

"Shut up," I whispered as the laughter continued. "Shut up!"

I lashed out again, mentally, with all of the fear and pain that I had in me. It was like when I fought the psychic vampire: I didn't realize how I was doing it, only that I was.

Brick, cement and steel erupted from the wall across from me, directly in my line of sight, as a huge dent appeared, as if a large invisible fist had punched it. I was dimly aware of patrons screaming, running past me, mass chaos ensuing. They were panicked, afraid that a terrorist had attacked, that a bomb had gone off, that a villain was going to try to take them hostage. Of course, it was all too much. I couldn't take any more.

"Mindy, what the hell?" Toby's voice was the last thing I heard before the world went black.

CHAPTER FIFTEEN

I woke to the sound of raised voices. Groaning, I opened blurry eyes to try to pinpoint who exactly was shouting. It sounded like Paul, but I had never heard him use that much profanity.

"Oh, good, you're awake," Lainey said, and I rose up in bed to see that Lainey and Emily had made themselves comfortable in my room and were settled in a chair pulled up next to my bed, watching a cartoon that seemed to revolve around a yellow square wearing a chef's hat. Regardless of the cartoon and the fact my door was closed, I could still hear the argument, which, now that I was more aware, seemed to be going on between Paul, Toby and Wesley.

"It remains to be seen as to whether or not that's good," I said. "What's going on?"

Lainey turned her attention to her baby, who was drooling and alternately pounding her fists on a plush version of the square on television. With every blow, the toy let out a high-pitched giggle. Socialized sadism at its finest.

"Em, stop. You're giving Mommy a headache."

"Mommy's dodging Aunt Mindy's question," I remarked.

Lainey sighed. "Your, um, incident made the news."

I winced. "Oh, no."

"There were multiple injuries, both when the building got damaged and in the aftermath. People were trampling each other to get out."

I felt my stomach flip. *I* had caused people to get hurt. "I didn't mean to. It was an accident!"

"I know, Min. But Luke told Paul that you had something similar happen earlier, and that he told you to go home and have it checked out."

That explained the yelling. Paul had to be furious with me.

"It doesn't help any that Simon held a press conference this morning saying he was going to address 'problems caused by heroes in matters such as this' in committee, and that he'd 'investigate the incident further.'"

Paul was probably going to go nuclear on me. I'd be lucky to keep my job after this.

I felt a tear slide down my cheek. I rarely cried, but the pain and trauma of the last month or so was really starting to kick in. "I really screwed up, Lainey."

"Oh, Mindy." My friend reached over to squeeze my hand. Emily frowned, like she couldn't figure out why there was water running down my face.

"I don't know why this is happening," I said, giving in and letting the tears come. If you can't cry in front of your best girlfriend, who can you cry in front of? "Or why now. How can everything go seemingly normal for sixteen years and then just one day fall apart?"

"Paul and Wes know you can't control these new powers; you're just like any teenager. There's been plenty of collateral damage and even fatalities before because of the newly powered, and there have been plenty of messes to be cleaned up afterward, so it's not like this is a problem never before seen. The only thing different . . ."

"Is that it's me," I finished for her. "I'm one of the

A-list, and nothing like that is supposed to happen with us. The media's going to drag me and the rest of the team through the mud. And it's all my fault." I wiped my eyes.

"It's not your fault that aliens screwed with your DNA and then tried to make that disappear by blocking you, Mindy. That is not your fault. And Paul and Wes know that too."

"There's still going to be fallout. With the press. With Simon." I shook my head. "You know he's not going to let this go."

"He's not as bad as we all make him out to be," Lainey said. "He was a greedy, spotlight-grabbing opportunist, but that's all. He's not all bad. He did come back to help in our fight with the Dragon, and he saved you."

"He was in trouble with us and the government," I pointed out. "How do we know it was out of the goodness of his heart and not a way to generate good publicity for himself?"

Lainey shrugged. "You worked with him for a lot longer than I ever did. You tell me."

The door was flung open and Paul walked in, eyes burning. "Tell your boyfriend we'll take it, then," he was saying to Toby.

"You know, he's only trying to help," Toby retorted. "He's been back in Washington since last night running damage control."

"I know, Toby, it's okay," said Wesley, trying to play peacemaker, which was a bit of a weird change of pace. "Go ahead and call him, tell him we'll be there."

"Yes, sir." Toby turned and walked out of the room, phone at his ear. He never said a word to me.

"Good, she's awake," Paul said, finally focusing on me. I wished he wouldn't, though, from the looks he was giving me. "How can someone as incredibly brilliant as you make such stupid decisions, Mindy?"

I frowned. "I didn't mean for all of that to happen, Paul. I don't even know how I'm doing whatever it is I'm doing, let alone how to control it."

"No, but you were told by a teammate to go home and let me check you out. And you had a similar experience earlier, so even if Luke hadn't said something, common sense would dictate that you come right to me. Especially after I told you specifically to come to me should anything occur."

"I was afraid," I admitted.

"Of what?"

"That you'd take me off the team."

"What do you think is going to happen now?" Paul growled. "You don't honestly expect that I'll keep sending you out into action and among the general populace like this."

My blood pressure pounded in my ears. "You're firing me?"

"No, I'm sidelining you," Paul said, burying his hands in his jacket pockets and turning away.

"We have to, Mindy," Wesley said. "It's for your own safety and the general public's. And we need to talk about those mental blocks."

"We have to go clean this mess up in Washington first," Paul put in.

"Wait, what mess in Washington?" Lainey asked.

"Paul and I have to go meet with Simon and the rest of his committee," Wesley told her. "They're concerned."

"Like we're getting called into the goddamn principal's office," Paul snapped, pacing back and forth in front of my bed.

"It's stupid political posturing," Wesley assured me. "Nothing we can't handle."

"We have to go kowtow to Simon Leasure, and that turns my stomach," Paul corrected.

"Do you honestly think *I'm* bowing down to Simon Leasure?" Wesley shook his head. "We'll let them know we're handling it and that's that." He frowned and turned to look at me. "I'm just going to check you, Mindy, see what can be done about these blocks."

As I lay still on the bed, Wesley closed his eyes and, speaking in soft Italian, ran a hand over the top of me without touching, like he was doing a medical scan. He concentrated most on my head. Still with his eyes closed, he said to me in English, "Try to reach those blocked memories, Mindy."

I did as he asked, and immediately a sharp pain burst through my brain.

"Is that like what happens when you access your new powers?" Wesley asked.

"No, it's totally different. It's like . . . when I'm upset or angry that they hit like that."

"Well, try to go there," Wesley said.

I thought of the pain I had brought on those poor people at the club, and of my anger that was out of my control. I felt my skin vibrate slightly.

Wesley nodded. "I think we need to take those blocks down," he said to the others. "She might be able to access the part of her mind that lets her control those new powers."

"How'd Mindy get new powers?" Lainey asked.

Paul gave me a look like I was a specimen on a tray. "It's possible that when the Kalybri were, for lack of a better word, tinkering with her, they accidentally unlocked powers that were latent, that were never meant to be accessed. It may have been genetic coding that should have passed down to her children that instead got yanked to the surface now."

Though I'd had similar lines of reasoning, I hated how he rattled that off, all cool and detached. It was my life he was talking about!

"The powers are currently being accessed in times of severe stress," Wesley said. "So it's subconscious right now, like her dream-memory retrieval. We take down the blocks, she might be able to control them consciously."

"Yeah, but after what happened yesterday, I'm afraid if we take down the blocks, she might get worse," Paul said. "Her parents were concerned that she would go insane, and that's *all* we need, for her to become insane and wield powers like a psychic hammer."

"The blocks are going to fail anyway," Wesley pointed out.

"We don't need to speed along the process, at least not right now with the government breathing down our necks," Paul said, barely sparing me a glance. "We need to just monitor her to make sure it doesn't get any worse and keep her out of the line of fire until we get this mess straightened out."

"I can't live like this anymore," I said, since they were ignoring me. "Not knowing what happened, and now having these powers I can't control and that I don't know where they came from . . ." I looked at Wesley. "You've *got* to take these blocks down."

He frowned. "I don't know if I can, Mindy. They were put in using alien technology and psychic abilities, neither with magic. I'm going to have to circumvent the system, and my power's not what it used to be."

"Just try, please, Wesley," I said, begging and not even

caring at the moment. "I would rather risk insanity than live white-knuckled, fearing that I'm going to accidentally hurt someone."

Paul looked at his watch. "We literally don't have time for this. We have to get to Washington ASAP." He frowned at me. "I know it goes against your rebellious attitude, but you're just going to have to accept that you're not in the position to make decisions on what's best, Mindy."

I stared at him, openmouthed. "It's my life. My mind."

"Your last decision caused more than ten people to be hospitalized."

That stung. I sat back, inwardly seething.

Wesley shook his head. "As much as it pains me to say so, I agree with Paul in that we have to deal with one crisis at a time."

Paul shot him a glare. "Thanks."

"Right now, we've got to deal with the aftermath of what happened," Wesley continued. "You're in the safest place you can possibly be—with your friends—and if the blocks fail, they fail. If they stay put . . . well, we can pick up where we left off once this matter is settled."

"Doesn't anyone care about what I think?" I asked.

Paul gave me a cold look. "Not right now, no."

"Wes, it might be safer to just take them down now," Lainey said. "Poor Mindy's a danger to herself and others, and if taking down the blocks will give her control . . ."

"But we don't know that it will," Paul argued. "And we have got to go."

"They'll wait, Paul," Lainey snapped, using a tone of voice I rarely heard from her. "Maybe the reason this happened is because you didn't deal with this crisis in the first place."

"What did you expect me to do, Lainey?" Paul growled.

"We're dealing with alien technology that not even your husband, the smartest man on earth, is sure he can fix."

"You can't just sit there and not do anything for her. She's in pain! If you—"

Selena tapped on the door and walked in, interrupting, giving cautious glances at all of us. "The car's here," she reported.

"We'll figure out the best course of action later," Paul said, and he turned to leave.

"Wes?" Lainey looked imploringly at him.

"I'll do what I can, when I can," Wesley said, leaning forward to kiss her and then drop a kiss on Emily's head. "I promise." He hurried out the door with Paul.

I burst into tears. I couldn't help it; I was scared and upset by the whole ordeal, and by how they had acted around me, like I was someone unstable and dangerous.

And maybe I was.

"They wouldn't listen," I sniffled.

Lainey's lips were a thin, determined line. "Wesley might be too busy, but I know someone who isn't. You feel up to a short trip?"

I nodded. "If it'll help get rid of these blocks, hell, yes."

She picked up Emily and headed out of my bedroom, dragging me into the main area of my living quarters. "Tobe? Selena?" she called.

Toby appeared from the kitchen. "What's up?"

"Mindy and I have to go out. I need you watch Emily."

Toby frowned. "Are you sure that's a good idea?"

I was crushed by his reaction. "What, you don't trust me? Are you going to be like Paul now?" I hissed.

Toby sighed, pushing his hands into his pockets. "You didn't see yourself, Mindy. It was scary."

Great, now my best friend feared me. I tried to stifle the tears that threatened to well up.

"Well, I'm trying to take care of her so she doesn't have another incident like that." Lainey handed over Emily. "Now, we'll be back."

"Where are you going?" Kate asked. We bumped into her while trying to leave my quarters. I was a bit surprised to see her; ever since the start of whatever problems she and Paul were having, the normally outgoing goddess had turned inward and begun avoiding contact with the rest of us.

"Out," Lainey said. "To get some help for Mindy."

"Uh-huh." Kate eyed me. "Sounds like she needs it."

I glared at her. "Thanks."

Her cold glance swept over me. "Well, what would you say if *I* put ten people in the hospital?"

"Actually, why don't you come with us, Kate?" Lainey suggested. Both Kate and I reacted like she had suggested something perverse, but she continued: "If Mindy does lose it after the blocks come down, I could use your help."

"Why her?" I asked.

Lainey addressed Kate. "Your powers of making people fall in love with you and do what you want—does it only work on men?"

"Not necessarily," Kate admitted. "As long as they're not already in love, I can enchant a man or a woman."

"Hold on, I'm not wired that way," I said, holding up a hand. "And even if I was, Kate certainly wouldn't be my type."

"Romantic love isn't the only type," Lainey suggested. "What about parental love?"

Kate shrugged. "I guess. I never really considered it before; I just assumed it was limited to romantic love."

"And you're not that close to your mother," Lainey

said to me. "So it could work. If nothing else, it will help to have another superstrong person there to hold you down."

"True." I gave Kate a fake smile. "And you are old enough to be my mother."

Kate sighed. "Why not? I'm not doing anything else tonight." She frowned, then asked, "Wait, what did Paul say about it?"

"He doesn't know," Lainey admitted. "He wanted to wait until this crisis with the government was settled."

"So he didn't approve?"

Lainey shook her head.

Kate grinned, the first such expression I had seen from her in a while. "I'm definitely in."

CHAPTER SIXTEEN

"We're going to a biker bar?" Kate asked, looking around.

Lainey shook her head. "No. We're going down an alleyway *by* the biker bar."

"Sorry to disappoint," I said, stepping up next to Kate. "I know you were looking for a date for Friday night to make Paul jealous."

"Please. Like Paul cares anymore," Kate said with what sounded like a hint of sadness. But when she turned to face me, her face was blank. "We're through."

I was shocked. Even though they'd had problems, they'd been *the* power couple for a while now and I didn't doubt their feelings for each other. I didn't think they'd ever break up for real and this news rocked me. "Serious?"

"As a heart attack." Kate's face was grave. "He wanted a commitment I couldn't give him. I needed to let him go since it wasn't meant to be."

"I'm sorry," I said, actually meaning it. I liked to torment Kate in a weird little-sister to big-sister way, and while I might be jealous of her good looks and the fact that she could get any guy she wanted—including the one I did—I'd never harbored any ill will. And it was a bit sad to think that, with her powers, she knew their love wasn't meant to last.

She shrugged. "Gods know it's my fault. He deserves better."

I didn't know what to say about that, so decided to change the subject. "Lainey, where are we going, exactly?"

"To visit the most powerful magic user since Wesley's rebirth," Lainey said, walking down the alley and scrutinizing the wall.

"The most powerful magic user is a bum?" I asked, glancing around.

"Or a biker?" Kate put in.

"No, the most powerful magic user lives in a pocket universe," Lainey explained. "Ah, there it is. Almost missed it. Here we go. Hold on to my hand, you two."

We each took one of her hands and started walking, seemingly into the wall, and suddenly we were somewhere else entirely. Kate and I exchanged surprised glances and took in our surroundings.

We were in a bar that looked like it had been decorated by someone with serious fetishes. The walls and floors were covered in thick red velvet, contrasting with black leather chairs around slick metallic and dark mahogany tables. Patrons perched in those chairs. The only light came from the flickering candles dispersed across every available surface, which meant the faces of the patrons were concealed to the casual observer, which was probably the point.

Lainey stopped one of the twig-thin and unearthly pale waitstaff. "We're here to see Fantazia."

The androgynous waiter smirked. "You and everyone else, miss."

"She'll see me."

"In due time." The waiter started to pass, but Lainey stepped in front of him.

"Tell her Lainey Livingston-Charles is here."

The waiter nodded. "Take a seat. Someone will be with you shortly."

"Thank you." Lainey took the table he pointed out, and Kate and I filed in next to her. Kate was just as silent as I, which was comforting: At least I wasn't the only one who felt out of her element.

"What is this place, Lainey?" I asked.

"Switzerland for the magic set," she said, waving away the goblet of wine a server offered. "Fantazia doesn't take sides amongst the magic community. Good or bad, she'll do anyone a favor. For a price."

Kate smiled at the server and took the wine. "I've heard of her, but I've never met her in all these centuries."

"According to Wes, she dropped out of polite society a while back," Lainey said. "Just likes to stay here and have the magic users owe her."

"You think she'll take these mental blocks down for me?" I asked.

"If we agree to her price," Lainey said. "Who knows what she'll want, though. Or when she'll want it."

I didn't know if I liked owing someone so much. "We don't have to do this, Lainey. We can wait until Wesley can give it a go."

"Wesley isn't sure if he can take them down," Lainey pointed out. "Besides, he trusts Fantazia."

"She'll see you now," the androgynous waiter said, appearing out of nowhere. We all stood up to follow him back into the VIP suite, which was a back room curtained off from the rest of the bar.

This time the walls and floor were black velvet, with two bright red couches facing one another in the center of the room. A spotlight hung over them, giving a weird feeling like the area was floating in space.

A woman that rivaled Kate in gorgeousness lounged on one of the couches, sipping wine from an elaborate goblet. Her long brown hair and dark eyes only set off ruby red lips. She was wearing a black corset and leather miniskirt that showed off her assets, and fishnets and black boots that seemed like they should come with a whip. Her skin seemed to glitter, and it was only as we came closer that I saw that was because her skin was adorned with symbols and letters painted in gold. Seeing us, she handed the goblet to one of the men who were silent walls of solid muscle on either side of her— bodyguards or boy toys, I couldn't tell.

"Well, well. Hello . . . Mrs. Charles, is it? I can never remember the name." She stood up and walked over to us and gave Lainey a cool embrace. "I'm sorry I missed the wedding, but I've never been one for ceremony." She motioned for us to take a seat on the couch opposite where she'd been sitting. "To what do I owe the unexpected pleasure of a visit from the Old One's current group of cronies?"

"My friend, Tekgrrl, has been the subject of memory blocks," Lainey said, motioning to me. "They were put in place using alien technology, and Wesley believes they might be circumvented and taken down with magic."

"But he wasn't sure he could do it anymore?" Fantazia's lips curled into a strange smile. "See what your life cost him?"

Lainey's expression was fierce, but she asked simply, "Do you think you can do it or not?"

Fantazia stood up and glided over to me. As she approached, I shrank back in my seat. The aura of power radiating from her practically burned. She might look as young as any of us, but like Kate, her eyes practically screamed that she was ancient and powerful.

She bent over me and cupped her hands around my

head without touching. *"La mia mente ad il vostro,"* she said, like Italian was her native language. Now that I thought of it, it probably was.

I felt a faint buzzing in the back of my mind, like hearing a badly tuned radio. A spike of pain ran through me, and I groaned.

Fantazia straightened and looked at Lainey. "Yes, I see it. It would normally take quite a number of magic users to circumvent such strange, otherworldly work."

"But?" Lainey prompted.

"I can do it if the techno mage will help," she said. When she motioned for one of her henchmen, he stepped forward and she directed: "Go find the Virus." With a slight nod, he disappeared into the other room.

"So, what's this going to cost?" Lainey asked.

Fantazia took her seat across from us again. She tapped one black-polished nail upon her red lips. "Something fairly simple for you, Mrs. Charles. I want to be able to spend some time with your child."

Lainey's lips thinned to a straight line. "Why would you want that?"

Fantazia's hand fluttered to her breast. "A better question is why wouldn't I? It's not every day one gets to be in the presence of a person who will decide the fate of the world."

We all knew about the prophecy that said Emily would either bring about the apocalypse or save the world from it, but it had never sounded more serious than when this ancient magic user said it. A shiver ran down my spine. Lainey seemed taken aback.

"And besides," Fantazia continued. "She *is* my half sister."

Kate and I both turned to gape at Lainey. The Reincarnist was this strange woman's father?

Lainey ignored us, keeping her eyes fixed on Fantazia. After a moment of silence, she said, "If your father doesn't care, fine."

Kate and I exchanged glances. What other surprises were we going to be hit with?

The bodyguard Fantazia had sent into the other room reappeared, escorting a stocky bald man whose arms were covered in binary language tattoos. "Cyrus the Virus," the bodyguard said, and then resumed his position next to Fantazia's couch. I thought I vaguely remembered seeing the bald guy in our criminal files.

"Cyrus. Good to see you're lurking about, abusing my hospitality," Fantazia said.

"Whatever this is, it had better be good," the newcomer replied, seemingly unimpressed and uncowed. "I had a great hand in the poker game you just interrupted and I've got rent to pay." Seeing Lainey sitting there, he grimaced. "What's the Old One's wife want?"

"It's time for you to return my favor," Fantazia said. She gestured to me. "You'll like the job."

Cyrus the Virus was a techno mage and a classic villain—one who had used his powers to steal money so he didn't have to hold a conventional job. And like every other villain who got into the game out of laziness, he was eventually caught by another team and sent to jail. He had already paid off his debt to society and had supposedly gone legit—if playing poker for your rent is legit.

Cyrus looked me up and down like I was a treat. "Very nice. If the job involves me, her, and a can of whipped cream, I think I love you, Fantazia."

An involuntary gasp escaped me, and I fought revulsion.

Fantazia gave him an exasperated look. "No, idiot. She's had memory blocks erected using alien technology. We're going to break them down."

"Really?" The Virus looked interested. "Wicked cool."

"Have a look around," Fantazia said, with a wave of her hand at me.

"Don't mind if I do." Cyrus approached. I gave Lainey a hesitant glance. After a moment's consideration, she nodded. Glumly, I leaned forward to accept my fate.

Cyrus the Virus copied Fantazia's earlier movement, cupping hands around my head but not touching. Looking directly into my eyes, he spoke softly: "I open my mind to the technological world. I speak its language; I see its pattern." His eyes glowed with a strange green light. Nothing else seemed to happen, and then I felt a buzzing in the back of my mind, only louder.

"Oh, yeah, I see it," he said. "Wow. That's some handiwork." He peered into my eyes, but not at them, looking almost through me. I twitched uncomfortably in my seat.

"Excellent," Fantazia said, getting up. "Ladies, I need you to move so that she can lie down, and I need one of you at her feet and one at her arms. We'll probably need you to hold her in place."

At that bit of good news, my heart started pounding furiously, but I did as I was told, palms sweating, head pounding and already feeling more than a bit nauseated.

Fantazia and Cyrus took their places on either side of my head.

"I won't lie," Fantazia remarked. "This is going to hurt like hell. And I can't guarantee what you'll be like when we're done. Are you sure you want to do this?"

You'll go insane from what they did to you, my mother had warned. I wanted to scream no, that I could just wait until the blocks broke down naturally or something else happened, but I knew in my heart that I had to go through with this.

As I couldn't find my voice, I nodded my acceptance.

Fantazia patted my head like a small child, which I guess to her I was. "It'll all be over soon, one way or the other . . ." She looked up at Cyrus. "Ready?"

He nodded, eyes glistening. "Oh, hell yeah."

Fantazia grinned. "Let's do this. *E' ora di abbatterie i muri.*"

Both of their hands plunged to my temples and forehead.

I started screaming.

CHAPTER SEVENTEEN

I sat at my desk in the formal classroom, chairs lined up in a row facing the teacher. I particularly stood out, looking like a ghost in my improperly fitting white linen, wide-sleeved unisex shirt and pants, the requisite uniform of every student.

I wanted to make a good impression for all of humankind, so I sat quietly at my desk, spine ramrod straight, glancing at the holo-pad in front of me, mentally changing the swooping curls and symbols of Kalybrian script into English numbers and letters.

It was a lovely, inviting spring day outside, and I had the misfortune to be seated next to an open window. With every breeze, spicy and exotic scents wafted in, practically begging me to go romp in the lovely weather, perhaps play with my foster brother and sister a game of drakenball, a sport somewhat like football and baseball combined that all the young teens my age played. Or perhaps I could spend the afternoon with my foster mother making likchen, an ice-cream-like delicacy of Kalybri.

Despite the fact that I was on an alien planet, my life here was the most normal it had ever been. I had brothers and sisters, I went to school and did homework before helping my mother prepare dinner, and was currently learning from my father how Kalybrian transportation vehicles worked. I was happy.

"Man-dei, do you know the answer?" As always, the teacher spoke in Kalybrian, and my name sounded foreign with her strange accent, but my mind translated.

"That was in stardate twenty-three, one-eighty-nine, madam," I responded.

She nodded. "Thank you, Man-dei."

The wind blew harder now, like a storm was coming. Sure enough, as I glanced outside, the formerly bright day had darkened, like a group of clouds had suddenly appeared. Strange, but I didn't think anything of it until a few seconds later when harsh sirens sounded. Everyone looked up, concerned.

Our teacher looked the most worried. "Probably just a drill, children," she said, but her voice quavered. "Let's conduct ourselves in an orderly fashion. You need to return to your domiciles immediately. Do not go anywhere else. Curfew has been instituted for everyone."

We had never been told to return home before in our drills, or had a curfew, and I noticed the ripple of excitement and worry in the student body. This was out of the ordinary and strange, but like all children, we were thrilled to be getting out early.

As I followed the other students out into the hall, I heard my name being called, and turned. Anyoska, my foster sister, came up to me.

"I wonder what's going on," she said.

"So, this isn't usual?" I asked, even though I knew it wasn't.

"Maybe father will know," Anyoska mused. "My teacher said they called curfew for the whole village."

"Sounds serious."

Anyoska nodded. "Maybe there's a bad storm coming."

As soon as we stepped outside, we knew why it was

dark. There was a giant black spaceship hanging in the sky overhead.

"Maker save us," Anyoska breathed.

"What the hell is that?" I said.

"Come on!" She grabbed my hand, knocking my data pads out of my grasp and yanking me toward her home.

"Wait, my schoolwork!"

"Leave it!" she hissed, dragging me along.

"Anyoska, what's going on?"

"We're being invaded."

We ran.

"Anyoska, Man-dei! Thank the Maker," said my foster brother, Dyvinsher, appearing out of nowhere. He was headed back the way we had come, and it was unsettling to see him carrying a weapon. The Kalybri never carried weapons; this was only the second time I had ever seen one in a whole year on their planet. "You've got to get inside."

"Who is it, Dyvinsher?" Anyoska asked.

His expression was grim. "It's the Vyqang." My foster sister's face drained of color, and I knew this was a bad thing.

And that's when the screaming began.

Men of varying colors and shapes suddenly rounded the corner of the town square behind us, dressed in ragged leather, torn flight suits and loaded up with a variety of weapons. I watched in horror as one rammed a sword through a townsperson, while another set a building ablaze with his flamethrower.

"Go!" Dyvinsher screamed, turning to face the invaders, unleashing a spray of bullets from his weapon. Anyoska's fingers bit into my arm as she pulled me away and toward her house.

We skidded to a stop near the front door. A body was lying across the front lawn, in pieces.

"Father!" Anyoska screamed, and I felt bile rise in my throat. This intelligent and kind man had met a terrible end.

A strange man-creature covered in scales and with dirty dreadlocked hair and what looked like horns coming out of his face, but on second glance turned out to be bones actually piercing his skin, stepped out of the house and caught sight of us. He raised his heavy gun and pointed it.

"Run!" I screamed to my foster sister, and we both took off. I heard a strange blasting noise from behind, and a second later the sound of a body hitting the ground. *Anyoska!* Then came another noise, and a sizzling pain hit me in the back. My body and mind went numb.

When I came to, I was lying on a cold metal floor that was also itchy. Forcing my eyes open, I noticed it was because someone had halfheartedly tossed straw down, I guess to make up for the lack of a bed. There was the sound of crying, and I looked up to see I was in a small cage barely high enough to sit up in, let alone stand.

"Man-dei?" A small form crawled toward me, and I noticed it was my foster sister.

"Anyoska!" I embraced her. "I thought that creature killed you."

She shook her head, and I noticed her eyes were glassy and dull. "The Vyqang do not kill females."

I didn't like the sound of that.

I looked around, seeing other small cages surrounding us, with weeping figures inside. Some of them housed familiar Kalybrian faces; other prisoners were strange alien species I had never seen. All of them were female. All looked scared out of their minds.

"Anyoska, where are we?" I asked.

"Aboard a Vyqang hunting ship," she said.

"Hunting? What are they hunting?"

"Us."

I shook in terror. "What do you mean, us? What's going to happen, Anyoska?" I clung to my sister in fear.

"The Vyqang are plunderers, warriors—males. No one knows their planet of origin. They travel the galaxies, raiding whatever planets they like, taking their crops, fine metals and technology for their own use." She met my eyes. "And their females."

Her unspoken meaning settled in. *"No."*

"There are no female Vyqang. They have no way to reproduce." She swallowed harshly. "For that reason, they round up the women of the planets they raid. Some become slaves or bed warmers to the Vyqang or are sold to other brutal species. The rest . . ." She broke off in tears. "The rest they turn into breeders."

I felt tears run down my face. "Stop."

"But first they . . . tinker with them," Anyoska continued, as if she had to speak the whole horrible truth. "They're not only brutal, they're smart. They study each female's genetics, the gifts of her species, and they modify her to suit their needs. They seek to produce the perfect warrior. Many females do not survive the process. The ones that do . . . well, the Vyqang take the needed reproductive matter and grow their new children in special incubation tubes. Then they either destroy the female or send her off to the slavers." Anyoska shuddered. "I don't know which is worse."

As I stared at her in horror, the sound of a door opening could be heard, and the imprisoned females all around us starting shrieking. Someone slammed a metal club against one of the cages, clearly in warning.

A pale being, almost ghostly white except with a vaguely feline look to the eyes and nose, bent in front of our cage and opened its door. He reached in with one clawed hand and grabbed Anyoska, ripping her from my grasp. I screamed and clawed after her, only to be dragged out myself and made to stand. Another creature, this one green-furred, walked down a quickly assembling line of released women, inspecting them like cattle, grabbing and pawing but with a vaguely detached, mechanical air. When he was finished, he pointed to one side of the room or the other, clearly separating them for slaving or breeding, though I couldn't tell which.

Anyoska didn't make a sound, her eyes dead as he checked her over and then pointed for her to be dragged off to the right.

Then it was my turn. The green-furred creature grabbed me by the hair and inspected my tear-filled eyes, then squeezed my jaw open to inspect my teeth. It pulled my shirt up to expose my barely developed breasts, squeezed one. I stiffened. Frowning, it reached between my legs to cup my genitals. I whimpered. It turned and said something in a harsh language to its companion, who replied, then turned back to me.

"What are you?" it asked in broken Kalybrian. "Not Kalybri."

I shook my head.

"What are you?" it repeated, harsher.

"Human," I said, voice barely above a whisper.

The alien spoke in rushed tones to its companion, and the other handed over a small mechanical device from which a blue light radiated, and the first Vyqang pointed the light at me, running it up and down my body. The device beeped, and the alien looked down at the results. With a grunt, it pointed to the right. The other alien ushered me forward, where I clung to my foster sister and wept.

The women on the left side of the room were tossed back into their cages. The women on the right side were led out into a hallway where gunmetal grey walls gave way to a series of doors. One woman was pulled from the group and taken into the first room. We all stiffened as we heard screaming, and then the alien returned alone, slamming the door behind him. It was like that at each door, my sense of dread building with each shriek of a vanished female.

At the next door, the white alien reached out and grabbed Anyoska. I held tight to her, trying to pull her back, but the alien frowned at me and brought the butt of his gun down on my hand. I screamed in pain and fear, but released her, and my sister was led into a room to disappear. No scream emerged.

I was dragged into the following room. It held nothing but a bunch of machines and a long flat steel table with all sorts of horrible-looking technology surrounding it, needles and knives and the like. I suddenly knew what we had been chosen for.

I fought for all I was worth, screaming, biting and kicking as the alien dragged me over to the table. I felt a sharp pain in my neck and then the world slid into blackness.

I couldn't figure out where that strange humming noise was coming from.

I blinked in the blinding light coming from above. How had I even fallen asleep with such a bright light right over my eyes? And what was that obnoxious humming? I tried to move my head so I could pinpoint from what direction it emitted, but found that I couldn't; I was being held still by something cold. Metal, perhaps. I tried to reach a hand to brush away whatever it was, but discovered my arms felt heavy, weighted down by something, almost like they had been numbed through anesthesia. I was aware my arms existed, but they weren't responding. A quick check determined my legs were suffering a similar fate.

Panic rose up in me, made all the worse by the blinding light and the fact that I couldn't escape it. I concentrated, that unnerving humming threatening to break my focus, and tried to move something, anything. A soft groan burned deep in my throat, and I felt pain somewhere. The more aware I became, the more my body was registering that something wasn't right, and pain rocketed through me like lightning. I moaned and tried to writhe, to get away from the discomfort, but in my state I couldn't get far.

A hydraulic hiss permeated the air and I heard heavy footsteps, followed by heavy male voices speaking harsh and guttural. The Vyqang. Instantly, I remembered where I was and why. They were doing something to me—specifically to my head—to make me better breeding stock.

The Vyqang moved toward my bed, the white one and the green one from earlier, this time joined by one whose skin was covered in dark, almost obsidian scales. I tried to scream but my throat caught.

The obsidian Vyqang leaned over me and spoke in Kalybrian. "Do not be afraid, little girl. It is all a bad dream." And then there was nothing but pain and terror and cold metal biting into my flesh.

It was like I was having an out-of-body experience, dimly floating above my body but not one hundred percent certain of what they were doing to me as they took my brain and my DNA apart and put it back together. At some point, I realized that there were explosions sounding far away, that my captors seemed worried, and then suddenly there were golden-skinned aliens all around, speaking in soft Kalybrian: "Don't worry, child. You are safe."

But once I became aware of my body again, the only thing that greeted me was agony and mind-numbing terror—and awareness of how I had been violated. I screamed until I didn't have any voice left, distrustful of even these quiet, reassuring golden-skinned creatures who perhaps had rescued me. Even when they brought to me a familiar-looking woman with blue eyes and dark hair so like mine, and a man with glasses and kind eyes, I still screamed and cried and lashed out at anyone that came near, seeing only monsters come to hurt me again. The woman and the man cried and begged the golden ones to do something.

"They're going to take away the pain, Mindy," the woman said, in a shaking voice, trying to be soothing. I screamed and bucked against the harnesses that held me down to the bed as I was wheeled through a long, white corridor to another room behind another door and—

I sat up, disoriented and sweaty like I had been fighting a battle, and looked around at the frightened eyes around me. Gradually I came back to myself, remembered where I was.

I was sitting on a red leather couch in the middle of a sea of black velvet, a bright spotlight blazing down on me. It was irritating to no end, reminding me of the bright light back on the Vyqang ship, and I lashed out with my mind, wanting it gone. I heard a soft pop overhead and the room was plunged into darkness.

"Illuminati," I heard a feminine voice say, and the room was lit by a ghostly green glow coming from a glowing ball held aloft by a glamorous woman. Fantazia, I remembered. A bald man stood next to her, arms

covered in tattoos of ones and zeroes, and he was looking at me like he wanted to be anywhere else. Cyrus
the Virus.

Lainey stood to one side of me, Kate on the other.
Both of their arms were covered in long red scratches,
like they had fought some sort of clawing wild beast.
Looking down at my hands, I saw blood in my nails.
My throat was raw from screaming.

"I remember," I croaked.

CHAPTER EIGHTEEN

"Where have you been?" Luke greeted us as we walked back through the door at EHJ headquarters. "Paul and Wesley have been looking everywhere for you." He eyed the fading scratches on Lainey and Kate's arms, and since their innate natures help with faster healing, I'd hate to see what they'd look like without powers. "What happened?"

I barely gave him a glance. I felt like I had been put through the wringer, regaining my memories by experiencing them afresh, then managing to relay them to the people who'd helped bring them back. My life had made a hardened criminal like Cyrus the Virus look sick to his stomach. Go me.

"Never mind, Luke, I'll take care of it," Lainey said, motioning for Kate to attend me. "Go lay down, Mindy. Try to get some sleep."

"I don't want to sleep," I said in a sharp voice, shaking Kate off and causing everyone in the room to stare. I softened my tone. "If I sleep, I'll dream, and I'd rather not dream right now." I straightened. "I'd rather deal with whatever's going on with Simon."

"No, you wouldn't." Paul popped in from around the corner. "Now that we're all here, meet in the conference room. Right now."

"Yes, sir," Kate said, giving him a smart yet mocking

salute. His cold blue eyes narrowed, but he motioned us inside.

I noticed Lainey walk over to embrace Wesley, who was already pacing the conference room, dressed oddly enough like his former life, Robert, in a suit and tie. Whether she needed comfort after the episode with Fantazia or had a bad feeling about what was happening with the government, I wasn't sure; I only knew I wished I had someone to whom I could turn.

Fortunately, my headaches had weakened as soon as the blocks came down. But my returned memories left me feeling like I was spiritually drained.

"Can we order coffee or something?" I asked as we took our seats around the large conference table.

Paul shot me a dark look. "We're in the middle of the biggest crisis of our lives and you want a coffee break?"

"Leave her alone, Paul," Lainey said. "She's been through a lot today."

"Well, *we've* been through a hell of a lot more," he said.

"I seriously doubt that," I snapped, not bothering to adjust my tone.

Paul narrowed his eyes and frowned. "All right, let's sit down and discuss what Wesley and I went through with Simon and his cronies in Washington. After all, it concerns all of you."

Wesley cut in. "Simon has raised concerns that Lainey and I have endangered people with the Dragon's vendetta against us."

"But we stopped the Dragon," Lainey said, looking plaintive. "We did that. Simon knows. He was there."

"Mindy almost died in that fight," Luke put in. "Simon almost died."

Lainey looked like she had been punched in the

stomach. "Of course, the Dragon was after me because of that stupid prophecy. Because of Emily." She shook her head. "They're right, I did endanger people."

"Don't blame yourself, love," Wesley said, reaching across the table to take her hand. "You have no control over what some psychopath does to try to kick-start the apocalypse. You can only stop whatever he tries, which we did."

"Which we pointed out," Paul put in. "If it hadn't been the Dragon and this prophecy, it would have been some loser with a chemical bomb. There's always someone wanting to blast the whole population to kingdom come. We always stop them. And this is the thanks we get."

"They questioned our fitness as parents," Wesley remarked to Lainey, his voice full of quiet rage, "having Emily in this environment."

Lainey's face drained of color. "What?"

"It's just Simon being a jerk because he's always hated you," Toby said to Wesley. "Because you didn't give him the attention and praise he thought he deserved."

"It's not just about Wesley," Paul put in. "Simon's also saying that Mindy is a problem. Having a psychopathic villain set on revenge and trying to end the world is one thing, but, well . . . Mindy not only put a villain in the hospital last month but turned around and caused injuries in over ten innocent bystanders the other day."

I felt my face burn, and I kept my head down and gazed straight ahead. Like I was ever going to forget how much of this was my fault.

Lainey spoke up. "It's not like Mindy meant for that to happen."

"I'm not saying she did," Paul replied. "I'm saying that Simon has called for us to terminate her employment immediately."

That statement ripped my gaze up to him. "W-what?" I managed, a cold pit in my stomach. If I didn't have my job or my friends, what did I have but estranged parents who couldn't look at me without regret and horror?

"What did you tell them?" Kate asked.

Paul frowned. "I told them—or more specifically, Simon—to go to hell."

"He told Simon and all of Washington that you were an asset to this team," Wesley said quietly. "He staked his career and reputation on you being able to pull yourself together."

I stared in shock at Paul. "You did that?"

Paul shrugged. "You *are* an asset to this team, and these new powers aren't going to change that. Besides, we make the decisions about who to hire and fire on this team, ourselves, not them. We aren't owned by the United States or any other government. We've done work for them over the years, but we're an independent agency and will remain so."

"And that's when Simon announced he is forming his own hero team," Wesley spoke up, running a hand through his hair.

"So? What does that mean for us?" Selena asked. She had been sitting quietly next to Luke, her hand in his the whole meeting, I'd noted with a twinge of jealousy.

"We don't know yet," Paul admitted.

"Probably nothing good," Wesley said. "Simon's looking for any excuse to stick it to us."

"Anything that Simon Leasure leads is going to crash and burn," Kate predicted.

Paul looked at Toby. "Forrest defended us at every turn. Simon practically made it sound like we were becoming villains, and Forrest kept citing how many times we've helped the country."

"See, I actually am a good judge of character," Toby muttered, perhaps reminding himself.

"So, what are we going to do?" Luke asked Wesley. I noticed the shift of focus in the room as everyone turned to look at the Reincarnist. He was, by common consensus, our leader. Not Paul. That decision was made.

"It is business as usual," Wesley said. "We are not owned by the government, and we need to remind them of that. We continue to patrol, help out when needed, and act like the heroes we are. I've never abided bureaucracy, and nothing's changed."

"So, what was the crisis you three were handling?" Paul asked Lainey, Kate and I.

I stared fixedly at the table in front of me, still reeling from both my newfound memories and the effects of my screwups in Cozumel's.

"I helped her take down her memory blocks," Lainey said, her voice hard, as if daring Paul to challenge her actions.

"You did what?" His voice rose with incredulity. "After I told you not to?"

"Did you succeed, love?" Wesley asked, sounding impressed.

I looked up to see Lainey shake her head. "I took her to Fantazia to do it."

"Who?" Paul asked. Wesley sat back in surprise.

"That ancient magic user?" Luke looked worried. "She's dangerous."

I was surprised Luke had heard of her, since he wasn't magically inclined, but he did hang with the shamans and yogis and others who might be.

"The one that has that parallel universe?" Toby asked.

"Pocket dimension," Lainey corrected.

"Isn't she a known criminal?" Paul said. "You took

Mindy to a known criminal to get mental blocks off that I specifically said not to mess with right now?"

"Fantazia's not a criminal," Wesley corrected, sounding a bit defensive. "I've used her information many times over the years. She's safe."

"Getting those blocks off wasn't," Paul said.

"I couldn't leave them on forever," I spoke up. Paul seemed to notice me for the first time.

"I took Kate along, in case things got out of hand," Lainey remarked.

"That was a good idea," Wesley agreed. "Fantazia's who I would have gone to about this, though I would have preferred dealing with her myself. I know how to handle her."

"It went okay," Lainey said. "And you have enough on your plate right now."

"So, what does she want out of it?" Wesley asked, putting his head in his hands, sounding very old.

"She wants to spend time with her half sister," Lainey said.

This piece of news got startled reactions from everyone at the table.

Wesley chuckled without humor. "Great, we have a new babysitter. So, she did it all by herself?"

"She brought in the Virus," Lainey admitted.

"Cyrus? Wonder what she has over him," Wesley mused. "Well, what's done is done, I suppose. Since Mindy's sitting here looking sane, I'm going to assume things went okay."

I didn't know if everything was okay or ever would be, but I wisely kept my mouth shut.

"That's all you're going to say?" Paul sounded put out. "'What's done is done?' We both told them not to do it and they disobeyed."

"Do you want me to spank them and put them to

bed without supper?" Wesley asked. "Lainey took the initiative to do what I would have done eventually. While I really would have liked to have been informed about the plan, I can't fault the results." He shot Lainey a pointed look.

She blushed. "Sorry."

Wesley turned his attention back to me. "We will have to monitor you for any changes since the blocks have been taken down, and someone will have to try to work with you about controlling these powers you seem to have acquired. That means: If you have any strange symptoms, you inform me or Paul immediately."

"Don't wait around and have a few drinks like last time," Paul clarified. "I went to bat for you, Mindy. Don't make me regret that." He stood up. "This meeting is adjourned."

I sat back in my chair. I couldn't believe Paul would really stake his career on me, but Wesley wouldn't lie about that. And Paul had called me an asset to the team. In all the years I had known him, he wasn't one to give out meaningless praise. I waited until everyone else filed out. Paul was clicking buttons on the terminal in front of him, obviously forgetting I was still there. Finally I cleared my throat.

"Why did you do that?" I asked.

Paul didn't look up. "Do what?"

"Stake your career on me? You don't even like me."

He gave a short snort of a laugh. "Yeah, well, you're one of my teammates. I would do it for any one of you."

So I'm not special in any way. Thanks, Paul, I thought. Out loud, I said, "I appreciate it."

"Well, you're welcome." He clicked a few dials. "How do you feel now that the blocks are down?"

"No headaches."

"That's good, I suppose." He eyed me critically. "What about those memories?"

I shivered. "They were . . . bad."

"How bad?"

"I witnessed a peaceful race slaughtered by invaders," I said. "My foster sister and I were captured and tortured. I was . . ."

Paul's face drained of color. In a voice just above a whisper, he said, "You were raped."

I shook my head and looked down, not wanting to see his expression or judgment. "Not in the way you're thinking. They experimented on us, changed us, to get various types of DNA they wanted. And then they extracted it. They cut us open over and over again." More memories were resurfacing, and without my realizing, a soft moan escaped my lips. A strange buzzing was reverberating in my brain. I raised my head to see several chairs around the desk floating in the air. I started to panic.

"Paul!"

He grabbed me by the shoulders and looked into my eyes. "No. Look at me, Mindy, don't look at them. You need to force yourself to relax. Close your eyes if you need to. Take a deep breath and let it out slowly. Try to clear your mind and concentrate on something peaceful, like waves on a beach. Try to make yourself hear those waves in your mind. Breathe out as they crash onto the beach and breathe in when they go back out again."

I did as he said, concentrating on slowing breathing and focusing on the mental picture of an ocean, not on the buzzing in my head or the memories that threatened to overwhelm me. I felt Paul's arms slip from around my shoulders to embrace me loosely as he patted my back. He had never touched me before, and for some reason I took more comfort than I expected.

"It's okay, Mindy. It's okay," he soothed.

I concentrated on his voice, on the feeling that someone cared what happened to me. The tension slowly melted away. A second or two later, I heard the chairs crash down around us. Opening my eyes, I saw them safe on the ground, back in place. I was still shaking.

"Thanks," I said.

He seemed to realize he was still touching me and quickly backed away. "I'm the one that wound you up, and I should have known better. I'm sorry."

"How did you know how to do that?"

"Your powers are flaring up with emotions, because you have no control over them yet. I was the same way when I first got my own powers." He shrugged. "I'm no telekinetic, but I can try to help you train your mind."

"Thanks," I said, and tried to focus on the here and now. It was bleak. The team was in trouble, and it seemed there was only one solution. "I think Simon might be right, Paul. Maybe I am a danger to everyone around me—more than a help. I hurt Lainey and Kate when the memories first came back. With these powers that just lash out . . . maybe I should tender my resignation."

He frowned. "Don't be like that, Mindy."

"Like what?"

"Don't be a scared little girl and balk at the first sign of a hard road ahead. You're not like that. You're strong."

"No. I'm not," I whispered.

"You just told me your past. You survived that and are still standing here before me, hardly a cowed shell, instead a woman who defines her life by helping others."

"I went insane for a while," I reminded him.

"You were young. You couldn't handle the memories then. But you can handle them now. And you will."

I was a little surprised that he was showing so much

faith. This was Paul, remember, who usually ignored my existence unless it was to dole out a reprimand.

"I said you were strong, Mindy. Don't prove me a liar. Especially in front of Simon Leasure. Not *that* guy." Was that a hint of a teasing smile on his face?

"Wouldn't want to do that," I agreed, giving him a half smile. "You can be nice when you want to be, Paul. I didn't realize."

"Gee thanks, Mindy." He rolled his eyes.

I ignored that, and asked the next question that immediately sprang into my mind. "So why don't you usually want to be?"

"I'm trying to lead a team that doesn't want me to be their leader, that is turning to someone who thinks we used to be nothing but glory hounds."

"Well, we kinda were," I pointed out.

"True, but we did good, too. We've all saved the day so many times, both individually and as a team. This group has trusted me all these years to lead them on the field, and frankly I don't understand why you wouldn't trust me to lead you out of combat, too. I understand Wesley's probably more qualified, what with his lifetimes of experience, but I'm getting pushed out more and more each day. Don't act like you don't see."

I nodded, having to concede his point.

"The United States government seems out to get us, and I only recently got up enough nerve to leave my girlfriend who has been boldly cheating on me since we got together. I know she doesn't mean anything by it and doesn't think it should matter because she doesn't love who she cheats with, but that's not how our society works and you would think she would have come to terms with that by now . . ." He stopped, looking embarrassed that he had let all of that slip. "Well, put all of that together and I've been a little cranky."

"You've been cranky since the day we met, Paul, and that was pregovernment and pre-Kate." I said this half teasingly, but it was true. Paul had been the textbook definition of a stuffed shirt since I first met him.

"Well, to be brutally honest, no one's ever respected me," Paul admitted. "I've tried so hard to earn more of a leadership role over the years, to be a true head of this team, but all my efforts get shoved back in my face. Everyone used to look to Rath and not me for guidance off the field. I was just the guy in the battle relaying orders from above. Now history's repeating itself, though instead of Rath it's Wesley. I just would think, after all of these years, you all might look to me off the field for once. I think I've done a good job."

I nodded. "You have, Paul. And I don't know that it's a matter of being qualified; everyone just wants to try the direction that the Reincarnist wants to lead us. Absolutely nothing against you or Rath, but we all felt we lost our way as heroes. It's not that we don't respect you . . ."

"Well, who could blame you if you didn't? Who respects a guy who can't keep his girlfriend satisfied?"

I didn't know if I wanted to have a conversation with Paul about satisfying anyone, but since he was all of a sudden opening up after sticking his neck out for me, I tried to make him feel better. "Paul . . . Kate is, well, Kate. We all know that. As you said, *she* knows she loves you and doesn't quite get why her poor impulse control would hurt. As much as I like Kate, you have to admit she's selfish. It's a god thing."

"It just sucks feeling superfluous in your team and your relationship . . ." He gave me a half smile and shook his head, clearly realizing what he'd said. "I'm sorry to dump all this on you. You didn't ask for it, and you've got your own problems to deal with. They're much worse than mine."

"It's okay," I said. "I like to exchange someone else's problems for mine once and a while. Keeps my mind clear." I hesitantly reached out to pat his arm. "And, for what it's worth, I think you should have left Kate a long time ago."

"Thanks."

"No. I mean, you were never going to be able to change her, Paul. There was nothing more you could do to make her stay faithful. It wasn't anything to do with you, really; it's all her hang-ups. She might be an immortal, but she has the maturity of a three-year-old. She does what she wants and doesn't think about who it hurts. If she didn't work so hard at doing good, she'd be a spectacular supervillain. No, Paul, it wasn't a matter of you not keeping her satisfied, it's that she's an emotional bottomless pit." I took a deep breath and fought a blush that had risen when I realized I was talking ill of a teammate, a woman who at heart I liked. "And now I sound like a daytime television psychologist."

"No, you're right. I know that. I knew it going in. I thought I could change her, and then . . . well, being with someone who cheats on you messes with your mind, makes you question yourself. But I appreciate what you're saying."

"No problem," I said, wanting out of this weird conversation. "Consider it the beginning of a payback for sticking up for me in front of the whole United States government."

He shrugged. "Like I said, no big deal. I would have done it for anyone."

"Wow, Paul, way to make a girl feel appreciated."

"Well, what do you want me to say, Mindy? That I'm

crazy about you and couldn't function if you left the team?" He glanced over my shoulder.

"I wouldn't go that far—" was all I managed to get out before he acted. He seized my face in his hands and crushed my lips with his. My immediate reaction was one of shock, stiffening and starting to pull away. But then I felt it: a spark. An ember burning deep inside me that started in my stomach and gradually spread through all the rest, singeing my nerve endings with delicious awareness. Maybe it had just been so long since anyone had kissed me, but it was like everything in me was awakening. It felt delicious.

I moved against him, fitting my body against his, sliding my hands—first raised in protest—against his chest, up around his neck, pulling him in tighter to me. I opened my mouth slightly, and he took the initiative to explore with his tongue. God, who'd known Paul was so hotly aggressive? I kissed him back, savoring the feel of his mouth on mine, the taste of him and the faint scent of his cologne. My head was threatening to spin.

Whoa. What was happening? Since when did Paul have the ability to turn me on?

Paul must have been coming to a similar realization, as he slowly, almost reluctantly, gave me my release. He was looking as if he had never seen me before. I blinked rapidly for a few moments, trying to reorient myself to just what was going on.

"Wow," I said, my voice thick and almost unrecognizable. "That was . . ." I trailed off as I noticed him looking over my shoulder. I turned to see Kate standing there, mouth hanging open, staring at both of us. She shook her head as if to make sure we weren't a mirage; then, when we didn't go away, she turned and walked off as fast as she could.

I glanced to Paul. Cold reality was setting back in,

slapping down my tingling nerve endings and telling them to shut up. This was freaking Paul I was with, not Luke, and not even some random hottie at a bar. In my normal voice I said, "That was all for her benefit, wasn't it?"

He seemed to be at a loss for words. Then he nodded and cleared his throat. "Initially, yes."

"Initially?"

"W-well, I saw her there and thought I'd show her I was moving on, but . . . you distracted me."

"I distracted you how?"

"You just . . . you have nice soft lips." Was it my imagination, or was he turning red? "I mean, you're a good kisser," he finished lamely. His eyes darted around the room, like he didn't want to look at me.

"Um, thanks." I didn't especially want to see him, either. Embarrassment was no fun for either party. "You, too, by the way."

"Thanks."

"I wouldn't have expected it." I didn't know if I meant the kiss itself, his kissing ability, or my reaction.

"Me, either."

I glanced up. He looked just as awkward as I felt. He fidgeted, didn't seem to know what to do with his hands or where to look.

"I think I'm just going to go before this gets any more uncomfortable," he finished.

"Okay."

"So . . . yeah." He straightened his suit jacket and headed toward the door. I stood where I was, watching him, unable to come to terms with what had just happened. Maybe my mind had snapped when the blocks came off and I'd hallucinated those last few moments.

The door had barely shut behind him before it opened again and he returned, striding with purpose, his mouth narrowed to a thin line of determination. He walked right up to me, seized my waist with his hands and pulled me in for another breath-stealing kiss.

All my nerve endings crashed to life again in a huge wave of intensity. My brain might have been confused as to how a person that I barely considered a friend under normal circumstances could make my insides melt, but other parts of me decided to override my brain. I wrapped my arms around his neck and deepened the kiss, tangling my tongue with his. One of his hands pressed into my back, pulling me tight against him, and the other got lost in my hair. The kiss was messy and imprecise, but it was full of heat and intensity.

We drew back from each other gasping for air. I leaned a hand on the table to steady myself and dared to meet his eyes. They were dark blue, unfathomable with some expression I wasn't used to seeing. I looked away.

"You're not going to tell anyone about this, are you?" he asked hesitantly.

"God, no!" I responded automatically, then realized I sounded disgusted when I felt the exact opposite. I softened my tone. "I mean, I don't even know what 'this' is."

"Yeah. Me either." He was switching back to being uncomfortable again. "So, I'll just . . ." He motioned to the door and I nodded. He turned and left without another word.

Waiting until he was gone for good this time, I sagged down onto a chair. The day had just become even more physically and mentally exhausting. And a lot more confusing.

CHAPTER NINETEEN

Sleep came to me, but in restless fits and with vague nightmares, whispers in the dark of monsters hiding in shadow. When I finally gave up and decided to rise the next morning, I felt like I had barely slept at all.

As I sat up in bed, yawning, stretching and trying to get my limbs to work, it occurred to me that Paul had shown up at some point in my endless stretch of alternately strange and terrifying dreams. That realization alone was enough to make me feel awkward, never mind the nightmares. What had happened between us yesterday? Was it emotional fallout from my rediscovered past, me reaching out for someone, anyone, for comfort? Had Paul really been trying to make Kate jealous and simply got a little too into his role? Or was this something else entirely that neither of us were prepared to handle?

I brushed such thoughts aside and pushed myself up and out of bed. There was nothing between me and Paul, of all people. We had both been suffering from personal and team crises and had shared a weak moment. That was all. I would get up today and our relationship would be strictly professional.

Maybe it was in reaction to my memories, a defense mechanism to once again rebel, to hide the pain even from myself, or perhaps it was in reaction to the weirdness with Paul, but I found myself pulling out an old and pleated black miniskirt and knee-high boots. I added a soft blue sweater that made my eyes stand out but was also a bit conservative. It was a mix of the old and new me.

Satisfied, I headed outside of my room and about ran into Kate, who seemed to be lying in wait.

I took a step back. "Kate. Hi. What's up?"

Even though she was dressed as usual to the nines, in a bright red silk kimono dress with matching lipstick, she looked a little less like herself. There was something hiding in her eyes, a sadness or pain that seemed to permeate her aura. Today she seemed tired and ancient and trying to hide it.

"Hello, Mindy," she said, and gave me a smile that didn't quite reach her eyes. Had Paul's jab really worked? "I just wanted to speak with you in private for a moment."

"Sure." I gestured around the silent corridor. No one was close. "Go ahead."

"I just wanted to say that I know I wasn't a good girlfriend for Paul," she remarked. The words hit me like a blunt object. "And I'm happy he's moving on."

"Uh-huh . . ." I didn't know what to say. After all, making Kate jealous was the whole point of Paul kissing me. Should I admit to the truth and undo the whole thing?

Kate continued: "I don't want you to feel awkward around me at all. We're grown-ups here. After all, this isn't the first time one of my exes has moved on to someone else on the team."

"Uh-huh," I said. It was amazing how Kate could somehow turn the fact that she'd had so many exes into bragging. Only Kate.

"And I couldn't be happier for you and Paul," she continued, giving me a friendly pat on the shoulder.

I grimaced. This was going too far. Paul could just

deal with the fallout. "Kate, I've got to be honest. There is no me and Paul."

"So it's all about the sex." Seeing the shocked look on my face, she added quickly, "Oh, it's okay, I understand completely. You both have needs and this is a stressful job. And after everything you've been through, Mindy, I can understand that you might need a release, someone in your bed to chase away those nightmares. Trust me, you live long enough, you find you always can use a distraction. And Paul might look like just another boring, staid academic type, but he's something else in the bedroom, am I right?"

She said the last in a joking, *we're all girls here* tone, like we were characters on that sitcom about overly sexed women, which was about the last thing I wanted to hear this morning.

"No, Kate. No, no, no." I rubbed my brow, already starting to feel the beginnings of a headache coming on. This was too much, too early, and without coffee.

She misunderstood my dismay. "Oh, well, Mindy, you know sometimes men in their forties need a bit of help getting started. There are pills for that."

"Jesus, no!" I practically shrieked. "There is no me and Paul, sexually or otherwise. We're just coworkers, that's all. *Coworkers.* What you saw was a total mistake."

She studied me for a moment, then grinned and winked. "Oh, don't worry, Mindy. I won't say a thing to the others. I'll keep my big mouth shut for a change. I know I've gotten a reputation around here for being a blabbermouth, but I can keep a secret."

I gave up. "Thanks, Kate." Paul wanted her to believe he had moved on, so as long as she didn't blab to the others, he could be the one to try to explain things to her. "I really don't want anyone to know about the incident you witnessed."

She smiled. "I won't say anything for now, Mindy."

"What's that supposed to mean?" I practically shrieked. I knew it! Kate was such a blabbermouth; she was probably going to want cappuccinos and shoes to buy her silence.

"It's going to start becoming apparent to everyone that you two are involved," she explained.

"What are you talking about?" I said, but then shut my mouth as Paul appeared. "Hi!" I squeaked in an overly bright tone.

"Mindy." He barely gave me a glance. So much for chemistry. It was like yesterday had never happened. "I need to speak with you a moment."

"I'm sure you do." Kate winked at me, then looked down at the delicate watch on her wrist. "I should go get ready; I have an interview with one of those entertainment gossip shows."

"I canceled that," Paul said.

She whirled on him, mouth twisted into a frown. "What? Why did you do that?"

"We need to regroup and figure out what we're going to say to the media as a team. All press contact is on hiatus."

"It was the cover story!"

"There will be other cover stories. And you were on the cover of every major magazine in February. How much more publicity do you need, Kate?"

She gave him a nasty look. "I'm going to see what Wesley says about this." Then she sauntered off down the hall like a runway model; and why not? She probably inspired their signature walks anyway.

Paul nodded to me. "See? It's what I said. My words carry no weight."

"I think that her reaction is more personal than professional," I said. "She's trying to stick it to you like you did her." Realizing too late how that sounded, I stammered, "I-I mean . . ."

"I know what you meant." He looked off in the direction Kate had walked, then back at me. "I was coming to see you, actually. I wanted to talk. It's about yesterday."

"Kate thinks we're having an affair," I blurted. "I tried to tell her we're not, but she wouldn't believe me."

"I can't blame her after what she witnessed," Paul muttered.

"What?" I was sure I had misunderstood.

"That's what she was meant to think. I mean, originally that's why I kissed you, only . . ." He ran his hand through his hair. "Look, this wasn't what I came here to talk to you about, but since the topic's out, can we just forget yesterday ever happened?"

I was surprised I felt stung. One minute he was practically pawing at me, and now he wanted to erase it from his mind completely? "No problem. I forgot already."

"Great." He physically sagged with relief.

"It wasn't that memorable anyway," I said.

His sharp blue eyes cut into me and then away. "Right. My thoughts exactly."

Ouch. I inwardly winced, but I guess I deserved that. That's what you got for smarting off.

"No, what I came to talk to you about is that Wesley and I discussed it, and we want to make sure you're physically sound."

"Not more hospital tests!" I groaned.

"We were thinking of having Wesley do a quick scan on you with the help of the machines in our infirmary. Then, if everything seems to be proceeding okay, he and I will both work on helping you learn to control your new powers. Neither of us are telekinetic, but as I said, I have experience learning how to control powers received late in life, and Wesley's had years of experience training the newly powered."

"Centuries," I mused.

He gave me a half smile. "Exactly. So I came to fetch you to get started."

"Right now?"

"No time like the present. We've got other troubles to worry about, of course, but since you couldn't wait to take those blocks down until after the government mess, we've got to take care of you now."

I'll say this: All of these snide comments between the two of us were making it easy to get back onto professional ground.

I followed Paul into our infirmary, where Wesley was typing on a data pad near the large, cold metal slab in the center of the room. In his jeans and an EHJ-logo T-shirt, his dress was a stark contrast to Paul's suit pants and dress shirt under a starched white lab coat.

He looked up as we came in and gave me a reassuring smile. "I promise this won't take long, Mindy. I just want to double-check."

"It's okay, I understand." I walked over to the table and slid up on it, careful not to flash too much bare thigh in my ascent. Was it my imagination, or did Paul's gaze linger on my legs as I crossed my knees? "I'm a liability now: the girl who could go crazy at any moment." I smoothed down my skirt, feeling self-conscious.

This time I saw Paul tear his gaze away from my legs with a frown. "We just need physical proof of your fitness for duty," he said. "Just in case."

I made out with you yesterday, I wanted to say. *I think that proves I'm mentally incompetent.* But I kept my big mouth shut and lay down on the table.

Paul adjusted the machine arm hanging next to the

table so that it hovered right over my head. Reaching over to the data pad, he typed in a few keystrokes.

"I thought we had to go to a hospital to do this effectively," I remarked. "I thought our machines weren't powerful enough."

"That's why I'm here," Wesley said. "I boost them enough that we can do a scan to compare to your results from earlier." He reached over and touched the scanner and muttered something in Italian that I couldn't catch. The machine clicked on with a hum, and I had a momentary flare of panic, hearing again that hum from the Vyqang machinery as they cut my head open.

No! I snapped to myself. *You're not there anymore, you're back home. You're with Wesley and Paul and they're trying to help you, not hurt you.*

"You okay?" Paul asked, checking the monitors. "Your heart rate sped up there for a moment."

"I'm okay. The noise freaked me out, but I'm okay now."

He nodded. "Well, try to hold still. We're almost done. Visualize the beach and the waves if you need to."

"No, I'm okay."

After a few more moments, Wesley switched off the machine. "We're done." He and Paul studied the monitor, and then held up the X-ray of my brain they had gotten at the hospital. I had a funny thought that I wanted to share it with my parents. *Yes, Mother, Father, I have photographic proof that there is a brain in my thick skull—one that you let get tampered with.* I fought down a panicky giggle as I sat up. Laughing like a maniac would not show that I was dealing with my recalled memories well.

"There's more brainwave activity, but that's to be expected," Paul said, studying several charts. "But otherwise, I say you get a clean bill of health, Mindy. Nothing for the government to worry about."

I breathed a sigh of relief. "That's great."

"Not that we need to prove anything to Simon Leasure. This was more for your own peace of mind, Mindy," Wesley said, giving Paul a significant look.

"Well, next time I see Simon, I'll be sure to wave these test results under his nose," I laughed, sliding off the table.

"You can tell him now."

We all turned to see Lainey standing in the doorway, cradling Emily. "Simon's here. And he's brought his team."

We were all silent as we struggled to process this information.

"Let's gather everyone in the war room," Paul said, his voice brittle. "Come on, Mindy." He ushered me out the door.

As I glanced over my shoulder I saw Wesley and Lainey hold back, speaking in hushed tones. I wondered what they were saying. Whatever Simon Leasure wanted, it couldn't be good.

CHAPTER TWENTY

"Hello, everyone," Simon said, a politician's smile painted on his naturally handsome face.

None of us returned the greeting, and instead we stared back at him. I had somehow ended up standing between Paul and Toby. Wesley and Lainey were on Paul's other side, and Luke and Selena near Toby. Kate stood off to the side, giving Simon a flirty look that I was sure was for Paul's benefit.

Simon Leasure hadn't changed in the year or so since he'd left us. He still had the same movie-star good looks, wavy blond hair, dark blue eyes, a faint hint of dimples when he smiled and a smile that had charmed the pants off of many a girl. Never me or Lainey, of course. We had been too smart for that.

Clad now in his standard Washington uniform, a dark suit with a red tie, Simon bore more than a passing resemblance to his senator father. I'm sure no intern in DC was safe.

His team stood in silence behind him, staring us down. There were eight in all, like the EHJ, four men and four women. They all wore uniforms emblazoned with the American flag.

"I'm sure the Reincarnist and White Heat told you all of our meeting yesterday," Simon said, surprisingly formal, using their aliases and not their real names, as if he had just met them and wanted to maintain courtesies. No one spoke, but unruffled he continued: "As I'm sure you are all aware, I have formed my own team that will ensure the safety and the interests of our country. Elite Hands of Justice, I'd like you to meet *my* team, the American Agents, or AA for short."

"Isn't the AA Alcoholics Anonymous?"

Selena, of all people, had spoken up. I bit the inside of my mouth to keep from giggling. I cast a quick glance at Toby, who seemed to be having the same trouble. Paul and Wesley just looked angry.

Simon frowned. "Not anymore. We bought the rights."

"Smart thinking," Kate said.

"I thought so." Simon preened, obviously unaware she was mocking him.

"So, what does this mean to us?" Luke asked. I noticed his muscles were tensed, like a snake ready to strike. He clearly sensed something was up.

"While the United States government does truly appreciate all of the work your team has done over the years," Simon said, "the president has asked me to relay that your services will no longer be required."

Paul laughed. "Well, since we don't technically work for you, that shouldn't be a problem. We just won't continue to work with your defense contacts or turn over our lifesaving inventions free of charge like Mindy and I both used to do. And the next time some maniac in a cape or a terrorist shows up to blow the White House to kingdom come, I guess that will just be your problem, won't it, Simon?"

"Yes, it will be," Simon agreed. "I'm glad you see it my way."

"Good luck," Wesley said. And it sounded like he meant it. He added: "None of those people behind you has an ounce of magic. I'll be interested to see how you defend against magical threats."

"The United States of America doesn't see any rising threat in the magic-using community," Simon said, as if reading off a press release. "They are a power, of course, but we have full faith in our abilities to handle them."

Wesley narrowed his eyes. "Next time the Dragon shows up, he just might kill you, Simon. Especially without one of us to pull your bacon out of the fire."

Simon frowned. "The Dragon won't show up again, because you won't be around to tempt him."

Wesley's mouth tightened. "Pardon me?"

Simon held up an envelope. "This is a cease-and-desist order signed by the president himself, after he and I had a little chat about what you're up to. You are to turn over to my team all equipment the Elite Hands of Justice use in their pursuit of evil." He looked directly at me and Paul. "And any inventions or patents currently in process become the immediate property of the United States government."

Everyone's jaws dropped. I felt a buzzing in the back of my head start up. Oh, no. That was usually a precursor to the episodes I had. *Hold it together, Mindy, hold it together,* I chanted to myself.

"Oh, hell no!" Toby blasted. "This has got to be some kind of joke."

Simon gave us a mirthless smile. "It most definitely is not."

"And if we tell you to go to hell?" Paul asked through gritted teeth. He looked as if he wanted Simon's head on a plate.

"If you tell me to go to hell, I will see it as an act against the interests of our country, and you will be taken into custody by my team," Simon said. "If you pretend to cooperate and still show up on the street at a later time, I will see it as an act against the interests of our country and you will be taken into custody by my team at that time." He gave us all a nasty grin. "I told you all that you'd be nothing without me."

It got deadly silent in the room. I noticed Wesley and Paul exchange glances. Lainey's mouth was a grim line. Wesley glanced down at Luke, who gave a barely perceptible nod, and Toby gave Paul a weary look. Kate cracked her knuckles. Instantly I knew what they planned.

"Simon," said Wesley, taking the baby from Lainey. "I'm afraid we're going to have to decline your offer."

Simon blinked. "Excuse me?"

"What he means to say," Paul clarified, stepping in front of me, "is 'Go to hell.'"

Simon's faced twisted into a terrible grimace. "Take them," he snarled.

His teammates stepped forward.

"No problem, boss," said one of the men. He charged straight for Luke. The others took the cue and launched themselves as well.

It only took a second for me to realize I was screwed. My only power was my design skill. Without my tech gadgets, I was nothing, and I had been too out of whack this morning, and felt too secure in our headquarters, to remember to grab a weapon. I was powerless.

The buzzing in the back of my head increased. That voice that crept into my thoughts hissed, *Powerless. Nothing.*

Simon's teammate jumped the table and came at me, claws literally out. Distracted by the voice in my head, I took a split second to react, but at the last moment I managed to evade the woman's blow, raising my arm just in time to ward it off. My sweater tore from her nails, and

I winced. Damn, these people were playing hard-core! Why would Simon be letting them use this much force?

She must have been expecting an easy victory; as the woman attacked again, I took her by surprise and palm-heeled her in the face. Thank God I had taken self-defense classes with Luke as an excuse to be near him when I was younger. My foe staggered backward, howling and holding her shattered nose, and then a foot caught her in the chest and sent her flying across the room.

"Mindy, get behind me," Paul snapped, turning to deal with one of the men.

I scrambled to my feet, hating to crouch behind him like a stupid, simpering girl. But that happens when you're a powerless nothing.

The voice in my head laughed. And then I had a flashback to lying on the table in the Vyqang ship, my head not even closed up again as they began to harvest more . . .

The voice in my head went silent, as did the rest of the world. My limbs felt heavy, like I was surrounded by water or some sort of other thick liquid. I stood up, moving as if I was in slow motion, pushing my way past Paul, who probably said something to me, and faced Simon's team.

Simon's lips were moving, but I couldn't hear. I reached out with my hand, as if I were physically picking him up, and made a throwing motion with my hand. Simon hurtled off his feet and through the wall behind him.

One of his teammates stopped trying to fight Wesley, who'd erected an invisible shield between them, and launched himself at me. I swatted my hand, like I was hitting a troublesome insect buzzing around my head, and he went crashing off into one of the women.

Then it was like someone had turned the sound back on. I could hear my heart pounding in my ears, my labored breathing, and the blasts of the other combatants all around me.

"Nice going, Mindy," Paul said, taking me by the arm as I swayed on my feet.

"Thanks, but I think I'm going to pass out," I replied.

"No time for that. Pass out after we're to safety." Paul put his arm around my waist. "Hope you still have that voice recognition software up. Computer, this is Paul Christian, White Heat," he yelled.

From over the din, I heard a beep and then a computerized voice said, "Confirmed."

"Initiate action: Fire sale."

"Initiation confirmed."

It was our contingency plan, should a villain ever get through all of our security and try to take over the building, so that no tech or information would fall into enemy hands.

Simon recognized the code name. "No! Someone stop it!"

"That's as good a distraction as anything," Wesley said. "Now, Lainey!"

"Everyone hold hands," my friend shrieked over the din. I felt Toby and Paul take my hands just as the sound of the bombs going off started in both my lab and Paul's.

"*Apri il portale*," I heard both Wesley and Lainey say at the same time.

Coldness washed over me, and then the whole world turned inside out.

CHAPTER TWENTY-ONE

We popped into existence outside of a familiar-looking dank alleyway, all of us an exhausted mess.

Lainey and Wesley were propped against one wall. I could only imagine how much will it had taken for them to magic the whole team here. Of course, the rest of us were suffering from the discomfort of interdimensional travel through magic means, and most of the team was doubled over fighting nausea. Lainey had always told me that magic teleportation had this effect on those whose bodies weren't used to it. Selena was actually vomiting, and Luke stood next to her, rubbing her back and speaking softly. My own stomach was tossing violently, and I wished I had someone to hold my hair.

Wanting to power past the light-headedness I still felt from whatever I myself had done back in headquarters, I focused on Wesley and said, "We could have used my teleportation system to avoid this."

He shook his head no. "They would have followed the tech signature. They have no magic users, so no way to trace us."

I nodded. That made sense.

"Where are we?" Paul asked, looking around.

"A safe house. Or at least it will be in a moment," Wesley answered, running a hand over the wall and speaking some words. He then walked through it.

Paul took a step back. "Where did he go?"

"Welcome to Fantazia's," I said, following Wesley, Lainey and Kate inside. The rest of the group stood staring, openmouthed.

As soon as they followed, and when the doorway between our world and Fantazia's closed, I felt a bit of the pressure in my head let up. I didn't know why it did, but I was grateful.

Surprisingly, there were no patrons in Fantazia's bar. It seemed like it was just beginning to open up. Did she have regular hours? I wondered idly as I watched as the rest of the team stagger in and look around.

"Fantazia!" Wesley yelled. A moment later, one of the usual emaciated waitstaff came scrambling out of a back room.

"Sir, you can't be here," the androgynous waiter said. "The establishment is not open for business yet."

"I don't care, she needs to see me. Fantazia!"

A moment later, a thundercloud in black lingerie erupted from the back, looking extremely angry.

"What do you think you're doing?" she growled, either oblivious or not caring that she was in front of a bunch of strangers in an almost see-through teddy. "You just can't barge in here like you own the place!"

"We need your help," Wesley said, keeping his eyes level with hers.

"And this is how you come to ask for it?" She looked behind her as a man with four arms and silver skin appeared, speaking some strange language. "No, you don't have to go, Qwuogidsh. These people were just leaving."

"No, we weren't," Wesley corrected.

The man shook his head, and to most of the room's shock, shimmered away. Fantazia just looked furious. She whirled on Wesley.

"Great! Just great! Do you know how long it takes for

Qwuogidsh's dimension to line up with this one? I'm going to have to wait another hundred years to see him!"

"The time will fly by." Wesley crossed his arms over his chest.

Fantazia looked murderous and started spouting off in rapid-fire Italian. Wesley spoke back to her in the low voice of a man trying to control his temper. Their tones started getting more and more intense and they looked like they wanted to strangle each other. Ah, family fights.

"Hey!" Paul interrupted the steady stream of Italian. "Do you want to talk so the rest of the class can understand?"

"So, what do you want?" Fantazia snapped at Wesley.

"Simon Leasure is abusing his power with the government. We had to turn over everything to his new team or Simon was going to consider us villains and take us into custody."

"We chose to leave," Paul put in.

Fantazia smiled. "*You're* a fugitive?" she said to Wesley. "That has to be the funniest thing I've heard."

Wesley frowned. "Glad we could amuse you."

"So . . . are you getting to the part where I find out what this has to do with me?"

"Simon and his team are going to be staking out our headquarters, just waiting for us to return. We need somewhere safe to stay. We need you to lock down this parallel universe so no one else can access it."

Fantazia's eyes narrowed. "No. No way. I'm not turning off my business so some fugitive from justice who used to be my father can have a hideout."

"You're the one who wanted to spend more time with Emily," Lainey suggested, holding up the baby in her arms. "Here she is."

"She's the one who's going to fight *the* world-ending

battle one day," Wesley said to Fantazia. "If we go to jail, she goes to foster care. You want to trust some ill-equipped stranger to raise her? Or worse yet, maybe one of the Dragon's minions will get her."

A trace of sadness worked through her bravado as Fantazia looked over at the baby. "Maybe I'm ready for the world to end. Maybe I'm tired of it all. Maybe I just want to sleep."

"Well, maybe this is what you need to wake up," Lainey suggested.

Fantazia regarded her and then the baby. "Maybe," she said. Then the sadness was gone and the bold and brassy Fantazia came back. "Okay. Fine. I'll do it. But you are so going to owe me for this." She pointed at Wesley.

He shrugged. "Put it on my tab. And for God's sake, put some clothes on."

Fantazia gave him a dark look and then snapped her fingers, willing her outfit to change from the most re-vealing lingerie to a black catsuit with a giant purple F emblazoned on the chest. "Better?"

"You're so funny."

She turned her back and raised her arms up to the sky. She spoke softly in Italian, something rhythmic and low like a chant. The floors began to shake and the glasses and bottles on the bar vibrated. A few shattered, spilling alcohol everywhere.

"Almost there," she said, her voice tight with strain.

Just then, the door opened behind us and we all whirled.

"Fantazia, what the hell's going on?" Cyrus the Virus said, and then saw all of us standing there, poised for a battle. "Oh, shit."

A muffled boom sounded, almost like a giant furnace kicking on, and Fantazia turned back to us, looking worn. Hers must have been a powerful spell. "What the hell, Cyrus? I put out the Do Not Disturb sign."

"And I'm disturbing anyway." He looked around at us. "What the hell are the EHJ doing here? Do you know there's an all-points bulletin out for them?"

"They're hiding out here."

"Really?" A gleam filled his eye.

Luke stepped forward. "We can't let him escape. He'll tell them where we are."

"So, what are you suggesting, that we kidnap him?" Paul asked.

"We're taking him prisoner. He's a known criminal," Luke pointed out.

"So are we, thanks to Simon," Toby said.

"And I'm a reformed criminal, thank you very much," Cyrus said.

Fantazia snorted. "You're not going to try to claim you're a good guy now, Cyrus."

"I helped your hot little friend over there when she needed some memory retrieval." Cyrus pointed to me. I felt Paul tense.

"You did that because you owed me one," Fantazia remarked in a cool voice. "A very large favor."

Cyrus frowned. "Don't go bringing that up, Fantazia. I mean it."

She narrowed her eyes. "Or what?"

The room started to shake a bit, and I could almost see a change come over Cyrus as he began to power up. Fantazia looked bored.

"Stop it!" Wesley snapped.

Cyrus gave Fantazia a sharp look, but he settled back down.

"See?" Luke said. "He can't be trusted. We need to hold him prisoner."

"We're not in the business of taking prisoners," Paul said.

"Besides, where are we going to put him?" I asked, motioning around. "It's a bar, not a jail."

"He'll turn us in!" Selena said, siding with her man.

"Everyone relax," Fantazia spoke up. "No one's getting in or out of this dimension without my say-so."

"He got in," Kate pointed out.

Fantazia narrowed her eyes. "Yes, before I got the walls up. They're in place now. No one's going anywhere. So if anyone's taking prisoners, it's me."

"Fantazia, there's got to be a big reward for turning them in," Cyrus said eagerly. "I'll go halfsies with you."

"Cyrus, sit down and shut up!" she snapped, and the whole room vibrated again. The lights in the dim bar flickered like there was a power surge. Judging from Fantazia's face, even for a non-magic user like myself, it wasn't hard to figure out where it was coming from.

She took a moment to compose herself. "I need a drink. Anyone else?" Not waiting for a response, she went over the bar and mixed a cocktail that started glowing red.

"So, now what are we going to do?" Lainey asked Wesley.

Everyone turned to look at him. I could almost feel Paul cringe.

"Lie low for now and hope everything blows over?" Toby offered.

"I don't see many other options," Luke agreed.

"We need to try to prove that we're not the problem and we're not doing anything wrong," Paul said. "We need to clear our names."

"How are we going to do that?" Kate asked. "In case it escaped your notice, Paul, we're on the run from Simon."

"Paul's right. We need to prove we're not doing anything wrong," Wesley said.

"I'm right?" Paul looked amused. "There's a first."

Wesley gave him a look. "We need to show Simon, the government, all the other teams and the general public that we are not controlled by anyone—and that our focus remains the same as always: helping people."

Everyone turned shocked looks on Wesley.

"What?"

"We can't do that!"

"We'll be arrested the moment we step out of this dimension!"

"We'll continue to patrol," Wesley continued as if they hadn't spoken. "We'll go out every night and fight the good fight."

"Wesley, I have no powers," I pointed out. "And now no gadgets."

"You have the telekinesis," he replied.

"That I can't control."

"We'll work to help you learn."

I was frustrated. "Yeah, well, I can't fight without any technology, and I don't see any spare engines or even a DVD player to take apart here."

"Technology's not exactly my friend," Fantazia admitted. "Television creeps me out."

Paul ran a hand over his face, clearly thinking about what was lost. "I blew up the labs so Simon's team wouldn't have our technology."

"All of our work, gone," I muttered.

"Not totally." He caught my eye. "As part of the program, all of our computers dump to a server at an undisclosed location. Any files you had are saved somewhere. That's something."

I gave him a grateful smile.

"Undisclosed," Cyrus scoffed. "Try the office building

across the street from the Elite Hands of Justice head-quarters."

We all turned to look at him.

He gave us an innocent look. "What?"

"If he knows, they'll know," Luke said.

Cyrus looked offended. "Hey! Do you know how long I worked to get that piece of information? That's no easy security system you kiddies have, and no way is some government flunky going to be able to hack it like I did. Give me some credit."

"The point is, we can get our information back and rebuild," Wesley interrupted.

"Mindy and I worked for years on a lot of those inventions," Paul said. "They're not going to rebuild themselves in a day."

"I'm not expecting that. And, we're not going anywhere." Wesley looked around. "You and Mindy can work to rebuild with whatever spare parts we can scrounge up, and we can patrol every night. This is how the rest of the teams do it, kids, unless you've forgotten. Few fancy gadgets to play with, no unlimited funds, and no time as media darlings, they're just people with abilities who want to help. That's all. That's how this team was founded way back when. Maybe this problem with the government is exactly what we needed to get back on track.

"Now, to see about accommodations. Fantazia, a word." He walked over to her and they started another conversation in rapid-fire Italian.

"Only the Reincarnist could see us being wanted by the law as a good thing," I muttered. Catching Lainey's hurt look I said, "Sorry."

She sighed. "He's displaying his usual lack of tact, but he's got a point. At the same time, Emily shouldn't have to live like this."

"No, she shouldn't," Paul agreed, shaking his head. "Sometimes I think you two are crazy for trying to raise a kid in our mixed-up world."

Lainey narrowed her eyes at him. "Are you saying Simon's right, she shouldn't be with us, Paul?" She looked ready to throw down.

Paul raised his hands. "No, not at all! I just don't know how you do it, that's all. Our lives are stressful enough on a normal basis; add a kid to the mix and my nerves would be shot."

It was a good thing I really wasn't interested in a relationship with Paul. He wouldn't be interested in my own hope of someday having a kid.

"We'll have a problem the moment we step out of the door and the authorities see us," Paul said, clearly trying to change the subject.

"We'll go to help the police round up a wanted criminal, and they'll round us up right along with them," Luke agreed. "Unless we fight our way out."

Selena nodded. "We need masks or something to conceal our identities."

"How's that going to demonstrate we're helping the world?" Paul asked.

"How's running around trying to help and getting caught by Simon Leasure going to help?" Kate retorted.

"Well, you all wanted Wesley to be the team leader," Paul exploded. "Now he's leader and the one making the big decisions. Ask him."

"I'm going to try to call Forrest," Toby spoke up. "Maybe he can get us in with someone who can straighten up this whole mess."

"Don't call him," Paul warned. "You don't know he won't tell someone where we are."

"What, he's going to tell Simon we're in a bar in another dimension?" Toby retorted. "I think we're safe."

He went to open his cell phone, but Paul made a motion and Toby dropped it. The gadget was smoking.

Toby turned incredulous eyes on him. "You melted my phone!"

"I'm sorry, but I can't let you jeopardize the rest of the team's safety to make a booty call," Paul snapped.

"You have got to be kidding! He can help us, and you crack wise with booty-call jokes?"

"This isn't a joke, Toby!" Paul glared at him.

"You're right it isn't. Maybe Wesley won't be stupid enough to turn down help when we need it."

The whole room shook violently, and we all turned to see Fantazia working some sort of magic. The tables and the bar faded and then disappeared, replaced by several couches and chairs. The room we were all standing in seemed to shrink as well. I stumbled into Paul, who reached out a hand to steady me as we all stepped closer, getting the disconcerting feeling of the walls closing in.

I glanced around. In the half of the room where there once was the bar and a few surrounding tables, now there was a long hallway that led off into new rooms. Wow. The fun of owning a pocket universe must be in changing it around however much you wanted. But then Fantazia collapsed into one of the chairs and started rubbing her forehead, muttering to herself, and I realized just how much it took out of her to do this.

"Wesley, I think we need to contact Forrest to see if he can help straighten things out with the government," Toby said.

Wesley shook his head. "We can't right now, Toby, not until we're sure we can get a secure connection to him. Maybe we can use magic to telepathically connect— that's harder to track. Let me think of some options before you try."

Toby nodded. "Yes, sir."

Paul shook his head, a frustrated scowl on his face.

"Now there are five extra rooms we can stay in," Wesley remarked. "We're going to have to share, and someone needs to keep an eye on Cyrus."

Cyrus was affronted. "Me? Why me?"

"Because you've been press-ganged into this little adventure, and I don't trust you not to go wandering off to try to collect some reward for our capture."

Cyrus shrugged. "You've got me there, Old One."

"He can't get out unless I let him," Fantazia remarked.

"Better safe than sorry."

She looked bored. "Do whatever you want. It's not my business."

"I nominate her as my warden," Cyrus said, pointing at me.

"Me?" I squeaked in surprise. Why was it the villain who had the darn crush on me?

Paul stepped forward in an almost protective gesture. "I don't think so."

"I'll do it," Toby said, wearily raising his hand. "I'm one of the strongest here, and I can always knock him out if he gets out of hand."

Cyrus eyed him. "Is that a threat?"

"No, it's a promise," Toby replied.

Cyrus nodded. "Good to know where we stand."

"We'll bunk together," Luke said, motioning to himself and Selena. My heart buckled. As if things weren't bad enough, I had to see visible proof that Luke and Selena had started sleeping together.

"So that leaves Mindy and Kate together, and Paul . . ."

"As the odd man out. Big surprise," Paul grumbled.

Kate nudged me and leaned in to whisper in my ear. "That's convenient for you two."

I closed my eyes and gritted my teeth to not say anything back.

"All you're getting is four walls and a bed," Fantazia said. "I can't provide new clothes, you'll have to go out and get those yourselves if you need them. We do have working plumbing here, but we're all going to have to share that, which is going to be a chore. I'm not reworking the whole system so you all can have private baths."

"We're not expecting that," Wesley said.

"Damn right you're not," she grumbled. "The refrigerator is unlimited, so you all can mooch food off of me as well."

"Thank you, Fantazia. We are grateful to your hospitality," Wesley said.

"Remember that," she replied. "Now I've got a terrible headache thanks to you people, so I'll take you to your rooms."

I hung back as everyone left, lingering in the open room. Paul leaned up against a wall, also watching them go and muttering to himself.

I walked over to him. "Thanks for building that escape route for our research. I'm sorry I never thought of that."

He cast his suit jacket off on the arm of the nearby sofa. With just his dress pants and shirt, he looked a little less fussy. Dare I think it, he almost looked cute. *Wow*, I realized. *That kiss really messed with my head.*

"It's something Rath and I discussed when you were first designing the system," he said. "We decided it would be best if it was something only the two leaders knew, so we went ahead and added it ourselves. I'm sorry for not telling you before. You could have built modifiers to the system to keep people like Cyrus out."

"It sounds like you did a pretty good job on your own."

He ran a hand over his head. "We tried." He looked tired.

"Well, it's still going to take forever to rebuild everything, especially with hardly anything to work with," I said. "The fire-sale action still dumps all of our funds to offshore accounts, right? Or did you change that too?"

"No, the money still goes to the Cayman Islands. Now we'll just have to figure out how to move it without raising suspicion," Paul said. "We can modify cheaper tech into bigger and better things, but it's going to take some time and labor."

"Joy," I said. "Good thing we've got time on our hands." Of course, I didn't know how I felt about the prospect of spending hours locked in a room with Paul.

"When we're not patrolling."

"You think it's a good idea to continue with our jobs as usual?" I asked.

"I do think it is a good idea, actually. But it's a good thing that Wesley made the call about patrolling. There's no way anyone would have listened to me. Like Toby wouldn't listen to reason when he wanted to call his boyfriend, but he turned around and obeyed Wesley."

"Aw, what's wrong, is Mommy mad that the kids are listening to Daddy?" I joked.

He frowned. "You saw what happened today, Mindy."

"Yeah, I saw you tell Toby what to do and then blow up his cell phone when he didn't listen."

"He could have led the authorities straight to us! I know he trusts Forrest, but it doesn't mean Forrest's phone isn't tapped or that he hasn't been forced to cooperate with his superiors."

"I know, but you could have reasoned with him instead of blowing things up."

"It's not like I enjoyed that." At my disbelieving look, he flashed a smile. He had a nice smile. Too bad he was always scowling. "Okay, it's not like I enjoy blowing things up any more than the next red-blooded American man. But I'm more concerned with keeping us safe than maintaining anyone's love life."

"His love life was not the reason that Toby was going to call Forrest and you know it," I growled.

"I'm sure it was to try to find out if he could help. But, come on, you can't tell me his reasons were strictly business."

I shrugged. "Whatever, Paul. I think you've forgotten what it's like to be in a real relationship and have someone you care about that cares about you. Toby's probably worried about Forrest, and vice versa." I softened my voice. "Look, I do understand why you were concerned about security breaches, but you could have handled it better."

"Like Wesley?"

I shrugged my shoulders. "You said it, I didn't."

Paul shook his head. "Sometimes I think I'm the only one who takes this team seriously."

"What's that supposed to mean?"

"The team comes first for me. Everything else is secondary. Wesley has Lainey, Toby has Forrest, and now Luke has Selena to be a distraction. And of course you've always had Luke . . ."

"That's been over for a long time," I said.

"Good." He spoke without looking at me.

"Good how?" I took a step closer to him, trying to catch his gaze.

"I didn't like seeing you following him around like some airhead when I know you're much smarter than that."

"Thanks, I think." Talk about a backhanded compliment!

"You're a much more interesting person now that you're not living in his shadow."

I decided to return the sentiment, since we were having a moment. "And you're much more interesting when you're not so uptight."

He let out a surprised bark of laughter. "I'm uptight?"

I laughed, too. "You say it like it's a shock. You're a control freak and you know it. That's what it really comes down to. You think because you have no love life, no one else gets one."

"Oh, that's exactly what it is, Mindy," Paul said, but his smile outweighed his sarcasm. "I'm a mean, bitter old man because I don't have a love life. Maybe if I had one I would become more understanding. Maybe I wouldn't worry when I'm sharing a bed about how to properly lead this team and try to fix its messes."

"Maybe," I agreed. And then, I don't know what possessed me, but on impulse I leaned forward, bringing my lips to meet his. Maybe I just wanted to see if sparks would fly this time around or if they had been a one-time-only fluke. Maybe I wanted to remind myself that typical type-A personality scientists didn't do it for me. Maybe I just wanted Paul to shut up. Or maybe something else.

The fire came back in a mad, dizzying rush. I had a moment to wonder why someone who could be so abrasive, who infuriated me and hadn't given me a second glance under normal circumstances, could practically make me melt. It was a soft, warm kiss to start, and then drifted into hotter territory as his hands slipped around my waist to pull me in close. I ran my hands up the planes of his chest, digging my fingers into his shirt as the kiss deepened. If I was losing my mind, I wanted to catalogue every experience: the smell of his aftershave, the strength of his arms around me, how his lips tasted.

Then reality came back and we released each other, drifting apart to stare as if we didn't know what to say.

"There," I said, my voice sounding weak and fluttery. "Are you going to be nicer to everybody now?"

He flashed me an awkward smile. "God damn it, Mindy."

I took a step back. "Not exactly the reaction I was wanting."

"I'm trying so hard to keep this on a strictly professional level." He started pacing.

"Sorry." I didn't know what else to say. I hadn't wanted these feelings either, and now they were just there. Like the proverbial elephant in the room.

"I was counting on you to act like yesterday had never happened so I wouldn't be tempted."

I quirked an eyebrow. "Tempted?"

"I mean, we have to work together. In close quarters."

I nodded. "Alone sometimes even."

"God forbid." He passed his hands over his eyes and pinched the bridge of his nose. "I know your parents, for God's sake."

"Is there a point to all of these strange ramblings?"

"I never thought you would do this!" he said, whirling to face me. "I've known you for so long, and I've never, ever looked at you once as anything other than a coworker."

"Well, Jesus, Paul, it's not like I've ever thought of you as anything other than my uptight boss. I'm as stupefied by this attraction as you."

"It's completely inappropriate." He went back to pacing.

"Completely," I agreed.

"When I was twenty-four and just starting to try to convince Rath to let me go on team missions, you were twelve!"

"Yeah, and you always glared at me as if I had no business being at the EHJ headquarters when I came there with my parents."

"You don't even like me most of the time."

"You don't like *me*."

"I don't dislike you! You've always acted like you think I hate you and I don't hate you. I've never hated you. I've always respected you and your work."

I smiled. "I don't think I've ever had a guy who's had his tongue in my mouth say that he respected me or my work."

"I think that's more of a commentary on the guys you've dated."

That was the final icebreaker. I burst out laughing. Paul looked at me for a moment, and then he started laughing too. After the tension-fueled last couple of days, it was a good release.

"Listen, whatever this is," I said, motioning between us. "It's not going to affect our work."

Paul gave me a disbelieving look.

"It isn't! I think we can both agree that this is temporary insanity. I'm sure it will just go away."

"Uh-huh." He looked like he didn't believe me. "I'm having extremely inappropriate thoughts about you right now, and that's just going to go away?"

I blushed. "It will. I mean, so we have a bit of a flirt, so what? At least we're getting along better now. And we're definitely not going to paw at each other right in front of everyone."

"Definitely not," he agreed.

"And we're not going to let it get out of hand. We're grown-ups."

"One would think."

"Why are you two still hanging around in here?"

I jumped about a mile, and Paul whirled to see Fantazia standing in the hallway between the main room and the others, tapping her fingers on her hip and looking impatient.

"We were just talking," I said.

"Well, come on, I'll take you to your room," Fantazia said to me.

I nodded. "I'll see you later, Paul," I said in all seriousness. "Thank you for discussing those tech ideas with me."

I saw the trace of a smile on his lips at my attempt to go back to normal, whatever that was. "No problem, Mindy. And we'll work on your telekinesis tomorrow."

"All right." I followed Fantazia down the hall, leaving Paul and the weird attraction behind. She showed me to my temporary quarters.

Kate looked up as I walked in. "I didn't think you'd actually be using this room."

"Why wouldn't I?" I stripped down to my underwear, suddenly exhausted and ready to curl up in bed and sleep for days if possible.

"I thought I was going to be your cover so you could sneak over to be with Paul. I'll swear you left early every morning for breakfast meetings with him if you want."

With a groan, I pulled the covers up over my head.

CHAPTER TWENTY-TWO

The next morning I dragged myself out of bed to find my roommate already up and around. Kate was a morning person. How annoying.

I threw on my old clothes from yesterday and made a mental note to try to convince Paul or Wesley that we needed to go out at least for basic necessities—like fresh clothes and a toothbrush, for starters.

Paul probably wouldn't be too hard to convince.

It was weird to think of Paul at all, let alone as the guy that made me feel tingly. I kept thinking I would wake up and things would be normal again: We would be back home, Simon's crew wouldn't have tried to arrest us, Paul would be just my stick-in-the-mud boss.

I walked into the new main room to find everyone hanging out, looking like they didn't know what to do with themselves. So far, we were still in a pocket universe and on the run from Simon. Things had not magically sorted themselves out overnight.

Kate was in one corner of the room, talking to Cyrus. (I wish I could say I was surprised.) Wesley and Lainey were holding some sort of conference with Fantazia on the other side of the room; Luke and Selena were sipping coffee and eating some sort of breakfast pastry a short distance away, obviously listening to the conversation. All voices were hushed, like we were living in a library or something.

I helped myself to a bagel and a mug of coffee, even though I wasn't all that hungry. I wondered how Fantazia got food into this universe. Had the bagels and that carafe just disappeared from other places in the regular world? Or were these magic bagels and coffee?

And, why was I pondering the origin of this food when our entire world had been turned upside down?

"You're up and about early," Toby remarked, reaching around me to nab a blueberry muffin. He was holding a delicate china cup of tea. From where had Fantazia conjured that?

"Couldn't sleep," I said. "As soon as I rolled over, I woke up and remembered what happened."

"I know what you mean," Toby said. "I kept expecting all of this to be a nightmare."

"We need a television or something in here," I said. "Something to take our minds off all of this."

"Tell me about it," Toby agreed. "Can you get cable in pocket universes?"

I laughed and then took advantage of the moment to ask, "So . . . I take it you're talking to me again."

He frowned. "Why wouldn't I?"

"You seemed upset with me after my incident at the club."

He put his hands in his pockets and looked down. "I might have been a little. I thought you were being irresponsible. But then Lainey told me what happened with taking off the blocks and what you remembered . . ." He looked back up at me. "I'm sorry, kiddo. That well and truly sucks. And then everything that happened yesterday probably doesn't help matters any. How are you holding up?"

If only he knew what crazy things I was doing to cope. Maybe that's what I could blame my strange attraction to Paul on: It was a coping mechanism.

"I'm doing okay," I said. Then my attention was drawn to the person walking into the room. Paul. He looked around as if he wasn't sure which group to join. I felt his eyes turn on me. Something was dancing in those blue depths—amusement mixed with worry, maybe?

I turned my attention back to Toby. "So yeah, I think we need to get a television. If for nothing else, just to kill time."

"We need something on which to monitor trouble," Paul said, overhearing and walking toward us. Nothing had changed about him, really; he looked wholly the same as last night, and yet somehow he was completely different. Maybe it was because his suit was rumpled, maybe it was the fact that he had dark circles under his eyes.

Or maybe it was that I was actually noticing that he really did have the darkest, bluest eyes I'd ever seen, and even though the suit was conservative, it really did show off his shoulders in a way that was very attractive.

He must have noticed me checking him out, because he gave me a half smile and pointedly asked, "Are you okay, Mindy?"

"Sorry." I tried to reorganize my thoughts. *Think of mean, nasty Paul*, I reminded myself, *not the unbelievably great kisser.* "My mind was wandering."

"About yesterday?" Toby nodded in sympathy. "It doesn't seem real, does it?"

I shook my head, watching Paul. "No."

"It's surreal—like something out of a dream," Paul remarked, and I felt my cheeks flush. I tore my gaze away from his.

"We need to do something to get back our sense of normalcy," Toby opined.

"Wesley's right. We need to focus on doing what we normally do—helping people," Paul said. "With that in mind, I think we need to get a television. Or at least a computer with Internet access. Something to let us know what's going on in the outside world."

"I was thinking we also need to get some basic necessities," I said. "Unless Fantazia has some sort of magic Laundromat going on here, these clothes are going to start smelling pretty ripe if we have to wear them day after day."

"I hear that," Toby said. "You can only turn your underwear inside out once, you know."

"Just go without," I said without thinking, and noticed Paul's eyes widen.

"Do what you want, Mindy, but going commando is not my thing," Toby said. He gave a slight shudder.

"Er, I think we're definitely going to have to discuss the clothing issue," Paul agreed. "Maybe we'll go in shifts of two or something to buy new stuff. Or maybe we should send a team. I don't think we need to go roaming the streets in a group right now, but I also don't think alone is a good idea."

"Here you go," Wesley said, walking up with Lainey and Fantazia, Luke and Selena in tow. "Fantazia's worked up a little something to make coming and going from here easier."

Fantazia dropped what looked like a coin on a string into each of our hands. I held mine up to the light. "Money?"

She shook her head. "It's a key and a *glamour* all in one. It will allow those of you not magically inclined to access the doorway to this world. This is the only thing that will allow anyone in or out now that I've locked the place down. If you lose it, you're on your own."

"And the *glamour* part?" Toby asked.

"It conceals your real appearance in the outside world. Of course, to anyone wearing one, you'll look the same as usual. High-level magic users can also see right through the disguise, so a degree of caution when you're out would still be a good idea," she warned.

Wesley nodded. "She's right. Even though we're going to still help people, we don't need to draw any unnecessary attention. The time for us as glory hounds is over. Save the day, but don't stick around for pictures."

We all nodded.

"How are we doing, Cyrus?" Wesley asked.

"All set," Cyrus replied, and I noticed he and Kate were surrounding a small laptop.

"Where'd you get that?" I asked.

"I was allowed out long enough to get my stuff—with the Old One," Cyrus said. "Can't be a techno mage without some techno, know what I mean? And if I'm going to be working for you . . ."

"Wait, you're letting him work for us now?" Luke asked. "He's a criminal!"

"He's a criminal who knows how to divert our funds into local banks without Simon's government connections finding out," said Wesley. "Unless anyone here knows how to do that?"

"For a small percentage, of course," Cyrus put in. He wouldn't want to look like he was out for anyone but himself.

"He's also a good source of information," Fantazia said. "Trust me, I've gotten some of my best dirt from him. If you want to know what Simon's cronies in Washington are up to, he'll dig it up. Probably with photographic evidence."

"I do PowerPoint presentations now," Cyrus joked.

Fantazia scoffed. "Pardon me for not knowing what that is—or caring."

Luke looked at Paul. "I still think this is a mistake."

"Kate's monitoring him. If he steps out of line, she'll turn on her power and he'll do what she wants," Paul replied. Did I detect a trace of bitterness in his voice?

"You knew about this?" Luke asked.

Paul nodded. "Wesley and I talked about it last night."

"And didn't include the rest of us?"

"We're the team leaders," Paul said, a hint of ire in his voice. "We can't run everything by you, Luke. Groups need heads to make these kinds of decisions. You never questioned Rath . . ."

"It's a good idea, Luke," Selena said. "We're all stressed. There's no need to snap at each other."

Luke took a deep breath. "You're right, baby." He gave Cyrus a nasty look. "I just don't trust him."

"And I'm wounded about that," Cyrus said. "Now, Old One, I dropped the amount you requested into each account across town."

Wesley nodded. "Great. I think we'll send a few people out to get necessities. How about Lainey and Selena go and get everyone some clothes and toiletries and the like. Oh, and a television, so we can monitor the news. Lainey can work a teleportation spell to send it back here."

"No problem," Lainey said. "I like how the former secretaries get the shopping duty."

"You're the ones who know all of our sizes," Wesley admitted. Was the Reincarnist blushing?

"Yeah, yeah," my friend said, and leaned forward to give him a kiss. "Even in a pocket universe, the more things change, the more they stay the same."

"I'd like to go get some bits and pieces of tech to start modifying," I said. "We at least need to get a communication system up and running."

"That's a good idea, Mindy," Wesley said. "Someone should go with you."

Cyrus put up his hand. "I volunteer."

"You've already been allowed out once with me. Count yourself lucky," Wesley retorted.

"First I'm a prisoner, then I'm a coworker, then I'm a prisoner. Make up your damn mind, will you?" the Virus grumbled.

"I'll go," Paul said. "She might need my help."

I bit down a retort. Like I'd ever needed Paul's opinion on anything for my inventions! But then I saw Kate smirking at me and decided to ignore the both of them.

"Sounds good," Wesley agreed. "Everyone try to meet back here at three so that we know you're okay."

Lainey edged close to me. "Is it wrong that I'm glad Wes is going to have to keep Emily for a while? This strange new place and everyone being stressed has stressed her out in turn, and she's done nothing but fuss all night. My nerves are shot."

"I seriously don't know how you handle all of this the way you do," I replied, and we stepped toward the door together.

Lainey shrugged. "You get used to it."

I took a deep breath and stepped forward toward the portal between worlds, and with a shimmering, queasy feeling I was back in the smelly alley behind the biker bar. Awesome: My headache had returned.

"You all right?" Paul asked, as I rubbed my head and groaned.

"Yeah, it's just this headache came back almost as soon as I stepped outside."

"That's weird." He frowned.

"I'll buy you some migraine stuff," Lainey offered.

"Thanks."

"Well, we'll see you ladies later. Let's go, Mindy," Paul said as he started down the sidewalk.

I followed after him. "You didn't have to come along, you know."

"No one needs to be going off alone right now. I'll be working on these projects with you, so it makes sense for me to come along." He gave me a sideways glance. "You didn't want me or something?"

"No, it's not that," I was quick to say. "I mean, it doesn't matter to me. I just meant you just don't have to if you don't want to." I was stumbling over my words. Why was I acting like such a spaz?

"Well, I want to. Now which way is the ATM?"

I looked at the paper Cyrus had given him. "It's that way." I pointed left. "Six blocks up. Think we can spring for a cab after we get some cash? I don't feel like walking around all day in the open like this. Or in these heels."

"Absolutely. If it wasn't daylight, I'd say we could fly. But since that would attract attention, it looks like we're going to have to hoof it until we get some money." He looked down at my feet. "I hope those boots are comfortable and not just for making your legs look hot."

I looked down. "You think they make my legs look hot?"

"Like you'd wear them if they didn't." He gave me a half smile. "And yes, I think they do. Now let's get down to business instead of talking fashion in the middle of the street."

I followed him. "I'm just not used to you giving me compliments."

"Hey, I said your hair looked nice after you had it done."

"No, you didn't. You said I was trying to remake myself into what I thought Luke would like."

"No, I didn't!"

"Yes, you did!"

"I did?" He gave me a sideways glance. "Hmm. That does sound like something I'd say. Well, I take it back. Your hair looks nice like that."

"Thanks."

"Even if you did do it to get some guy's attention."

I turned to give him a nasty look and saw his mouth twitching, so I settled for a light punch on the arm. "Jerk. I'm seeing a whole new side of you, Paul, and I can't decide if I like it or not."

"Well, let me know when you make up your mind."

My head continued to pound. I was beginning to think it was a reaction to the sun or something. Or stress. I glanced around as we walked up to the ATM. "Is it just me or does it feel like everyone's watching us?"

Paul looked around. "It's just you. No one's looking at us any more than at anyone else."

"I don't know." I ran my hands up and down my arms, feeling a chill that wasn't climatic. "I'm just getting that feeling you have when someone's watching you."

"It's probably because of what's going on with us. It's made you a bit paranoid. Understandable, but still paranoid." He got money out of the ATM and tucked it away. "But we're protected by magic, remember?"

"No, that's not it . . ." I trailed off as a sharp stab of pain burst through my head. "Ow!"

Paul reached for me. "Mindy?"

I swear I could hear my heartbeat in my head. I concentrated, trying to relax, to push the pain away, to breathe in and out and imagine the waves, like Paul had taught me.

There you are, the voice whispered in my head. It was pushing unwanted into my thoughts.

I mentally pushed back. *Shut up!*

The pain was suddenly gone, as if a cloud had lifted around me. I looked over to see Paul still holding my arm and my waist, looking concerned.

"Did I do anything? Did I hurt anybody?" I asked, sweeping a quick look around me. Everything looked normal.

"No, nothing happened. Except, you looked like you were having some sort of episode. Are you all right?"

"I'm okay," I said, feeling my heart rate return to normal. It was the first time that I hadn't lashed out during an attack. "I'm okay now. I visualized the waves like you told me. I think I'm starting to control things a bit."

"That's great!" He looked pleased but still concerned. "Are you sure you're all right?"

"Yeah. That feeling I had like I was being watched? Someone just spoke to me. In my head. And it's not the first time it's happened."

"Before your other attacks?" he prompted.

"I don't know." I thought back to all the times I had heard the voice. "I think so."

"A telepath," Paul said. "Trying to contact or harass you. Maybe the stress of having them brush up against your mind is kicking off your telekinetic bursts. We've seen them come on from stress." He frowned. "What has the voice said to you?"

"Not much. 'I see you,' 'There you are,' and 'You're all alone' . . ." I trailed off. I didn't want Paul to know some freak was playing on my sense of loneliness. "Whoever it was seems to have been looking for me. And found me."

"Now we just have to figure out what they want." Paul frowned. "Maybe if we figure out how to help you better control your powers, you'll be able to block this person completely. Their unwanted communications are—"

"Like mind spam?"

Paul gave a startled burst of laughter. "Like mind spam. Exactly."

"Great." I sighed. "Another project. As if we weren't busy enough with having to rebuild from the ground up and continuing to fight the good fight."

"You wouldn't want life to be boring, would you?" Paul joked.

"I guess not." I took him by the arm to lead him down the road. "Come on, I still feel up to shopping. Let's go find ways to turn a CD player and a dog's shock collar into a weapon."

"Great idea. Let's grab a toaster, too."

I gave him a smile. Paul had a sense of humor. It was just another one of the surprises about him I was discovering.

CHAPTER TWENTY-THREE

"So then I told him, if you can't figure out how a car engine works, I'm afraid the science of black holes is totally beyond you. I don't care if you did play the captain of a space exploration ship."

"That's what you get for dating a celebrity," Paul said. "They're paid to be pretty, not brilliant. Can you hand me that motherboard?"

"He wasn't so pretty, either." I looked around for the motherboard. Paul's new bedroom had become our impromptu workshop, and there were random bits and pieces scattered about like a tornado had hit. We'd come home from our shopping extravaganza and immediately dug in, constructing a new communications system. "I don't see it."

"It's under that portable radio there." He pointed again.

"How did it get under there?" I handed the piece over and went back to work.

"You scattered everything around like you were divining the future from the entrails of that poor radio."

I looked up with a grin. "Nice analogy, Paul. All highbrow and stuff."

He laughed. "Well, I have to live here, you know, so if you can keep the chaos to a dull roar, it'd be appreciated."

"At least you don't have to live with Kate."

He gave me a pointed look, and I winced. "At least you don't have to live with Kate *anymore*. I don't trust morning people. Who wants to wake up early?"

"I get up early," he remarked.

"And I don't trust you either," I retorted. "There's something sick about someone who doesn't need coffee to motivate them."

"Luke gets up early and doesn't need coffee."

"He's sick, too."

"Weren't you the one getting up early to work out with him?"

"Yeah, well, I'm not doing that anymore."

"Getting up early and working out? Not even if *I* ask you?"

"Absolutely not."

"I'm crushed," he said.

"You'll survive." I looked up to give him a teasing grin, and saw him watching me intensely. He flashed me a quick apologetic smile. He knew I had caught him staring.

"However," I continued, "if you want me to stay up late working on some invention, I'll be glad to, so long as more coffee is involved."

"Good to know you've got your priorities straight."

"That's right." I looked around. "Now, where did I put that . . . ?"

"What are you looking for?"

"Didn't we get a soldering iron? I've got to fuse these two wires together."

"Here." He got up and walked over to where I sat on the edge of his bed. "Which ones?"

"These." I held them up to the light.

He leaned over my shoulder and raised a finger. "Hold them still."

I did. As I watched, a small burst of heat shot out of his finger and into the wires, melting them together.

"Well, aren't you handy to have around? Thanks!" I turned to look at him as I said it, and realized too late how close he was. As I turned my head, our mouths were just a space away. It was almost too tempting to close that tiny distance and lean in for a kiss.

He didn't move away, but judging from his intake of breath he must have realized the same thing. "You're welcome," he said. His eyes went to my lips.

My breath quickened. "And it was going so well."

"Says you," he said. "You and your sexy boots." He tilted my chin back toward him with his fingertips, and brushed his lips against mine in a soft kiss that made my insides melt. God, what had happened to us?

A knock sounded on the door, and we scrambled away from each other like teenagers caught by a watchful parent. I picked up a random piece of plastic and started tinkering as Paul went to answer the door.

"Yes?" he said, and I hoped whoever it was didn't notice how flustered he sounded.

"Hi, Paul," Selena said, breezing into the room. "I just brought you some clothes and . . ." She trailed off when she saw me. "Hi, Mindy. I didn't know you were in here."

"Yeah." I held up my piece of plastic. "Working on the communications system."

"It's going to be a secure frequency," Paul promised.

"We're modifying Bluetooth technology," I remarked, holding up a piece. "So we'll look like every other random city person, yakking to no one but thin air."

"It won't look suspicious," Paul added.

Selena nodded as if she didn't notice the steady stream of babble. "Well, I won't keep you. I just wanted to drop this off. Mindy, Lainey left yours in your bedroom, is that all right?"

"Sure thing. Thanks, Selena," I said.

"No problem. Go back to work. Sorry for interrupting."

"That's fine. Thank you, Selena," Paul said, closing the door behind her.

I put my tools back down and laughed. "Oops."

He smiled. "Oops is right."

"Do you think she suspected anything?"

"Not a chance. Who would?"

"Kate."

"Besides Kate. Our dirty little secret is safe, Mindy."

"Good, because I wouldn't want anyone to know I have a hidden attraction for anyone who wears polo shirts. Yuck!" I held up the offending item from the bag that Selena had brought. "Really, Paul? Polo shirts?"

He stared at me. "What's wrong with polo shirts?"

"Besides everything?"

"I don't make snide comments about your clothing."

"No, because I have good taste and you secretly like it." I dug in further. "Ooh, jeans? If you wear these, it will be a first."

He took the bag. "Will you quit digging through my stuff, please?"

"Afraid I'm going to find out if you wear boxers or briefs?" I teased. "I can just ask Kate, you realize. If you tick me off enough."

"There are better ways you could find out," he said, completely deadpan.

I looked up, my mouth hanging open. "Paul Christian! I can't believe you just said that!"

"Got you to stop, didn't it?" He picked up some of the bits and pieces of tech lying all over his bed. "Now, we need to test this. Maybe we can take the prototypes out when we go on patrol. Leave the receiver here with Wesley . . ." He trailed off when he noticed me still staring at him. "What? I was just joking, Mindy. You know I would never take things that far."

He didn't realize the reason I was standing there gaping was that I was actually imagining what it would be like to slowly unbutton his shirt and then his pants, all the while getting one of his bone-searing kisses. For some reason I was picturing him to be a briefs man, but not one of those tighty-whitey types. No, they'd be a darker color. Black or dark blue. Or maybe he wore those boxer briefs . . .

"I'm sorry," I said, realizing he was speaking. "You were saying?"

"I said, maybe we've worked too long on that communication system. Why don't we take a break and maybe see what we can do about teaching you how to control your powers?" Paul was apparently back to business. "How are your headaches, by the way?"

"Oh, um, they're fine." I pushed aside thoughts of him undressing me next (Who would have thought I'd ever have to do that?!) and focused on work, not on my obvious extremely lonely and demented state. "It seems once we walk into this pocket dimension, whoever's trying to contact me can't."

"You're away from the real world," he said. "Hopefully we can teach you to put up walls of your own."

"But no one here has telekinetic or telepathic abilities. How is anyone going to teach me?"

"Well, I've thought about that." He cleared his throat. "I think I could maybe help you with your telekinetic abilities. As I've said before, your reactions have been stress-induced, and that's how it was with me when I first got my powers, so I'm hoping there's a similar mechanic. As for the telepathic part, I thought that perhaps Luke could work with you on cleansing and clearing your mind through meditation. It's all about focusing your thoughts and blocking the rest."

"That makes sense," I admitted. "So what do I do?"

"Well, for starters . . ." He set an empty pop can on the edge of the bed and came to stand next to me on the other side. "See if you can create a psionic wave to knock that can off the bed. Focus all of your thoughts and attention on pushing the can away from you, if that makes sense."

"Okay." I thought of the can and tried to think of pushing it, of knocking it away with my hand, except not doing it in the physical sense. "Nothing's happening."

"Well, it's not going to happen the first time. It will take a lot of practice," he said, practical as always. "You're not just going to wake up and be able to do it. Since your powers have been emotion-based so far, use that. Channel your emotion into using the power to your benefit. Think of something you are afraid of or angry at, and then make the can the focal point. That's what I did for a while. My heat powers were an expression of my anger or frustration."

"I'm shocked the EHJ headquarters didn't spontaneously combust a long time ago," I joked.

"I said for a while. I gained control eventually." He nodded at the can. "Go ahead and try."

I focused on the can. I was angry and scared that some creep was trying to talk to me in my head. I was angry at the memories that I had so recently recovered. I was angry that we had been chased from our home by Simon Leasure and his cronies. I tried to channel all of that into pushing that stupid can over the edge.

A dent appeared in the side of the can, but it didn't topple over.

"Well, that's progress," Paul said. "You just need to work on this every day. And when you experience anger or fear, you need to not panic and instead channel it inside for when you need to fight. Think of it as a backup system."

"So, bottle up all of my feelings like a man. Got it."

He shot me a look. "You're not as funny as you think you are."

"Oh yes I am," I said. "But you're not the stick-in-the-mud I thought you were. You can be cool."

"You just say that now because you want to solve the underwear mystery." A smile twitched on his face as he picked up bits of our project and started stowing it for later.

"See, that's exactly what I mean," I said. "When you relax and tease and joke, you're fun to be around. Kate must have told you—"

"I never acted like that around Kate," he interrupted in a low voice, picking up something else. "I always felt like I had to be on guard with her."

The full meaning of his words hit me. He had been with Kate for a long time but had never felt as comfortable around her as he did around me. Maybe that said something about how he felt about Kate.

Or maybe that said something about how he felt about me.

How did I want Paul to feel about me? I wasn't able to figure out this strange attraction and friendship we were forging. I would have never thought that I could be this comfortable around him, either. I had known him for so long, and yet we had never been all that close. Previous to this, he had been almost like a famil-iar stranger. But that was changing every day. I didn't feel like I had to impress him with how cool or how tough or how sexy I was, like I always did with other guys. I also didn't feel like I had to hide my intellect. I could relax. I could just be me.

How scary was that?

I looked up at the can. I channeled those churning feelings in the pit of my stomach at it. The can toppled over the edge.

Paul looked at the can and then at me. "Did you just do that?"

I nodded. "Uh-huh."

"Great! Whatever you were just thinking of, hold that thought for later. Keep it in the back of your mind."

I nodded again. "Oh, I will."

CHAPTER TWENTY-FOUR

"So how'd we luck out and end up having patrol with Paul?" Toby groused as we stood atop one of the office buildings in the city and kept watch for trouble.

"Just the luck of the draw, I guess," I said, giving a glance around.

When Wesley had mentioned patrolling tonight, Paul had immediately volunteered himself and me to test out our communications system. I had the vague suspicion he just wanted more time together, a thought that wouldn't have even crossed my mind a few weeks back— no, make that a few days back. So much had happened since Paul and I first kissed that it felt like weeks and not the day or so it had been. Toby was volunteered by Wesley to tag along. He didn't look any more thrilled by the prospect now. I remembered all the times Toby and I had made fun of our stick-in-the-mud boss. Now those jokes weren't so funny.

Pushing the button on the Bluetooth headset Paul and I had modified, I said, "I don't see anything up here."

"That's because you're too high up," Paul replied through the earpiece. "Move down this way a bit."

"Reading you loud and clear, boss," I said, with a bit of sarcasm. It had been Paul's idea for me and Toby to scout the rooftops while he followed the alleys, so what more did he want? And why was I, the one with no controllable powers and no current technology, crawling around on rooftops in the first place? "I'm moving down to the ground with you."

"Give Toby your earpiece," Paul said.

I unhooked the device from my ear. "Here you are. I'm going down with the boss man." Wow, that sounded pervy now! Good thing Toby didn't know the truth.

My friend took the Bluetooth without batting an eyelash. "Great," he complained. "I'll have to listen to Paul breathing into my ear constantly."

"It only works when you push the button," I said. "So you won't have to hear him all the time. Only when he wants you to."

"I'm sure that will be close to constant," he grumbled, and took a running leap over to the next building. I descended the fire escape as quietly as possible; I didn't want people in surrounding buildings to hear me clanging about and calling the cops. That was the last thing we needed.

After climbing down what felt like five billion stairs, I ended up on the ground, splashing into a puddle of muck and God knows what else. "Ew!" I said, lifting my boot and cursing Simon and his cronies for ruining a good pair of boots that I shouldn't have been wearing on patrol in the first place. Thanks to Lainey and Selena's shopping, I now had a pair of jeans and sneakers, as well as a tank top or two and a few other essentials. We had all ended up in black jeans and T-shirts for patrol. Not the most stunning of hero wear, but who was going to complain? Unfortunately, the sneakers I'd gotten were bright white. I made a mental note to buy a pair of practical dark shoes so I wouldn't have to wear these boots anymore—my "sexy boots" as Paul called them.

"You all right?" he said, coming over to me. I had to admit, seeing him in such casual wear as jeans and a T-shirt gave me a pleasant pause. He looked totally different, less rigid. And the girls had managed to find dark sneakers for him and Toby, the lucky jerks.

"Oh, it's these boots," I said, lifting one foot. "They're not exactly made for patrol."

"You should have worn the sneakers."

"My feet would have glowed."

"True." He motioned for me to follow him. "Well, we're almost done now. Only a few more blocks to go. How's your head?"

"No weird messages from beyond," I said, following him. "So far."

"That's good," he said, creeping along to the opening of the alley. "Maybe . . ." He paused and put a hand to his ear. Toby was saying something to him. "I understand. Proceed with caution." He glanced over at me. "Toby just saw AssaultR breaking into a building."

I froze. "What good am I going to be against him?" AssaultR was a notorious villain. He once picked up a bus and threw it at cops as a simple distraction. Here I was, nothing but a lowly human with possible telekinesis that I couldn't control. Paul and I had spent most of the day working on our communications system; I hadn't even begun to work on any technology I needed to fight.

"You can stand nearby and throw trash cans at him telekinetically," Paul said. "Or garbage trucks."

I gave him a look. "I don't think I'm quite there yet."

"Just stand by in case Toby or I need you to call for backup," he replied, taking off his communicator and handing it to me. "We have it wired to call our base of operations, so in an emergency just hit that switch."

"I remember, I'm the one that helped design it," I said, taking the headset and putting it on.

". . . going into the bank," Toby was saying. "I think

the silent alarm has been tripped. Should I follow him in?"

"Toby wants to know if he should follow AssaultR in," I said to Paul.

"Tell him to hold back for a moment," Paul replied, looking around. "I don't want him going into a building to fight when he can't see what's coming up behind him. Better to wait until AssaultR comes out."

"Unless he leaves through the other side," I pointed out.

Paul frowned. "Good point. Tell him we'll cover the rear exit, have him stay out front."

As I relayed the directives to Toby, I couldn't help but be worried. What exactly *was* I going to do if he came blasting out at us? Hide behind Paul?

We skirted the building, sidling around the back. From inside I could hear muffled thumps. It sounded like AssaultR was going to pummel his way through the safe.

"Paul," I whispered.

"Yeah, I know," he replied. "It sounds like he's destroying the place."

"So guys, what are we doing?" Toby asked.

"Toby wants to know what to do," I relayed to Paul.

"Tell him to hold tight . . ." Paul trailed off, putting a finger to his lips. "Wait, did you hear that?"

"Hear what?"

"That high-pitched noise." He motioned for me to be quiet. "There it is again. It almost sounds like . . ."

I pointed to the sky. "Someone's coming!"

"Quick!" He pulled me along, behind the dumpster, for us to slip between it and the wall. It was a very tight fit. I ended up smashed against him, my face buried in his chest. It felt like every part of our bodies was touching. If it wasn't for the smelly garbage nearby, it might have been weirdly romantic. I certainly felt my entire body heat up.

"What are you doing?" I hissed, squirming against him.

"Shh!"

From around Paul, I watched as two heroes landed in the alleyway where we'd been standing. It was very dark, but I could just make out their faces as they passed the streetlamp. It was two of Simon's cronies.

"You guys, where are you?" Toby crackled in my ear. Paul yanked the headset off my head and buried the Bluetooth somewhere between my stomach and his. I felt his fingertips brush the edge of my skin, just barely peeking out from where my shirt had ridden up, and my breath quickened. I knew my face flushed. It was wrong to get turned on in a situation like this. So wrong. But I couldn't help it. I glanced up at Paul in the darkness and could see his dark blue eyes peering down at me. He shifted and ran his other hand down my bare arm. I shivered deliciously and, without meaning to, wet my lips.

The heroes in the alley paused and looked back our way. Paul's grip on my arm tightened—

A loud crash from inside the building tore their attention away, and they hurried to the front of the bank. Paul yanked the communicator back up and spoke into it. "Toby, get out of there now! Two AA members are heading in your direction!"

A dark figure sailed down from the sky to land in front of our dumpster. "Where are you guys?" I heard Toby whisper.

I eased myself out from beside Paul. "Right here."

Toby frowned. "What were you doing back there?"

"Didn't you hear me?" Paul hissed. "I said there were two AA members here." There were multiple crashes sounding from inside the building. The fight must have commenced.

Toby shrugged. "So? We're glamoured, remember? They can't see us."

From the expression on Paul's face, he'd forgotten about that. Or maybe he'd just wanted an excuse to press up against me. One or the other.

"We still don't want to attract their attention. If they're trying to arrest us, who knows what they'll do to people lurking around a crime site, dressed all in black."

"Good point," Toby said.

I could now hear sirens blaring. The police were here. And there were shouts coming from the front of the building.

"I'll go check it out," I whispered, and broke away from the guys.

"Be careful!" Paul hissed after me.

I crept to the edge of the building and peered around the corner. There were Simon's new team members, one of the women and one of the men, standing there in triumph, holding a bound AssaultR between them like he was the catch of the day. Several of the police had their guns drawn and pointed. Then "the Cage" pulled up: the steel truck used to transport powered villains to the appropriate jailing facility. The policemen clapped as Simon's cronies led AssaultR over to the truck and tossed him in.

"That should be us," I sighed. It looked like no one was missing the EHJ. Simon's crew had replaced us in our building, in our stature with the government, and now in the public eye, and probably no one was going to even blink.

Depressed, I turned back to find the guys.

"They saved the day," I reported glumly.

Paul nodded, as if unperturbed. "Let's head home.

We'll take the long route so we can swing a full patrol on the way."

"Great, maybe more AA members can show up and beat us to the punch," I said.

Paul glanced at me. "Toby, why don't you go on ahead? We can test out the range of the communication system. That way the night won't be a total wash."

Toby nodded. "Sure thing." He looked at me again. "Are you okay, Mindy?"

I shrugged. "Just seeing them like that made it more real, you know?"

He patted me on the shoulder. "I know. But we're going to find a way to clear our name and get back on top again. You'll see."

"That's right," Paul said. "Now we better get moving before the police start investigating back here. Let's go."

We walked in silence toward home, Toby bounding over rooftops above, while Paul and I took the alleyways. Toby and Paul would randomly speak through our communicator, which I gathered was working as it should. Yay. This was one bright spot in a pretty lousy evening.

I couldn't explain why seeing the AA members there had bothered me so much, but it had. I had been chased from my home and begun living in a pocket dimension; I knew that, but I couldn't help but continuing to hope it was all a bad dream. This just proved it wasn't. It was all real.

And my head was hurting.

You're nothing now, a voice in my head whispered. *And when I get there, I'm going to finish wiping out your very existence.*

I froze, rooted to the spot. "Shut up," I whispered. "I don't know who you are or what you want, or why you're messing with me, but just shut up!"

Paul must have noticed that I'd stopped, because he came rushing back. "What's wrong?"

I couldn't pay attention to him. The voice in my head had gotten more insistent. *You're weak and I'm strong. There's nothing you can do to stop me. Any of you. You want to save the world, but it's because of you it's going to end.*

"My friend went through this already," I growled. I felt something warm and wet run from my nose and I brushed it away in bemused irritation. "She had some weirdo invading her dreams, wanting to use her to end the world. Well, we put a stop to the Dragon's plan, and she and Wesley sent him to some scary hellish dimension, so unless you want to end up there with him, shut the hell up!"

"Mindy! Mindy!" I heard Paul shout, but it was like he was in a tunnel far away. I ignored him as the voice spoke again.

Silly girl, do you think this is some sort of game with interdimensional gods? My people eat those self-proclaimed gods for breakfast. We don't play apocalypse games. We destroy worlds, well and truly. Which you're going to find out. Very soon.

"We'll stop you," I vowed. The wet heat was running down my lip now. "Me and my friends. I don't care if the government wants our help or not, we'll find a way to be around and help."

You'll do nothing but allow it to happen. Every time we speak, I get closer to you, the voice promised.

"Mindy, stop talking to it," Paul was saying. "Concentrate! You've got to block whoever it is out, it's killing you!"

I looked down at my hand and saw in shock that it was covered in blood. There was blood trickling from my nose! I wiped it away in horror.

I won't kill you, not when I'm still finding you . . .

"Shut up!" This time I focused my rage and fear and pushed as hard as I could, mentally. The pressure in my head started to let up.

"You're doing it," Paul said. "Keep pushing!"

So alone. What do you want to save this world for anyway? the voice asked, but it was getting softer, almost a whisper.

"I'm not alone," I said between gritted teeth, pushing harder. I angrily wiped the blood away. "People care."

Paul grabbed me by the arms and looked directly into my eyes. "You have friends that care. People that care. *Fight.*"

My mind swam. The pressure in my head eased, but I felt weak, tired, like I could slip away and sleep forever. Then I wouldn't have to deal with being a homeless wanted criminal with some freak-job messing with my brain. I wouldn't have to deal with being alone.

Paul crushed me to him and kissed me, almost bruising my lips with his fierceness, and suddenly I felt more awake than I had all night.

I kissed him back, hard, opening my mouth to his, tasting his lips, his tongue, and his breath. He smelled faintly of sweat from walking around all night, a scent that was earthy and masculine. I ran my hands up his chest, feeling the muscles hidden beneath his shirt. My hands came to rest against his neck, and I ran my fingertips up to the stubble of his close-cropped hair. As I pressed my body against his, I felt all of my fears from earlier melt away in a haze of lust. The police could come by right now and arrest us and I wouldn't care. I was beginning to understand the appeal of darkened alleyways, like that couple Luke and I had happened on what felt like a lifetime ago.

Paul's hands were doing a bit of roaming on their

own. They slipped down to my buttocks and stayed there, pulled my hips into him. I gasped slightly with arousal and moved to kiss his neck. His five o'clock shadow was prickly under my mouth. He groaned in a way that was good.

"Wait, wait," Paul was saying, trying to disentangle us. "This was meant to snap you out of it."

"I feel pretty out of it," I said, my voice husky to my own ears. It was like I had developed some sort of strange addiction to kissing him that, once I started, I couldn't stop.

He laughed, a strange deep sound unlike I'd ever heard. It was a secret laugh, one that probably only Kate or the other women who'd shared his bed had heard. "I meant snap you out of fainting, not turn this into some sort of grope-fest in a back alley."

I blinked. I never thought I'd hear Paul use a term like grope-fest, much less participate in one. With me. "See what you started?" I said in a light tone. "I'm beginning to see a certain appeal to back alleys."

"Guys? Guys? Where are you?"

I could hear Toby's voice crackle through the speaker attached to Paul's ear; that's how close we were standing. I sagged in his arms and said, "I think we're developing a pattern."

"It's probably for our own good we were interrupted again," Paul said. "Back alleys aren't the most sanitary of places."

I laughed. "Well, thanks for snapping me out of it." Inside I was crying out for him to keep kissing me, touching me. I was more than a little shocked to realize how much I wanted him.

"Glad I could help," he said, giving me a wink. "Let's go find Toby."

CHAPTER TWENTY-FIVE

"I spoke to Luke about starting your meditation training today."

I looked up from the new shocker I was working on. "Really?"

Paul nodded. "Yes, I think it is important to start immediately after what happened last night with whoever is messing with your head. You need to learn how to block them as soon as possible."

"What, and no longer require your 'snapping me out of it' services?" I flashed him a flirty grin.

He returned it, which warmed my heart. "I will continue to offer those services whenever necessary. But I thought that, for your peace of mind and my own, it might be nice if you could block enemies yourself and not rely on me or other distractions."

"Very good point," I agreed.

"And I don't want to see you bleeding like that ever again. Once is more than enough for a lifetime."

A flush of pleasure swept my body. "Aw, shucks, you don't have to worry about little ol' me," I said, teasing, then looked up to see him staring at me in concern.

"I'm serious, Mindy," he said, his voice soft. "I don't ever want to see you like that again."

My heart began pounding in my ears. I'd started off glad to have someone worried about me, concerned for my well-being, but now I was a bit freaked out. His intensity was intimidating. My feelings for him were a confused and muddled mess; I didn't know what exactly I wanted. What did he want from me?

I was still weighing those heavy thoughts when Wesley barged in without knocking. Good thing there was no make-out session in progress, I thought as I said, "Hi, Wes. Knock much?"

He glanced at me. "I knew it was just you two in here working. It's not like I'm interrupting anything. Was I?"

I shot a quick glance at Paul, who raised a hand to his mouth to hide a smirk. We wisely looked away from each other.

"Paul, I need to see you for a moment out in the common room," Wesley continued. "You too, Mindy. Actually, this is probably something the whole team needs to hear."

"Something wrong?" Paul was back to business as usual.

Wesley shook his head. "Just something . . . interesting." He focused on me. "Paul told me what happened last night."

I shot a horrified look at my boss. "He did?" I thought we had mutually decided we were never telling anyone about our momentary leaves of rationality! Everyone except Kate, of course.

Paul was giving me a slight shake of his head.

Wesley continued, "Yes, we'll have to see about stopping the telepath who is threatening you."

I shot a relieved look at Paul, who rolled his eyes. I had to admit, I should never have worried. Wesley was probably one of the last people Paul would choose to confide in about feeling me up in an alleyway.

"Yes, it wasn't pleasant," I said. "But I came through okay, thanks to Paul."

"I think his idea of having Luke work with you is a

good one," Wesley went on. "And Lainey and Fantazia and I are going to look into magical means of blocking. There's a spell I know that could help. Unfortunately, the bulk of my spell books are back at the EHJ headquarters, and my memory is not what it used to be."

I nodded. "I understand."

"Hopefully Fantazia will remember how to work the spell. She's not plagued with memory loss like her father." He gave me a reassuring pat on the shoulder. "I'll see you two outside."

As soon as he left, Paul shook his head at me. "As if Wesley is going to be the one to whom I read the '*Penthouse* Forum' letter I'm writing."

I cracked up. It had only taken mass chaos for Paul to grow personality and a sense of humor. "'Dear *Penthouse*,'" I said. "'I never thought this would happen to me! I have this annoying coworker that I now find myself unable to keep my hands off of.'"

He held up his hands. "I'm doing a fair job of it right now."

I put down the shocker and stood up and stretched. "Yes, you are very close to going back to your old ways of snapping at me and being a stick-in-the-mud."

"Tell me how you really feel, Mindy," he replied, opening the door so we could walk out of the room and down the hallway to the common area.

"Just stating the facts as I know 'em," I said. I looked around at the full house. Even Cyrus was milling around.

Paul leaned close to whisper in my ear. "Yeah, well, would the old Paul say your butt looks fine in those jeans?"

I know I turned red, and so I tried to concentrate on Wesley.

"There's been a development," Wes was saying, addressing all of us. "As some of you may or may not know, I've hired Cyrus to do a bit of an investigation on the members of the American Agents. He's uncovered something that I thought needed to be brought to your attention. Cyrus?"

The Virus turned his laptop around so we could see the pictures there. "Half of these people were low-level heroes, graduates of that school you all attended but who never really joined any teams or did anything of importance. But these four . . ." He pointed out two of the men and two of the women. "They're a bit shady."

"They're criminals?" Luke looked aghast.

"Not exactly, but they hang around questionable people," Cyrus said.

"They've been seen with known associates of the Dragon," Wesley said softly.

The room settled into horrified silence as Cyrus changed the pictures on the screen to what looked like surveillance photos of Simon's four team members speaking with people wearing the Dragon's mark.

"Those team members are not tattooed with the Dragon's symbol that we can tell, but it could be somewhere hidden. Or it could be the Dragon's cult only marks magic users. Who knows? We're still learning about them." Wesley looked at us. "The question is, what do we do with this information? Do we go to the authorities, or do we investigate it ourselves?"

"I say we go to the authorities—or the media," Luke said. "People need to know about this."

"But we don't have anything concrete yet," Paul said. "They could have been trying to infiltrate the Dragon's cult for all we know. That's all we need, to blow a sting operation and give Simon more ammunition against us."

"I don't know," Kate said. "We have known associates

of criminals *working for the government in positions of power*. That's awful. We have a responsibility to warn the people before something bad happens. Just in case."

"Washington, DC, is full of known associates of shady people," Selena remarked.

"I don't want anyone hurt on our watch because we didn't speak up," Toby said. "Especially since it has to do with the Dragon." He cast Wesley and Lainey a look.

"What good's it going to do to tell anyone when all we have is grainy surveillance photos?" I asked. "It's just going to look like a smoke screen or sour grapes coming from us, a bunch of renegade ex-media dolls. Who's going to believe us?"

I could tell from the looks on their faces that I had a valid point.

"Forrest will," Toby suggested.

"Well, maybe now's the time to contact him," I said, turning to look directly at Paul.

He ran a hand over his head. "They already said they didn't need our help. Who are we to interfere?" he asked.

I stared at him. "Who are you, and what have you done to Paul Christian?"

"I don't know. Maybe being hauled in front of the government to defend ourselves and our methods, and then being treated like a criminal by Simon Leasure brings out my inner rebel," he replied.

I laughed and then said, "It's nice that you're channeling your inner teenager, Paul, it's a fun new side of you, but come on; you know as well as I do that we can't turn our backs on the world."

"Well," Lainey said, "I'd like to keep an eye on it ourselves for now. Besides, if Cyrus found out, the news media will likely find out."

The Virus shot her a nasty look. "It took me a lot of time to track all that down! I only make it *look* easy, damn it!"

I turned back to Paul. "I think we need to put a bug in someone's ear about it. The Dragon and his people are not just our problem; he wants to start the apocalypse. That's going to be everyone's problem if he gets out and gets his wish."

"He won't," Lainey said sharply.

I winced. "I didn't mean he would get it with Emily; I just meant in case he finds another way to start the end of the world."

Wesley nodded. "I think Mindy is right: We need to make someone else aware of this. What do you think, Paul?"

"Oh, Mindy's full of bright ideas," Paul replied, but I could tell it was a teasing remark.

"Spoken like a true surly teenager," I responded.

"You should know."

"I haven't been a teenager in years."

"But surly . . ."

"Leave her alone, Paul," Toby said, coming to my rescue. "Just because she has a good idea that you didn't come up with, you're hassling her and going to be unwilling to do it?" Little did he realize the sparks flying between me and Paul were delicious.

"I think given that this is the Dragon, we should move forward on this," Wesley decided. "Toby, let's see about contacting your boyfriend."

"Hassler," I remarked sotto voce to Paul.

"Surly teenager," he replied.

"That makes you a cradle robber."

"Don't remind me," he said, and then in a louder voice: "Hello, Lainey."

I turned to see my friend. "Hey! Are you okay? I'm

sure this possible Dragon connection is stressful for you."

She nodded. "I'm saving up my worry until we know something concrete. But you'd better believe Wesley and I are going to check it out thoroughly. Are *you* okay? Wesley told me about the trouble last night."

"It's creepy but I'm dealing," I said, not wanting the chilly reminder of the voice. "Paul and Wesley are going to have me train more to block it."

"And I'll help out any way I can," Lainey offered.

"I know you will," I said, giving her a hug.

Paul touched my arm and cleared his throat. "I'm just going to go back to work. I think Luke's going to plan a meditation exercise with you after this, so I'll see you later."

"See how much power the shocker's getting," I suggested.

"You want me to shock myself?" he asked.

"Will you?"

"I think I'll find other means, thanks," he said. "I'll see you later."

Turning back to Lainey, I saw a strange look on her face. "What?"

She was staring after Paul. "I think you two have been working too much together."

My heart sped up. "Why do you say that?"

"You're establishing a rapport. It's kind of freaky." She smiled. "You're teasing each other almost like . . ."

"Like what?" If Lainey figured out what was going on with me and Paul, would she understand when I didn't even understand it myself?

"Like friends," she finished. "It's weird. In a way, I always expected you two to be friends. I mean, you're both supersmart and both scientists, but I know Paul's usually so uptight . . ."

"And I'm not."

"No, but I think some of your laxness is rubbing off on him," she observed. "Toby said you two were getting along on patrol too."

I shrugged. "He's trying to help me learn to control these powers, and we're working on our tech together. We were destined either to become friends or to kill each other." Or to stick tongues down each other's throats.

"Well, I think it's helping relieve a bit of the stress on the team," Lainey admitted. "Whatever you're doing, keep it up."

I inwardly grinned. "Yes, ma'am."

Luke walked up. "Hey, Mindy, sorry I've been kinda distracted lately. I know we discussed training together more."

I turned my attention to him. "That's okay, Luke, I understand. Training's kind of been the last thing on everyone's mind."

"Well, I think we're going to start up again. Paul asked me to start some meditation exercises with you today. Are you ready?"

"As I'll ever be," I said.

"Well, why don't you meet me in my room and we'll get started?"

"Sure, just give me a minute," I said.

Lainey nudged me as he walked off. "Bet those are words you've been dreaming of your whole life."

"Yeah," I said. But somehow being alone with Luke in his room didn't hold the appeal it once had.

CHAPTER TWENTY-SIX

"Now try it again. Clear your mind of all thoughts."

I was sitting cross-legged on the floor of Luke and Selena's room, facing Luke and feeling ridiculous. We had been working on this for what seemed like hours and my back was killing me. Clear my mind of all thoughts? That wasn't happening anytime soon. I had too many, the number one thought being: Why am I sitting here all alone in a room with a bed and Luke, and instead of being overjoyed I'm wishing I were with Paul, the two of us working and teasing each other, perhaps sneaking a kiss in here and there?

"Mindy, you're not concentrating on pushing all the noise out of your head." Luke was giving me a knowing smile. "You're off, lost in your thoughts."

I shook my head. "Sorry. It's just hard to wrap my mind around this think-of-nothing concept."

"Well, you don't have to think of nothing, but you need to learn how to clear your mind of unwanted thoughts. Concentrate only on the thoughts you want. Like, picture a beach, or a park, or a quiet room, somewhere serene, and concentrate on making that picture more and more real until you can smell the ocean and taste the salt in the air."

I closed my eyes and concentrated. *Right. The ocean. The blue waves, the color of Paul's eyes . . .*

Yikes. Don't think about Paul! I told myself. An unwanted thought.

So . . . the ocean, the blue waves, the salty sea air and the taste of it on my lips. The taste of Paul's kisses . . .

Stop it!

"It will come to you. Don't worry, Mindy," Luke was saying, watching my discomfort.

"I just . . . have a lot on my mind lately," I finished.

Luke nodded. "Don't we all."

"I just keep thinking about Paul—er, how I should be helping Paul right now instead of sitting on the floor trying to connect to my inner child or something. No offense, Luke."

Luke frowned. "Yeah, Paul. You two seem like you're getting along well."

"As I told Lainey, it was that or kill each other. We need each other's expertise to help rebuild."

"It's just a bit strange," Luke said, giving me an embarrassed smile. "I got used to you . . . being there."

I stared at him. "Pardon me?"

"You know, when you had your crush on me, you were always following me around. I got used to you being there. Even when I was with Kate for that brief period, you were always there, like my little sidekick."

"Gee, thanks." I tried really hard not to be insulted.

"I mean it as a compliment, you know. Like, backup," Luke said. "And I hate to sound like, well, Simon, but I couldn't help but be flattered. It *is* a bit of an ego boost to have someone think you're so cool, you know?"

"Uh-huh." I was starting to feel sick to my stomach.

"But then I started dating Selena and things fell apart between us, and suddenly I turned around and you weren't there anymore."

"Things didn't fall apart between us. We're still

friends," I said. "Just like I promised at Wesley and Lainey's reception. I simply moved on, and I don't feel the need to keep trying to grab your attention. But all the 'we' there ever was . . . that hasn't changed."

He shook his head. "I'm sounding like a complete jackass now, I know, but what I'm trying to say, very poorly, is that I miss you, Mindy."

I knew I should say, *I miss you too*, but the words stuck in my throat. "That's nice," I said instead. "But I'm still here, Luke. It's not like I left the team or anything. We still live together and work together every day."

"No, I know, but you're spending all that time working with Paul on those inventions, and even patrolling together now—"

"Toby went with us," I inserted quickly, defensively.

"—when you used to go patrolling and work out with me," Luke finished. "I know we had Selena come along all the time, and maybe that made you feel awkward."

"Three's a crowd," I admitted.

He sighed. "Look, this is totally my own hang-up, but I can't help but feel a bit, I don't know, jealous." He was flushing. "I know it's arrogant and stupid, but it's how I feel."

I was shell-shocked. Luke was jealous of Paul? Over me? And he didn't even know all of the making out that had been happening lately!

"And I know you're over that schoolgirl crush on me, you've made that clear, but I've got to come clean about something." Luke took a deep breath. "The night of Lainey and Wesley's reception, when you told me you were over me, I was getting ready to tell you that we should try to take our relationship to the next level. That we should give dating a try."

My mouth fell open. "No freaking way."

He nodded. "You're gorgeous, Mindy. You know you are, and like I said, it was flattering you were so into me. That fight with the Dragon, when you got hurt, I realized how much your friendship meant. And I don't know how well we would have worked out, we have next to nothing in common except the team, but I was willing to give it a shot." He glanced up at me and then said, "I'm still willing to give it a shot."

My head was spinning, and I felt like I was going to pass out. I stared at him in horror.

Luke looked worried. "And I'm freaking you out now, aren't I?"

The truth was I was more than freaked out, and not just by the utter shock of Luke's words. What was most freaky was my reaction to them. A few weeks back those words would have put me on cloud nine. I would have felt like I'd won the lottery or finally gotten my heart's desire. Luke Harmon wanted to be with me!

But now I couldn't help but wonder: If he had discovered he had feelings for me after the Dragon incident, why had he never made a move on me in all of those months before I finally decided enough was enough? Why had he never shown any interest when I was still hanging around him like a groupie? I couldn't help but wonder if he was simply missing my attention and wanted me fawning over him full-time again.

"I'm no more freaked out than you were when I had a crush on you," I said softly. "I'm flattered, Luke, really. But you're with Selena now."

"I know," he said. "And Selena's great. She really is. She's a really great person."

"She's better suited for you," I reminded him. "Better than me."

He shook his head. "I don't know about that. She's great, but I don't see myself with her for the rest of my life."

Ouch. Poor Selena! Was our team turning into a soap opera?

"Look, I know I'm making a fool out of myself here, but I wanted to clear the air. Kind of like you did the night of the reception. So it's all out in the open and there are no hidden secrets between us."

I nodded. "I understand. And I do value your friendship, Luke. I told you that before."

He smiled. "It must be some sort of weird karma that we never had feelings for each other at the same time."

I gave him a sad smile. "I think it's the universe trying to tell us something: That we wouldn't work out and we're better suited as friends."

"You're probably right," he said.

I stood up. I had to get out of the room. "Look, I really should probably go help Paul with the new Shocker. I made him promise to test it, and if I'm not there to help him . . ."

"He's going to get upset." Luke nodded in understanding. "Let me know if I can help you any more with the meditation thing, Mindy. You just need to try to remember to focus your thoughts on what you want and block out the rest."

There were all sorts of thoughts flooding my head, and none of them could focus. "Thanks, Luke." I turned and left the room, shutting the door behind me.

Paul looked up as I walked in. "Do you feel more centered now?" he asked. He wore a semisarcastic grin.

I made a face at him. "Ha-ha. So funny." I picked up my Shocker. "How did it do?"

"Good. I tested it on Cyrus."

I looked up. "Did you really?"

"He volunteered." At seeing the look of absolute shock on my face, he broke out into a grin.

I threw his pillow at him. "You've turned into such a smart-ass."

"As opposed to a dumb one." He tossed the pillow back to me and I plopped it back on his bed, eyeing him. Never had I been more aware that we were in a bedroom than at that moment. "So, how'd the training go?"

I shrugged, watching him. "Blah, blah, blah, centered chakras, blah, blah, blah, go to your happy place. You know. All the usual stuff."

"Doesn't sound like you were too impressed." Paul went back to work.

"Yeah, well." I sat down on the edge of the bed. I had to see him to see how he reacted. "But some rather enlightening things came into play."

"How's that?" Paul kept his head down.

"Luke told me he's jealous that I'm spending more time with you now than him."

Paul's eyes flashed up to meet mine, and I saw shock. And was that pain in there too?

"What?" he asked.

I nodded. "And that he misses me hanging around him all the time. That he's had feelings for me since the Dragon fight when I was injured, but just never said anything. And he pretty much said he'd dump Selena for me."

Paul had his head down again, but I noticed his hands shook as he picked up a tool. "Well," he said after a long moment, and his voice sounded heavy and dead to my ears. "You must be in seventh heaven. You've finally gotten what you've always wanted, the love and devotion of Luke Harmon. Congratulations."

I could tell it all in that moment. He was sad. He was jealous. He was hurt.

In contrast, I might not be able to identify how I felt about Paul. Or it might just be that I wasn't *ready* to identify how I felt about Paul, considering how quickly the feelings had overtaken me. But they were there and real; I was sure of that. It was nothing like what I'd felt for Luke, but something more and much stronger.

And if I wanted to be honest with myself, it started in the exact moment when he'd said he stood up for me against Simon and all of the government. He had *defended* me. And that delicious kiss afterward had just further cemented it.

Oh, yeah. I had definite feelings for Paul. And it seemed he did for me too.

"The thing is," I said softly, getting up and walking over. "When he said that, it didn't affect me at all. I am well and truly over Luke, and not just pretending anymore."

Paul looked up, almost seeming shy. "Really?"

"Really," I said, swinging his chair around so that I could straddle his lap, facing him.

Paul eyed me. "I never thought you two suited. Would you really have wanted to spend hours talking about fight coordination and differing workouts and meditations?"

I shook my head, stretching my arms out over his shoulders. "Absolutely not. Who cares?"

Paul settled his hands around my waist. "I never understood what had you so over the moon."

I shrugged. "He's pretty."

Paul snorted. "Well, yeah."

I leaned forward so my forehead was barely resting against his. "But you're pretty, too."

He gave me a disbelieving look. "Yeah, right."

"And a lot more fun."

"I think that telepath is messing with your brain again." He was looking at me a bit warily, but with amusement. It was obvious he thought I was teasing.

"God, Paul, take the compliment already," I said, and brought my lips to his.

I might have taken him by surprise, but his male instinct clicked in quickly and he shifted, pulling my hips in tighter, causing my already short skirt to ride up to indecent levels. My mouth opened and he deepened our kiss, teasing my tongue with his. But this was all territory we'd explored before. In all of our stolen kisses in this room and darkened alleyways, it seemed by unspoken mutual agreement we wouldn't deny our strange attraction, but we wouldn't move it further. I was ready for that to change. I dropped my hands from his shoulders down his chest, and began to unbutton his shirt.

He clasped my hands in his to stop me, and pulled back. With a teasing grin he said, "This is a new twist to the game."

I wrenched my hands free, leaping to my feet and standing in front of him in one lightning-quick motion, feeling as if he had slapped me. "God, Paul, is that all this is to you? Some sort of game?" I felt betrayed and even stupider than usual. I had misjudged him. This was only what it had started out as: a distraction. I was a way he was choosing to distract himself from the pain of losing Kate. And why shouldn't he behave that way? He probably thought it was the same for me. I had never been exactly nice to him over the years, so now I was using him as a distraction from never being able to get Luke. How was he to know that he was wrong, so wrong? Something had changed in me, though it wasn't easy to define.

Tears brimmed in my eyes, and I whirled and started

to move toward the door so he wouldn't see me cry. At the last second he reached out and caught my arm.

"Mindy."

Something about his tone caught me, and I glanced back to see an expression on his face I had never seen before.

I took a step back, and he came forward, taking me by the waist for a kiss that stole my breath away. It was soft and sweet and passionate and gentle all at the same time. I was crushed against his chest, felt the quickened rise and fall of his breath and the awareness of his arousal, as mine began to seep through my body like liquid fire.

I began unfastening his shirt again, and this time he didn't stop me. A tingle ran through my body as I undid every button. We were really going to do this. And what's more, if we didn't soon, I was going to explode. I'd stop to ponder the strangeness of it all later; for now, I was going to enjoy myself.

I drew off his shirt, hands exploring his broad shoulders as I did, mentally cursing him for having to wear an undershirt underneath and maintaining another layer of clothing I'd have to take off. And then I noticed his right shoulder.

"Oh my God, you have a tattoo?"

He looked embarrassed. "Yes, I have a tattoo."

"You? Seriously?" I ran a finger over it. It was a white shield with a sun on it, and a sword overlapping. Some words were written below it in Latin. I translated. "Protect and defend."

"Yeah, well, I was young and thought it would be cool." He looked really awkward.

"It *is* cool." I was impressed. "Definitely not the stuffy scientist you appear." With a mischievous grin, I leaned forward and ran my tongue over that patch of skin.

"I . . . Jesus." He shuddered as I delicately nipped him. He pulled me back up to reclaim my mouth in a devouring kiss. His hands lightly skimmed the skin where my tank shirt met my skirt, and then he moved up under my shirt, to my breasts. My breathing quickened.

His hands moved away as he grasped the hem of my shirt and pulled it over my head, tossing it somewhere to the side and then reaching for the zipper of my skirt, finding it and letting my skirt fall into a pool around my feet. Not to be outdone, I yanked his undershirt up, and he helped me by pulling it off the rest of the way and tossing it off with my shirt.

I was met with a very pleasant surprise: Paul was built like he worked out constantly, something I didn't realize. With a grin, I moved my hands along his flat stomach, defined chest and arms, as if to assure myself I wasn't imagining this. Why had he been hiding such a killer body behind all of those terrible clothes? I guess because it wasn't so important to him.

"Very nice," I said, trailing a hand down his stomach.

"I was thinking the same thing," he said, looking at me, his voice rough with desire.

With a wicked grin, I stepped back and away, toward his bed, and reached behind to unhook my black lace bra. Enjoying seeing the heat burn through in his eyes I slowly drew it off, then held it by one strap and tossed it onto the pile on the floor. I gave him a daring smile as I did.

I was just reaching for my black lace panties when he started unbuckling his pants. I drew one leg out and then the other, tossing the garment off to the side; then I slid onto his bed, him following me with every bit of his warm, bare skin covering mine as he moved atop me.

"Tattoos and a wicked sense of humor, not to mention a hot body you've been hiding for some unknown reason. There is definitely a wild streak hiding behind White Heat's serious exterior," I said against his mouth.

"Just you wait, babe," he said. "I'll show you how much fun I can really be."

CHAPTER TWENTY-SEVEN

I woke up to someone kissing my neck. I stretched with a smile, my mind flashing back to the events of the previous night. All of them. I giggled as a male hand slid down my stomach and I said, "Good morning to you, too," still not turning over and keeping my eyes closed.

Warm breath rustled near my ear. "You're a terrible overnight guest." Paul's deep voice was a purr, sending hot shivers of pleasure through me. "You slept late. How's a guy supposed to make the grand romantic gesture of breakfast in bed when you sleep the whole time?"

"Get me some when I wake up," I suggested with a sleepy smile, snuggling against him without opening my eyes. "You can serve me lunch in bed if you want."

"Your boss is going to be really mad at you for being late for work," he warned. But even with my eyes closed I could tell he was smiling.

"Oh, is he?" I rolled over and opened my eyes. He was lying next to me, his head propped on his arm, dark blue eyes twinkling with amusement and something else. Heat and desire, yes, and something even more. Something that gave me a bit of a chill.

I pushed away my fears and smiled at him. "I better get to work then. My boss is really strict. He once yelled at my friend, Lainey, for being late to this boring meeting because she was in bed with her boyfriend that she hadn't seen in months."

"Sounds like a real ballbuster."

"Oh, he is," I agreed, with an impish grin.

"You'd better think of a way to distract him from your being late, then."

I bit my lip. "Well, there are a few things I could think of. But I'm afraid I'd be charged with sexual harassment if I did any."

"I think you should call in sick, then."

"Oh, really?" I raised an eyebrow. "You think I should just skip work today?"

"Yeah, I mean, if your boss is going to be mad you're late, you might as well just call off." He ran a hand over my hip. "Stay in bed all day."

I smiled. "How very irresponsible of you, Paul."

He leaned forward and kissed me, stealing my breath with his sweetness. Getting out of bed today was looking less and less likely.

A knock sounded on the door and we froze.

"Oops," Paul said in a whisper. Then, louder: "Hang on."

We both scrambled up, throwing on clothes in a hurry. I was rocking a major case of bed head, my makeup was a mess, my tank top was inside out and I still couldn't locate my underwear. Paul had just thrown on jeans and a polo shirt and was opening the door when I spotted my underwear on the other side of the bed. I dove for them, hiding them and myself effectively out of view as I heard Wesley say, "There you are. Are you all right?"

"Sorry. I didn't get a lot of sleep last night," Paul said, and I had to cover my mouth to keep from giggling. *Gee, I wonder why?* "I was contemplating going back to bed. What's up?"

"I know I said that Lainey and I'd take patrol tonight, but is there any way you can go instead?"

"Sure," Paul said. "Why, where are you going to be?"

"I'm taking Fantazia with me to do a little investigating about Simon's people and the Dragon. We're going to see what information we can scare up through the magic community. I'd like to believe that it's just a sting operation, but my gut says otherwise."

"I know what you mean," Paul replied. "We'll keep our ears open when we're out on the streets too. Don't worry about patrol; I'll take care of it. I'll see if Mindy wants to tag along and test her Shocker. Maybe even test her powers."

"Take Toby too," Wesley said. "Just in case she has another episode."

I bristled.

"She's doing a lot better," Paul said, coming to my defense. My hero!

"Better safe than sorry. Where is she, anyway? Has she shown up yet to work on your projects?"

She's currently crouching behind the bed in yesterday's clothes, I thought.

"She hasn't shown up for work yet," Paul said. "She's probably slept in or something. She can be a bit lazy at times."

I could hear the teasing in his voice, but he was going to pay for that.

"Well, tell her you're all going on patrol tonight when you see her," Wesley said. "I'll talk to you again before Fantazia and I leave. Maybe we can try to sneak into our headquarters when we're out. I'm sure Simon's got the place under heavy surveillance, but if we go in with an invisibility spell for a quick jaunt, I doubt we'll be detected. I'll try to grab a few of yours and Mindy's inventions while we're there. If there's anything left that wasn't incinerated."

"Unlikely, but it wouldn't hurt to check," Paul said. "Thanks."

I waited until I heard the door close again before I got up, stuffing my underwear in the pocket of my skirt. "Lazy, huh?"

"Oh, Mindy, there you are. Wesley says we're going on patrol tonight," Paul said with a smile. "So glad you decided to show up for work, finally."

"Yeah, this really hot tattooed guy I know? He suggested I call off today."

"He sounds like a bad influence."

"He's the worst," I agreed.

"Well, now that you're finally here, how about we go to breakfast? Or lunch? Whichever one we're closer to."

"Sure. Give me a minute to go change my clothes and get into some semblance of order," I said.

"Yeah, I know what you mean," he remarked, gesturing to his clothes, which were barely rumpled. "I'd like to get cleaned up before going out in public again too."

"Hey, on that subject, can I ask you something personal?" I said.

He shook his head. "Absolutely not. Nothing personal whatsoever. I don't think we're on that level." He rolled his eyes. "Yes, Mindy, you can ask me whatever you want."

"You obviously work out. You've got a really nice body hiding behind those layers of dress shirts and undershirts and jackets. So, why do you hide it?"

He ran a hand over his hair. "Ugh. I have to work out to not make an embarrassment of myself in our uniforms, but that doesn't mean I want to flaunt it the rest of the time."

"Well, why not? 'If you've got it, flaunt it,' as they say."

"Yeah, well, I didn't exactly have it when I was thirteen, and I think the ghost of that fat kid has followed me around for the rest of my life, all right? I was the typical science geek: chubby, thick glasses, bad acne, the works. And God, that's probably something I shouldn't be admitting to you right now."

"Oh, come on, Paul, everyone's hideous when they're thirteen. You saw me then, remember?"

"Trust me, you weren't hideous. And please, let's not go bringing up the fact that I knew you then. I was twenty-five at the time. That creeps me out."

I put my arms around his waist. "Paul Christian is a terrible, evil cradle robber."

He grinned. "Shut up."

"Make me."

He kissed me hard, and I responded in kind.

"Do me a favor," I said when we broke apart. "Wear something a little more casual to breakfast. Preferably something that shows off the tat."

"I'd have to buy a new wardrobe," he complained.

"Don't tempt me." I winked at him. "I'll see you in a few."

"Don't take too long, babe," he said, watching as I walked out the door.

Once in the hallway, I looked around. Ugh. Time to do the walk of shame. *Please God, don't let anyone come back this way*, I prayed, and hurried as fast as I could without drawing attention to myself to my room.

I had my hand on the door handle, ready to open it when it opened on its own and Kate stepped out, almost bumping into me.

"Gods, Mindy, I'm sorry," she said.

"It's okay," I replied, starting to bolt around her.

Her viselike grip caught my arm and I looked up, alarmed. She was staring at me as if seeing me anew. Or like she was looking right through me.

"Kate?" I said, a bit spooked.

"Oh, my," she breathed. She looked like I had punched

her in the stomach. "I knew you two were having a bit of fun, but I didn't know . . ."

I blanched. "Um, Kate? Can we talk about this inside? And can you let go of my arm?"

She looked down at her hand, as if for the first time noticing she had it in her grasp. "Sorry. Go ahead." She stepped aside so I could pass.

I stripped off my clothes and threw on a fresh tank top and hip-hugging jeans. I wasn't wearing those killer boots anymore, and I stuffed my feet into the sneakers. Since I didn't feel like messing with the magic showerhead, I pulled back my hair into a ponytail and noticed Kate watching me in the reflection of the mirror. I sighed. "It just happened, okay?"

"I know," she said, her voice soft. Was it my imagination, or did she sound like she was in pain? "I didn't see it on you until now."

"It's no big deal," I said, even though it was. I made a halfhearted attempt to repair my makeup in a hurry.

"I'm happy for you two—really," Kate said. "I'm glad he finally has someone that deserves him. Someone who loves him like I never could."

I paused, lipstick poised in front of my mouth. "Pardon me?"

She gave me a sad smile. "Oh, Mindy. Don't try to deny it. Remember who I am. I can see when love has blossomed, okay? You two are in love, I can see it. And I really am happy you're able to give him what I never could."

I stared at her in shock. Don't get me wrong, I really liked Paul. That much was clear now. And I knew he really liked me, too. And last night had been the most incredible night of my life. I half wanted to ask Kate why she had been crazy enough to cheat on him and toss him aside. Because, wow. But love?

"I, uh, gotta go," I said to Kate, throwing the tube of lipstick down. "Paul's waiting for me."

She nodded. "Of course."

"And don't say anything to anyone yet."

She nodded again. "I understand. You want to tell them yourselves."

"Something like that, yeah." I headed for the door. "I'll, uh, see you later." I closed the door behind me, my stomach flipping. It was way too early in our relationship, and there was way too much insanity going on right now for that kind of intensity.

I stepped into the common room, and Paul was standing there talking to Luke. He was wearing jeans and a polo shirt, looking somewhat casual. When he saw me, he absently scratched his arm, pushing up his sleeve to reveal the tattoo. He shot me a grin and then said something else to Luke before heading in my direction.

I shook my head at him, sharing a small smile. Now was *not* the time to be falling in love. Not with anyone. We were outlaws, and I had crazy people talking in my head.

So why did I get a giddy feeling in the pit of my stomach just from Paul smiling at me?

CHAPTER TWENTY-EIGHT

"I feel like a ninja dressed like this," I complained.

"Ninjas are silent assassins," Toby reminded me over the headset as we patrolled. "You couldn't be silent if your life depended on it, Min."

"Hardy-har-har," I responded, brushing my hair back as I pressed the button that allowed us to talk completely undetected on any frequency.

"Toby's right, let's cut the unnecessary chatter," a stern voice said over my headset. And then over my shoulder in a low voice, "Ninjas don't wear bright red lipstick when they're working, either."

I depressed the button to speak into the headset and said, "We're heroes. We're supposed to quip." Then I turned and asked Paul, "What exactly's wrong with the lipstick?"

"It comes off, for one thing," he replied, wiping his mouth with the back of his hand. "It looks hot on you, but not so much on me. Leave it off next time we're out."

He leaned forward to kiss me again, but I ducked. "We're supposed to be working, remember?" I said with a teasing smile. "I have this mean boss who'll be on my case if we don't at least attempt to catch some bad guys."

"You really shouldn't talk about Wesley like that," Paul said, catching me by the waist and trapping me. "He's not so bad, really."

"Okay, seriously, how long do we have to be out

here?" I asked, both over the headset for Toby's benefit and to Paul in person.

"What's wrong, Mindy, you have a hot date tonight?" Paul retorted over the headset. At the same time, he slid his hands places entirely inappropriate for work.

"As a matter of fact . . ." I replied. Then I leaned close and whispered in his ear, "I want to go home and rip your clothes off."

Paul's eyes widened, and a mischievous smirk broke out on his face. He started to say something in return, but Toby's voice over the intercom interrupted.

"The only thing Mindy has waiting at home is her latest erotica novel, but I've got an actual man coming to meet me at some point, so I agree: Can we wrap this up?" Toby groused.

"Wait, I thought Forrest wasn't coming until tomorrow," Paul said.

"He's not. He's meeting me here. Nearby."

"How nearby?" Paul asked.

"Relax. He's at a nice hotel about ten blocks over. You know, the kind that has champagne and strawberries for room service. And whipped cream . . ."

"Getting a little too detailed there, hon," I said. To Paul, I whispered, "I know this store nearby that has chocolate body paint."

"I've never been into food products," Paul said, shaking his head. "However, scented massage oil . . ."

"Ooh, I know where we can get this great sandalwood one that heats on contact."

"The champagne sounds like a good idea," Paul mused. "Do you think Fantazia still has some left?"

"Maybe, but I don't want to ask her for it. She's cranky and scary." I shivered. "Let's offer to make sure Toby meets up with Forrest okay, then we'll go to the store."

"Yeah, what's up with *them*?"

"Um, they're in love?" I shrugged. "Did you need me to explain the details? When a man and another man really care about each other . . ."

"Are you guys still there?" Toby asked over the headset. "Where are you?"

"Is it a good idea to be having liaisons with Forrest before we find out what he knows?" Paul asked him.

"We're going to *find out* what he knows. If you want, I'll ask him straight off and then we'll continue our reunion. You'll be the first person I report back to afterward. Besides, I thought we had decided we were going to trust Forrest."

"We hadn't decided anything yet," Paul said.

"By the way, thanks, Toby, for your commentary on my love life," I put in, trying to defuse the tension building between the two men.

"You're the one still holding out for Luke, sweetie."

I turned red under Paul's gaze. "Totally not the case, Tobe, and you know it."

Paul shook his head. "You're never going to live that down."

"Whatever. It's dead out here tonight. I think even Wesley would agree to that, and he's the one who's so gung ho on us patrolling. No offense, Paul."

"None taken. Up until Wesley and Lainey starting pushing for it, I thought nightly patrols were a big waste of time too." Paul sighed. "But I want it known that it's not my job to handle your personal lives . . ."

"Duly noted," Toby said.

"Um, it kind of is," I whispered to Paul. "Since you're the one debating the virtues of chocolate body paint versus scented massage oil."

"But I'm okay with wrapping this up and letting Mindy get back to whatever her big plans are for tonight," he said into the microphone. "Massage oil and champagne definitely," he told me.

"You're the boss."

"That's right." He leaned in and kissed me again, obviously no longer caring whether or not my lipstick would smear off. All I could think about was getting rid of Toby, seeing him off safely to Forrest, and getting Paul home as soon as possible. How sick was it that Fantazia's world was rapidly becoming home?

That's when the whole world seemed to shake.

I moved slightly away from Paul. "I've heard of kisses making the earth move . . ."

"Great. Just great," Paul said, looking over my shoulder. "Toby!"

"I see it, I see it." Toby cursed over the headset. "There go my plans for the night."

I turned around to see what they were gawking at, and my mouth fell open as something giant and green went running past. "Mine too."

"I'm calling the others at headquarters," Paul said, flipping a switch on the headset and speaking into it.

We followed the growing sounds of chaos. There was a giant man-lizard wandering the city streets, knocking over cars and making a general mess of things. As we turned the corner of one building, we could see it break a light pole in half.

"What is that?" I breathed.

"It's got to be one of Doctor Chaos's creations," Paul said, referencing a notorious villain whose human and animal hybrid experiments were his modus operandi for taking over the world. "No one other than him is so Hollywood."

"I thought he was in jail."

"A lot of people are supposed to be in jail, including

us and Simon Leasure," Paul said. He kissed me again. "Be careful, babe."

"You too," I said, and we turned to face the monster.

"Hey, ugly!" Toby called. As the monster turned, he punched it in the face. The creature reared back but didn't fall. It growled, flashing sharp teeth, and swiped a clawed fist at Toby. Toby just barely dodged, and his chest caught part of the blow, his shirt getting torn to ribbons.

"Stay out of its range," Paul commanded me, and then he ran forward to blast heat at the monster.

I wondered if it would just enjoy the attack (didn't lizards prefer humid areas?) but the creature hissed and howled, trying to get away. It picked up the nearest object, which was a car, and hurled it.

"Paul!" I shrieked. He dove out of the way at the last moment, ducking behind another car as the one the lizard hurled crashed down. The lizard, hearing my shout, turned its attention to me.

"Stay back, ugly," I commanded, holding up my Shocker. "I have a modified Taser and I know how to use it."

The lizard growled and hurled itself at me. I pressed the button and let the Shocker blast hit him at full power. What would normally paralyze a grown man simply knocked the lizard guy off his feet. He got up, shaky, but still able to move.

"What does Doctor Chaos *do* to these people?" I snapped, looking around for something, anything to stop the rampaging beast.

Toby stepped in, swinging what looked like a flag-pole as a baseball bat. The blow knocked the lizard man into a building across the street.

I looked at him. "Nice property damage, Tobe."

"Hey, circumstances being what they are . . ."

Paul popped up behind us. "I'm going to hit it with everything I have. Mindy, concentrate your telekinetic powers on trying to keep that thing back. Toby, while we're doing that, sneak around behind and hit it with something heavy."

Toby looked around. "Like that dump truck over there?"

"Sounds as good as anything else," Paul said. "Ready, team?"

"As I'll ever be," I muttered. The lizard man was getting up.

"Let's do it, then," Paul said, and he set to work.

The lizard man growled as the heat started to build on its skin, burning. It howled, hate raging in its eyes. It started to push past the pain and move toward us, however.

I concentrated, focusing all of my energies on this freak of nature in front of me. Poor sap, he had probably been some rent-a-thug the villains managed to dig up who couldn't hold a steady job and make enough money to pay the bills, and he'd likely turned to thug work to make ends meet. And this is how he ended up: a rampaging mutant creature that we had to take down before it hurt somebody. Somebody like us.

I concentrated, trying to push the lizard man away from us and toward Toby, who wasn't as strong as Lainey and was still having a bit of trouble hefting the rather heavy truck. My head started to pound and I felt a strange sort of light-headedness as I let go. I was there, but it was like I was floating outside of my body, experiencing only that which was around me, but all of it at once. I could sense the creature's struggle against myself and Paul, Paul starting to weaken from the use of his powers, powers he hadn't exercised in a while, and Toby's strain in lifting the car, hefting it to smash it on top of the animal.

I'm going to be a lot harder to get rid of than that animal. Mindy.

I practically shrieked. The voice had never used my name before.

That's because I'm close now. I'm almost there, and our bond is growing stronger.

"Bond? What bond? The stalker voice bond?" I snapped. "Now go away, I'm busy!"

You and I, we have a connection you can't even begin to realize. Or sever.

"Shut up!" I snapped and focused my anger with the voice upon the lizard man. I lashed out with everything I had.

The lizard man suddenly went flying back into the building behind him, crashing to the ground in a heap. Toby delivered the coup de grâce by dropping the entire truck atop him. I watched as Paul went over and, using his heat powers, fused the metal together, making a combination cage and handcuffs.

"Great work, everyone!" Paul said, just as sirens sounded and cop cars pulled up. The police, they were always a day late and a dollar short. Either that or they just liked hanging back, waiting for us to do our jobs so they could come in for the clean-up.

I'll be seeing you soon, Mindy, the voice said, and then it departed.

"If you show up, I'll kill you," I growled under my breath.

Paul looked over at me. "Are you okay?"

I shrugged. "Voice problems again. But he went away without too much trouble after babbling something about bonds and connections."

Paul's face clouded. "We'll figure out a way to stop it, Mindy."

"You know how villains are, Paul, they like to hear themselves talk. We're bonded, blah, blah, blah." I shrugged. "It's the usual. I'm not worried."

The police stepped up in front of us, looking worried, checking one face, then another. "Thank you for helping. This creature escaped from four of the American Agents earlier tonight."

I looked at Paul and burst out laughing. "Now that is priceless."

"Never send a second-rate team to do a first-rate job," Toby said.

"W-who are you people?" one of the police officers asked as reporters appeared seemingly out of nowhere and started snapping pictures. They were filming the creature and the police and us.

I realized they were seeing our glamours and not us. "Just people that want to help no matter what," I said.

"Forget that," Paul said, ripping off his glamour key and tossing it on the ground. He didn't look any different to me, of course, but the rest of the crowd around us literally gasped. "We're the Elite Hands of Justice, and we're not going away because the so-called American Agents say so."

"White Heat," I heard the reporters murmur.

"Who's that with you?" another one called out.

I pulled the key from my around my neck and tossed it to the ground. "Tekgrrl and the Magnificent," I said, as Toby did the same. "We're still here, and we're still doing our jobs."

"We are here to help the public, not to be slaves of the media or any government," Paul said. "We're here to save people and we'll continue to do so, even if we have to do it as outlaws because a politician says so."

The police started clapping. "About time you showed back up," someone called out.

I turned to Paul. "I don't think I've ever wanted you more," I said softly. "Rebellion is hot on you." And in front of an unconscious lizard man, the police, the reporters and Toby, I kissed him.

CHAPTER TWENTY-NINE

"So I guess you all are pretty shocked," I said the next morning as we sat around the couches in the common area at Fantazia's, watching the television Lainey had acquired for us.

The news coverage of our capture of the lizard man last night and the aftermath was on every channel. The aftermath was played just as much as the capture. From the serious networks, there was speculation regarding where we had been and what this would mean for our future. Political pundits were arguing over whether or not Simon should step down from his post. Forrest and Wesley were still investigating the Dragon connection, but everyone in Washington was alarmed that four members of the American Agents had a connection to a so-called "terrorist" organization, especially since those four members had disappeared last night. News of that had leaked, and the public was rocked, especially since it was coming out that several other high-profile villains had escaped when AssaultR got away, and the American Agents hadn't been able to apprehend them—and then Simon had done his best to cover that all up. The non-evil team members had tried their best, but they just didn't have the powers or experience we had. And since Simon was too busy playing politician to actually lead his team or go on missions, they had been practically on their own.

An investigation to see if Simon had abused his new government post for personal reasons was being called for, as well as to see how closely he was tied to the Dragon. Considering he had almost been killed fighting the Dragon, I doubted he had anything to do with the guy or even been aware of the connection. Simon could be pretty oblivious. But news crews showed people protesting the American Agents and calling for our return. The lobby of our headquarters had been taken over by protestors. Footage of a tearful teenage girl crying for our return was being played incessantly.

Meanwhile, the tabloid and entertainment shows and networks were having a field day about Paul's and my embrace. It was practically the kiss heard round the world. My dating history and his had been trotted out and compared by a talk-show host. The age difference had already been brought up several times, and there had been several unfavorable comparisons of me versus Kate. I knew I didn't stack up next to the gorgeous goddess, but did the rest of America have to rub it in? Judging by the way we spent the rest of last night and most of this morning, and by the way Paul sat next to me on the couch, hand on my leg, absently rubbing his thumb across my knee, he didn't care.

As I looked around the room at my teammates, I wondered at their reactions to our new relationship. Shock? Horror? Disapproval?

"Shocked?" Lainey said. "Not really."

I gaped. "Huh?"

Wesley gave me a kind smile. "You didn't exactly do such a good job of hiding when I showed up the other morning, Mindy."

"He asked me if there was something going on with you two," Lainey added. "And Toby mentioned his suspicions after patrolling with the two of you. Apparently you kept disappearing on him . . ."

I turned red. "And here I thought we were being subtle."

"It's been obvious to me since I showed up," Cyrus said, barely looking up from his computer. "It's all in the body language. So unfair. You could have done better, girl."

I looked at Fantazia, who shrugged, looking bored with the whole thing. "You think I don't know what goes on in my own pocket universe?"

Luke had been sitting next to Selena in silence on one of the couches. When he finally met my eyes, he looked hurt. "Guess I'm the last to know."

Selena gave me an embarrassed smile. "Lainey told me."

Kate had been sitting quietly through the whole ordeal, hands in her lap, eyes downcast. She seemed to be the nine-hundred-pound gorilla in the room at whom everyone kept shooting sideward glances. I hoped it wouldn't get awkward between the three of us now that Paul's and my relationship was out in the open. Although, if Kate made a habit of acting strange around her old flames and their current mates, the only safe person would be Toby.

"Well, then, if everyone already knows, there shouldn't be a problem," Paul said.

"I'm not going on patrol with you two anymore," Toby remarked, walking into the room with Forrest in tow. "It was awkward enough when you two were hiding it. Now that you're out in the open, it's going to be a million times worse. The image of you two making out is seared into my brain," he said, delicately shuddering.

"He was traumatized," Forrest put in. "I had to do a lot of consoling."

"I'm sure that was such a hardship," I said to Toby, who winked at me. It was good to know that our friendship hadn't been truly affected.

"So, it's obvious from what we've been seeing that at least a few of the American Agents weren't on the side of good," Paul said, getting down to business despite the fact that he hadn't removed his hand from my leg. "What's the talk in Washington, Forrest?"

"I've done nothing but field questions all morning," our liaison replied, taking a seat on an overstuffed chair. Toby perched on the arm and put a hand on Forrest's shoulder. "My phone didn't stop ringing until I stepped in here."

"This is a no-cell-phone zone," Fantazia explained.

"It's probably going to voice mail then." Forrest shuddered. "In light of everything, the higher-ups, including the president himself, are starting to wonder if they made a mistake by giving Simon so much power. They're suffering bad publicity over this. Not only is there a possible connection to a dangerous terrorist group with half of the team, the other half of the American Agents are vastly inexperienced and have barely been able to apprehend any of the villains they've fought. The American people are begging for your return, and the pols are starting to wonder if it would be better to disassociate themselves with Simon and his team."

Paul snorted. "They wonder, huh?"

"Glad they finally see reason," Wesley said.

"And of course, the four missing AA members are wanted for questioning. No one's seen hide nor hair of them. We think someone in the magic community tipped them off that you were asking about them," Forrest said to Wesley. "Simon has been calling all morning. The president has asked him to meet with you to see what can be done to resolve the situation. I haven't told him I've been in contact with you at all, and he certainly doesn't know where you are. *I'm* not even entirely certain where we are, but if the two of you"—he nodded to Paul and Wesley—"are okay with meeting him to discuss things, I will set up an appointment for this afternoon at a safe location."

Toby looked at Paul and Wesley. "Well? What do you think?"

Paul gave Wesley a look. "Do they really think they can insult us, let Simon try to arrest us, drive us from our home and then a minor apology is going to make everything all right?"

"They know it won't," Wesley said. "Especially not Simon. But don't we want to show that we are the better people and agree to at least discuss things like rational adults?"

Paul laughed bitterly. "I hate being the better person."

"It doesn't get any easier with age," Wesley agreed. He addressed Forrest: "Set it up. This doesn't mean we're coming back like everything is forgiven and back to normal, though. I doubt Mindy and Paul will be taking any defense contracts for a while, and we won't be offering to do security at any White House functions anytime soon. I think the clean members of the AA can handle that much."

Forrest nodded. "I will make sure they understand that. Thank you for agreeing to see Simon, though. A lot of people will be relieved, including myself."

"Most of the American public from the looks of it," Lainey said, motioning to the television, which was still showing sobbing people calling for our return.

"Does this mean I'm no longer a prisoner here?" Cyrus asked.

"No," Paul snapped.

"You're still working for me," Wesley reminded the former villain.

"Don't forget about owing me, either," Fantazia said to Cyrus. "One little favor isn't going to cut it for all I had to do for you."

"Don't believe a word Simon says," Luke told Wesley and Paul, as if they needed to hear it. "I don't trust him as far as I can throw him."

"No one does," Wesley replied. "I always said it was a mistake to have him on the team." He gave Paul a look.

"Yeah, yeah," Paul said, brushing this off. I was shocked; a few weeks ago and he would have been having a minor meltdown, now he just quietly acquiesced? God, how he had changed. How he had mellowed.

He squeezed my knee, and I smiled. He'd changed for the better. Definitely for the better.

"I'll set up everything and be back later," Forrest said.

"I'm going with him," Toby said, motioning to Forrest. Paul nodded, and the two other men walked out of the room and back into the real world.

"You guys *will* be careful around Simon, won't you?" I asked Paul.

"Why, Mindy Clark, are you concerned for me?"

My cheeks burned. Our kiss last night had outed our relationship before we had truly identified—at least in words—what it even was to us. I wasn't sure of how he felt, though I knew in my heart this was more than a fling for me. Kate had confirmed it before I was ready to hear: I was in love with Paul Christian. It was strange how it had happened in a matter of days after so many years; but there it was.

Something kept holding me back from voicing this, however. "Of course I'm concerned for you," I murmured. "And Wesley, for Lainey's sake. But I'm more concerned for you."

"Not that I don't appreciate your concern, but the day I'm scared of Simon Leasure . . ."

"Is the day you get a tattoo and hook up with me?" I teased.

"Neither of those turned out to be unlikely, now did they?" he asked, brushing a light kiss against my hair. "Looks like Lainey wants to talk to you. I'd better speak to Wesley, anyway," he said, getting up. "She's all yours," he said to Lainey, motioning for her to sit down on the couch next to me.

Lainey did, settling Emily on her lap. I smiled at the baby and took hold of her chubby hand.

"Hey, Em. Keeping Mommy busy?"

"Of course." Lainey gave me an awkward smile. "I've got to admit, Min, I was a bit shocked at first. You and Paul were the last people I could ever imagine hooking up."

"As weird as you and the Reincarnist?" I quirked an eyebrow at her.

She shrugged. "Touché. But when I started noticing how you two were acting around each other, well, it wasn't a shock when Wesley told me he accidentally stumbled onto something he shouldn't have."

"It came out of nowhere," I admitted. "Both of us were surprised. But . . ."

"It's serious, isn't it?"

I nodded. "I think so." I didn't know what a future with Paul would hold, but I was suddenly starting to see it as a distinct possibility.

Lainey grinned. "I'm excited for you! Frankly, I always thought all Paul needed was the right person to draw him out of himself, and I can't tell you how thrilled I am you're finally over Luke."

"Yeah, speaking of that . . ." I lowered my voice. "Did I tell you he wanted to get together? With me?"

Lainey looked shocked. "What? No!"

I nodded. "He pretty much offered to dump Selena for me."

Lainey cast a glance over her shoulder to where Luke was talking to Fantazia, Selena in tow. "But he's still with her. What's up with that?"

I shrugged. "Who knows with guys? I think he got lonesome for my fawning adoration, frankly. I don't think he actually wanted to be with me, he just wanted someone to think he's awesome."

"Hello, male ego," Lainey said.

"Tell me about it." I gave Emily another halfhearted smile. "I'm worried about them going to meet with Simon, though."

"Welcome to my world," Lainey said. "It never gets any easier sending someone you love into combat, or any potentially dangerous situation, and wondering if they're going to come out alive. It's even scary when you know they'll come back one way or another, but that they just won't remember you." She nodded in Wesley's direction.

"It's just this feeling I have. Like, all the hair on the back of my neck is standing up," I said, brushing a hand there. "Something bad is going to happen."

"Mindy! You know you should never say that because . . ."

I couldn't hear Lainey anymore, as a searing pain went through my head. Clutching it in my hands, I cried out in pain as the familiar voice of my nemesis spoke two words:

We're here.

CHAPTER THIRTY

"So this voice has been talking to you for a while, but before this never in my place, and never this loud?" Fantazia said, taking her hands from my head and gazing down at me with a frown. Apparently my shrieks had drawn a bit of attention. Now she and Wesley were casting several spells to try to track down the source of the voice. Paul stood nearby with a worried look.

"That's right," I affirmed. "The basic villainous 'We're coming to get you' threat. No offense, Cyrus."

"I never went around threatening to go get anyone," Cyrus replied, affronted. "Now 'You'll never stop me,' or 'You're powerless to resist,' sure. But I'm not out to 'get' anyone."

"We stopped you," Luke put in.

"Yeah, you stopped me with the almighty dollar. Hiring counts as stopping. Good for you," Cyrus said.

Fantazia tapped a ruby nail on her lips, ignoring their babble. "So far the voice has only targeted Mindy. There are no reports of other telepaths with similar incidents, right, Cyrus?"

Cyrus shrugged from behind his computer. "If anyone's been contacted, they haven't been talking about it online. That's one of the things our grand leader told me to search for." He motioned to Wesley.

Fantazia looked at Wesley, too. "Knowing what I do about your background, Mindy . . . this has something to do with those communications we stumbled across at your headquarters last night."

Wesley ran a hand through his hair, disgruntled. "I was going to wait until we got confirmation from Simon before dropping that bombshell. Thanks, Fantazia."

"What are you talking about?" I asked, my nerves buzzing.

"The government stumbled onto an alien transmission," Wesley said. "They passed it along to the American Agents. When Fantazia and I snuck in last night, we caught it on our alert systems. It's a countdown to an invasion."

All of my nerves jangled at that moment. An alien invasion? Sure, there were many alien species out there, not just the Kalybri and the Vyqang, but were there any who would be telepathically harassing me? Not likely.

I slumped in my seat, feeling like the room was spinning. "Oh my God."

"An alien transmission that those of us in the know have had for weeks," Cyrus bragged.

"One that you should have shared," Wesley snapped.

"I didn't work for you then!" Cyrus said. "And I didn't know it was important. Come on, I'm no hero. Do you know how many end-of-the-world plots I hear about on a regular basis? And how many of those are all talk and no action? Who knew this was the real deal?"

"I didn't want to unduly upset you, Mindy," Wesley said. "I wanted to have all of the facts before I came to you."

"I need to hear," I said softly. "I need to hear what language they're speaking. I might know for sure all of what they're saying. I need the original transmission, not whatever the hackers or the government has already translated." I looked over at Cyrus.

He nodded. "Give me a minute and I'll see what I can do." He attacked his keyboard, and I could see magic radiating off his fingertips as he used his powers to move even faster.

After a few moments, he motioned to me. "Have a listen." He clicked a button on a Wave file and it immediately played.

The sounds that came out of his computer speakers were the same as those that populated my own personal hell, the ones that haunted my nightmares and my memories. The Vyqang had spoken largely in Kalybri to us captives, but I had a ghost of a memory of lying on that table, strapped down while they worked on my brain, and those grunts and growls in the background.

"Oh God, oh God," I started moaning, unaware of the fact I was unconsciously putting my hands over my ears. All of this time it had been one of them in my head, one these monsters of my past, whispering threats.

"Turn it off!" Paul ordered Cyrus, rising from his seat to stand by my side.

"No, no!" I held out my hands as if to ward off blows. "No, I have to hear." I listened, caught between nausea and terror, trying to see if I could make sense of the words and wondering if my invader was still present.

Yes, I am. A laugh echoed in my head. *Do you believe me now that we're coming to get you, or will it take ripping the guts out of your little friends to make it real, Mindy?*

I tried to tune out his words and the terror he inspired by speaking my name. Instead I focused on him, trying to make him more real to me. After all, he had tracked me down using this link the Vyqang had probably installed in me for this very purpose. I was part of a catch-and-release program and . . .

No, we don't make that habit, the voice said. *If it was*

*anyone other than me, well, they might have left you and
this backwater world of yours alone.*

His words were horrible but our link was real. It only
stood to reason that I could track him. I focused on that
voice, and on his thoughts that I could almost reach out
and touch.

What are you doing? Stop it!

He was sitting on one of those cold metal ships headed
toward my world, blue eyes glittering in the darkness.

Stop!

The connection was immediately severed, and I stumbled backward, falling against Paul, who steadied me.

"Turn it off!" Paul snapped, and Cyrus immediately
complied.

Paul turned me to face him. "Are you all right?"

"It's them," I whispered. "The Vyqang. The aliens
that . . . tortured me. It's them. They're coming here.
They've just hit our solar system, but with their ships,
they will be here in a few days. Maybe less." I focused on
Paul. "They're coming here because of me. I thought
they were gone, destroyed, but I should have known
they'd come back." I started crying.

Paul held on tight to me. "They're not going to hurt
you. I promise."

"You can't promise something like that, Paul. You
don't know them!" I said.

"Yes, I can," he replied, a steely edge to his voice.
"Because we will stop them."

Forrest and Toby stepped into the room, and we all
jumped.

"Jesus, it's just us!" Toby held up his hands. "What's
wrong?"

"Alien invasion," Cyrus said.

Toby and Forrest looked at each other. "Invasion?

But I thought they wanted to help," Toby said, looking confused.

"What are you babbling about?" Luke eyed him.

Forrest stepped forward. "I just got another call. From Senator Leasure."

"Simon's a senator now?" Kate asked.

"Simon's father," Paul corrected. "What did he want?"

"To meet us without Simon knowing. He was saying that 'Simon screwed up' is the understatement of the millennium," Toby replied. "Apparently this group of aliens heard how something bad was going to go down on planet Earth and wanted to help. Simon told them to stick it, that he had everything covered. The government is adding his poor diplomatic skills to a long list of things they're upset with Simon about, and wants us to help."

"They don't want to help, they want to kill us all," I murmured to myself.

"The Kalybri?" Toby looked really confused. "I thought they were the good ones, the ones who rescued you."

"Wait, what?" I was lost. "The *Kalybri* are here? Were here?"

Forrest nodded. "I just found out they came to lend their assistance. Until Simon turned them down."

"How do you know it's them? Were they speaking Kalybrian, because don't believe that. It could just be the Vyqang pretending to be Kalybri."

Forrest shrugged, looking out of his depths. "You'll have to talk to Senator Leasure about it, Mindy. He was one of the people who heard the original transmission. You're mentioned in it, actually, and you're the one he wants to talk to. The only one. He doesn't want news about this getting out."

"Too bad," Paul growled. "They put their foot in it,

now they're going to have to play by our rules if they want our help."

"From what I'm told, the aliens are refusing to speak to anyone other than Mindy."

"If it's the Vyqang, this might be a trap to get Mindy alone to brutalize her," Paul suggested.

"Or it could actually be the Kalybri," I said. "They know I'm the only one who knows how seriously to take this threat. I'm not afraid of Simon's dad, of course. He's the least scary person in all of this." I met Forrest's eyes. "Set it up. I'll do it while Paul and Wesley are talking to Simon."

"No!" Paul shook his head. "I'm not letting you do this, Mindy."

"You're right. You're not *letting* me do anything. I'm doing it, end of story," I said, narrowing my eyes at him. "Excuse me, but I have to go change." I spun on my heel and went back to my room to put on something more serious than jeans and sneakers for my meeting with the senator.

Paul barged into my room without knocking just as I'd finished undressing. "What do you think you're doing?"

"What do you think *you're* doing?" I snarled. "I'm kind of getting naked here."

His eyes flicked over me. "Yeah, nice. But I've seen it before, so I'm not going to be shocked out of having this argument. You are not going down there to offer yourself up willingly to Simon's father or some aliens who may or may not be the Kalybri and may or may not be the Vyqang."

I yanked a sweater on. "I'm just going to see Simon's father, and to find out for sure what he knows and who he's talking to. I'm not meeting with any aliens yet."

"What if when you get down there it's just a diversionary tactic or a trap? I wouldn't put it past Simon, and I'm not putting it past his father."

"The aliens said 'speak to,' not 'meet.' I won't go any-where to meet them without talking to you first. I promise." I zipped up my skirt and boots. "Why won't you trust me, Paul? Don't you think I'm as qualified as anyone else in this squad?" It was a fear I'd always had.

He faced me, hurt and fear in his eyes. "I do trust you, Mindy. It's everyone else I don't trust." He began to pace the room.

"You don't trust me to make the right decisions to keep myself safe," I accused.

I had him there, and he knew it. His eyes narrowed. "If I don't, it's because I'm worried. You're acting rashly. I can understand that; you've had a terrible shock. You're looking for help against the aliens who hurt you. But you're not acting as smart as your IQ."

I glared at him. "Thanks."

"I'm sorry, but it's true," he replied.

I gave him a nasty look. "Well, I guess it's too bad that you don't get a say."

"That's where you're wrong." He stepped in front of me. "I'm your team leader, and I do get a say."

"Team leader? So's Wesley."

"Wesley will agree with me."

"Don't go there," I snarled. "That's not the real rea-son you're acting like you can tell me what to do. This is because of *us*."

He threw up his hands. "Excuse me for being con-cerned."

"I hate this," I said, breaking. I crossed my arms over my chest. "I hate it that just because you've been in a guy's bed, he thinks that gives him the right to order you around."

Paul shook his head. "Tell me you didn't just say that to me."

"Oh, so I'm wrong? This has nothing to do with the fact that we're sleeping together?"

Paul rolled his eyes. "Don't you dare take my concern for the woman I love and pervert it into some macho head trip! You should know damn well I'm not like that, Mindy." He turned his back, obviously furious.

But his words had taken the wind out of my sails. "W-what?" I said.

"I said that you know damn well I'm not like that. At least you should. Jesus." He ran a hand over his head.

"No, before that." I took a step toward him, hesitant. "It kinda sounded like you said . . . like you said you love me." Maybe I had misunderstood his meaning.

"Well, I guess that's because I did. I do." He turned around to look at me, and his features softened at the obvious shock on my face. "You hadn't figured that out yet?"

"Well, it's just . . . y-you never said anything," I stammered. I'd known I was falling for him, and I'd hoped that my feelings were reciprocated, but to hear the words . . .

"Well, not to put too fine a point on it, but neither have you," he said, leaning back against the closed door. He held up a hand as I opened my mouth. "And I don't want you to feel like you have to now. I know this came on fast and under terrible circumstances. It's not totally out of the realm of possibility that this is some sort of stress reaction to everything that's going on with the team. I don't think it is, but I didn't want to pressure you too soon." He sighed and continued before I could say anything. "I'm making a mess of this. Look, Mindy, I do trust you. I really do. I'm just very concerned, and I think I have a right to be, both as your team leader and as the guy who's in love with you. I'm only asking you to do two things in consideration of that."

"And that is?"

"First, you'll wear a communicator in case you need to get in touch with our home base," he said. "So if you're in trouble, you can let us know. And . . . along similar lines, I want you to take Luke along."

I started to protest, but he held up a hand. "He doesn't have to go into the meeting with you, just be in the same area. Wesley and I are going together to meet with Simon; you need someone with you to meet with his father. We haven't been going anywhere alone so far as a team, and we're not starting now. That's an order from the team leader side of me. And since he offered to dump Selena for you and also judging from his reaction today, Luke still has feelings for you, so I know he'll look out for you."

I sighed. He had a point. "Fine, okay. I'll take Luke and a communicator. Happy?"

Paul nodded, looking grave. "Happier."

"Was Luke the last thing or was there something else?"

"There's something else. This is from the personal side, not the team leader." He took a deep breath. "Promise me that when everything gets back to normal, when there's no more alien invasion and we're back home where we belong and not outlaws, that you'll consider making our relationship something real. Something permanent." He looked really nervous. "I'm not asking for any sort of commitment now, and I'm not even asking for it when this is over. Only that you'll give it some thought. That it'll be in the back of your mind. On the radar. That kind of thing." He sat down on my bed. "I'm not trying to scare you off, but I'm being honest, Mindy. This thing with Kate really screwed with my head. I'm too old to play games like that and I don't want to ever do it again. I just want to make sure we're on the same page, and since this started out so strange . . ." He sighed. "I just want to make sure we both know where we want this to go. Or we should get out of it now."

I looked over and felt something I had gotten used to feeling around him: I was happy. Despite the evil aliens knocking on our door, despite being an outlaw, despite the craziness surrounding us, I was happy. With him. Come what may, no matter what the future might hold.

I sat down next to him and slipped my hand into his. "Okay," I said.

He brought my hand to his lips and kissed it. "I know I sound crazy right now, but as long as we can talk about it after . . ."

"No," I shook my head. "You're misunderstanding me. I don't have to wait until the dust settles. I mean, I can if you really want, but I already know what my answer is going to be. It's not going to change between now and then. It's still going to be okay." I squeezed his hand. "I love you, Paul. Depending on how you look at it, this relationship moved really fast or really slow, but it's been real to me since the night we were together. Maybe even before then. And it's stupid, but I was nervous that it wasn't real for you until you said that you loved me too."

"The same," he said, almost like he was in shock. "About everything you just said."

"So, you're stuck with me," I promised, squeezing his hand again.

"Until you come to your senses."

"You're in for a long haul, buddy. Now, what time do you have to meet with Simon?"

He checked his watch. "We have to leave in about twenty minutes or so."

"Not a lot of time, but it'll have to do." I pushed him back on my bed and whipped off my sweater.

CHAPTER THIRTY-ONE

"Do you see them yet?" I asked Luke, glancing around.

We were the only two people standing in this secluded area of Megolopolis's largest park, where people generally went jogging and picnicked with families in the mornings. At night, however, it became a different place, where drug deals went down and no one went walking for fear of muggings or worse. We'd patrolled in this area for years, and the police tried to keep up surveillance, but there was only so much they could do and we had been working from more limited resources lately. I was glad Paul had insisted Luke come with me; it was nearing dusk and, hero or no, even I didn't want to be alone here. This was that strange in-between time, after the moms took their kids home and the businessmen finished their evening jogs and before the dangerous people showed up. I suppose it was the perfect place to have a clandestine meeting with a senator about the possible fate of the planet.

"Not yet," Luke said, keeping an eye out.

"I hope the meeting with Simon is going okay for Paul and Wesley," I remarked.

"They're probably telling him where to stick it right now," Luke said. Then: "It's none of my business, but there's just something I've got to know."

"What's your question? Who Simon's sleeping with to keep his job?"

"No. Are you in love with him?"

"Simon?" I asked.

He gave me a look. "You know who I mean. Is it just physical, or is it more?"

I frowned. "That's an awfully personal question."

"We're friends, aren't we?"

"I don't ask you about your relationship with Selena."

"Because you know it's not serious."

I wasn't sure why he wanted to know what he asked, but I told him anyway. "Yes. I love Paul."

"It's just so strange to hear you say that." He shook his head. "But if you're happy, then I'm happy for you, Mindy."

I smiled, thinking about it. "Given the vast weirdness of this whole situation, I can say without a shadow of a doubt that, yes, I am happy, Luke. Thanks. And I think this is them." I nodded to the figures starting to approach. Considering they were in conservative suits and ties, I had a feeling they weren't local drug dealers showing up early for work.

"Mindy Clark?" The oldest gentleman reached out with a hand. "Jackson Leasure." A silent bodyguard stood in the background. Good to see I wasn't the only one who brought backup.

"Nice to meet you, sir," I said, taking his hand and shaking it. "Yes, I'm Tekgrrl. This is my teammate, Sensei. Luke Harmon."

"Luke." The senator shook his hand. "I'm glad you decided to meet with me, young lady. I'd just like to apologize on behalf of the Senate and myself. I'm afraid my son led us to believe your team was starting to become a threat to national security, and that his team was better suited to be the premier team of this country." He shook his head. "Now we find out how wrong he was."

"You said it, I didn't, sir," I said.

"Those people linked with that Dragon cult were influencing him too," Jackson defended his son. "They were trying to convince him that your friend's baby was in danger so they could get close to her for their own reasons. Simon realizes that now."

I wondered if he did, or if that was just an excuse Simon was using, but I didn't say anything.

"These Kalybri showed up a week or so ago, telling us that a warrior race of raiders was on its way to our planet. They've been fighting a war with them for many years and thought they had them finally beaten back until they intercepted transmissions showing a countdown to the first strike on Earth, and they wanted to warn us and help."

I swallowed down the bile that threatened to rise in my throat. "Yes, their planet was subject to an invasion back when I was living with them. I was one of the prisoners taken. The Kalybri joined forces to save us, and to put a stop to the Vyqang. I believe they took down one of the Vyqang's largest marauding ships, but apparently they didn't take out the whole race."

"And now they're here."

I nodded. "Yes, sir. Or coming."

"Well, if these Kalybri stopped them before and have been fighting them for a long time, I would say these are people we want on our side," he mused.

"Yes, sir. If it is actually them contacting us and not the Vyqang pretending to be them to lure us into a trap to lower our defenses . . ."

"He suggested you would say as much."

"Sir?"

"The emissary for the Kalybri, their leader. He said you would refuse to meet with them."

"And wisely too," a familiar accented voice said. I

whirled to see a shimmering glow surround the bodyguard as the image inducer he was using switched off.

Luke bolted forward, putting his bulk between me
and what had been the senator's bodyguard.

The newly revealed alien smiled. "Hello, Man-dei."

I gasped. "Oh my God!" I maneuvered past Luke.
"Dyvinsher! Is it really you?" I hugged my former foster
brother.

He smiled. "Yes, it is me, Man-dei. You have grown
up."

"So have you!" I hugged him again. "You look great.
What about Anyoska? How is she?"

The Kalybri's face darkened. "She was never the
same after we got her back. She doesn't go outside of
the house, just sits in a chair in front of her reader. She
thinks she is still in school." His face cracked with
sorrow.

"Oh, Dyvinsher!" I felt tears rush down my cheeks.

"Our people left Earth alone to continue our fight
with the Vyqang, yes, but also because we were afraid
of what would become of you. Your people entrusted us
with you, and we failed that trust. We did not want to
be a constant reminder . . ."

"Dyvinsher, that wasn't the Kalybri's fault!" I pro-
tested.

"We tried to help in any way we could, but we
thought you would end up like Anyoska. But you are
strong, Man-dei. You are strong."

"Well, I don't know about that."

"Yes." He nodded emphatically. "You are a warrior,
like me."

I recognized the symbols on his robe. "You're a com-
mander now!"

"Yes, I am leading the expedition to help this planet.
Once I heard they were making their way to this region,

I knew he was coming for you." He made a sound like a sigh. "I knew it was only a matter of time."

"He? Who is 'he'?"

"The current leader of the Vyqang." Dyvinsher's face looked pale. "Your son."

"W-what?" I felt like the bottom had dropped out of my world. My head swam. "What are you talking about?" I didn't want to hear this, but I especially didn't want to hear it front of Luke, and Simon's father.

Dyvinsher reached out a hand to steady me. I didn't even realize I was swaying. "When they took you and Anyoska, they took you for breeding stock. They harvested from you."

"Oh God." I whispered, remembering what I had seen during that hazy point in time during my capture, when I had watched them take apart my brain and tinker with it . . . to steal my DNA to make the perfect soldier. A soldier who was now coming this way to do to my planet what they had once done to the Kalybri.

"That's why he's been able to talk to me and only me," I said. "The telepathic bond only works between us because we're linked by DNA." I don't know how I knew that, only that I did. Perhaps because *he* knew.

"We have been fighting them in deep space, Mandei," Dyvinsher explained. "We have learned much about their tactics, though they are still strong. We will work with your people to try to defend your planet. Hopefully they will not even make it to orbit. But if they do, and they send out a landing party . . ."

I nodded. "We have to be ready. I understand. But he's been contacting me, warning me that they're coming. Why?"

"I think he wants you to know who he is. I think he wants to see you."

"Does he think I won't try to stop him because . . ." I

couldn't bring myself to say the words. He wasn't my child. Not really. He was a scientific by-product of experiments done in a lab, grown in a tube by creatures who had violated me. His birth wasn't brought on by the usual style of rape, but it had been rape nonetheless. "Because of what he is?"

"The Vyqang have no care for the females that spawn them," Dyvinsher said. "Had we not taken back you and Anyoska, you would have been disposed of without a thought."

"So, why?"

"I think he is curious. He is part human, and human curiosity is great. Your race is technologically backward, but you managed to interact with us—and with the Vyqang."

"Well, as we say on Earth, curiosity killed the cat."

"In this case, I hope so. And that cat is a Vyqang." Dyvinsher studied me. "We will stop them, Man-dei. Are you a strong enough warrior to face them?"

"I'll do what I can," I vowed, feeling the weight of those words. "We all will."

But . . . could I help kill a thing that had grown from a part of me?

I thought of all of my friends in the EHJ, of tiny little Emily who was going to—I had to believe—grow up to save the world from certain destruction. I thought of my parents. And mostly I thought of Paul and the future we could have together.

Yes, if it came down to it, I would choose to save all of them. I could be just as cold as the Vyqang.

"Come back with us, Dyvinsher," I heard myself saying. "My team leaders will want to make a plan with you."

The senator looked startled. "We were going to have talks with them as well."

"He said he wanted to help *my* people," I said. "The last I checked, we aren't welcome with yours."

"Th-that was a mistake," Simon's father stuttered. "My son was bitter about his rejection from your team; I know that now. We made a mistake."

"Don't worry, Senator," I said. "We'll save the world as per usual. But we'll take any help that is genuinely offered—unlike others, who are glory hounds and poor sports." I turned back to Luke and my foster brother. "Let's go."

Hours later, we were back home. Our real home, not Fantazia's pocket dimension. It seemed as if several months had passed since we left, even though it had only been weeks. I wandered the halls of the Elite Hands of Justice, thinking. Simon had graciously offered to drop all false charges. He had also been gracious enough to offer us a place on the American Agents team. Paul and Wesley had graciously told him to go to hell. But we were no longer outlaws. We were back home. Just in time to prep for the battle against my evil offspring.

We'd gone over the plan several times, and each time, part of my mind had paid rapt attention. The other part was numb, cut off, distant.

Since the leader of the Vyqang wanted to meet me so much, he was going to. I was going to be the distraction, the bait to draw him out. I would give him the chance to leave. If he didn't, everyone was waiting to destroy him. My foster brother's people would fight his minions in space. The Elite Hands of Justice would fight any that came Earthside. The military had nuclear weapons they were willing to bring to bear. I hoped it wouldn't come to any of that, but I remembered the only way the Vyqang were stopped before was destruction.

I surveyed a different destruction: my lab, totally incinerated when we had our fight with Simon. As I sorted through the debris, making piles of trash and of other things I could probably repair, I sighed. Dyvinsher, whose own ships were in orbit around the Earth as our first line of defense, had estimated that the Vyqang would arrive any day. It didn't matter. It could be one day or one month from now; I was still ill equipped to deal with this painful reminder of my past who wanted to enslave my planet.

I heard the sound of a door swishing open behind me and turned to see Paul. "Hi," he said.

"Hey." I motioned to the pile. "Just sorting some stuff out."

"I can see that." He stood with his hands in his pockets. "Feels weird to be back here, doesn't it?"

I nodded. "Yeah."

He looked over my pile. "Anything salvageable?"

"A few pieces here and there." I felt like we were having this conversation on multiple layers. "What's up?"

"I just wanted to check on you. You were really quiet all through the meeting."

"There's just a lot to process."

"I understand."

"Do you ever feel like this team is cursed?" I asked. "Maybe Simon's right. First Lainey and Wesley are part of some ancient prophecy that might destroy the world and has the Dragon going after Lainey. And now . . ."

"It wasn't Lainey's fault she was targeted by the Dragon. And what's happening here isn't your fault. They violated you and stole part of you to make him. You had no control over that. It's not your responsibility."

"It's not my DNA running rampant out there?" I asked.

"Well, not just yours. Something else's too," he said.

Trying to cheer me up he added, "That's how it works. You need me to explain Biology 101 to you?"

"But if it wasn't for me—"

"It would have been someone else who was violated."

"Then the Vyqang wouldn't be coming here," I pointed out.

"But they like to conquer worlds. Murder and rape and ruin, right?" At my nod, Paul continued. "We can stop them, Mindy. Maybe this battle is all that stands in the way of them running rampant and conquering whole galaxies. Your foster brother is here to help *you*. If it had been someone else, maybe the Vyqang would never be stopped."

I gave him half a smile. "Interesting way of looking at it."

"I'm a scientist. I look at things in interesting ways." He gave me a reassuring smile.

Wanting to change the subject, I motioned around us. "Is your lab the same?"

He nodded. "Pretty much. Simon has cost us a lot."

"We should send him the bill."

"We should," he agreed.

"Is everyone else getting settled in?"

"I think everyone's glad to be back in their own beds," Paul remarked.

"Except Cyrus, who didn't live here."

"Yeah, well, we still need him, so while he's freelance working for us, he's living with us," Paul said. "I'm thinking of turning my lab into a bedroom. Have a cot set up or something."

"For Cyrus?"

"No, I gave him the spare room I was staying in while Kate and I were splitting up," Paul said. "And I'm not bunking up with him, so don't ask. We might kill each other."

"You're not staying with me?" I said.

He looked shy. "I wasn't sure if you'd want me to."

"Didn't we already have this conversation?"

"I know you said you were in this for the long haul, but with us coming back home and the Vyqang—"

"Nothing's changed for me, Paul. Nothing." Now I was nervous. "Has something changed for you? I understand that you were shaky about kids in the EHJ anyway, and this revelation isn't helping, I'm sure."

"You think I don't like kids or something?"

"You said once that Wesley and Lainey were crazy to have a kid in our environment," I reminded him. "And now that we see what my DNA mixes into, I can understand if that makes you not want to chance anything."

He shook his head, frustrated. "Like I said, this Vyqang leader isn't your fault. And yes, I did say that about Wesley and Lainey, but I also understand why they are crazy enough to do it." He smiled. "I could see having a child someday . . . with the right person. If you're suggesting Emily should have a playmate in the EHJ family."

For a moment I could see a child with Paul's smile and my eyes. "Not anytime soon," I quickly amended. "But someday. Since we're getting all of our relationship expectations out in the open. Wow," I realized. "That's the quickest way to scare off a guy, huh? Talking about future babies."

"Well, I think a more permanent relationship is called for first." Paul sounded hesitant, nervous again. But also more than a little hopeful. "Maybe a little bit of paperwork, too. In the form of a license."

Was he suggesting what I thought? "I'm not opposed to it," I admitted. I didn't want to overreact.

He scratched his head. "Are you being serious, or are you just teasing?"

"I'm serious—but remember I'm a cold-blooded scientist. If you're cool with a little ceremony in front of a judge, just the two of us, then you've got yourself a deal."

His face broke into a bright smile. "You're completely serious?"

"Yes, I'm completely serious! What do I have to do to prove I'm saying yes to your unasked question? Yes, Paul, if you decide to ask me to marry you, I'll say yes. If that's what you're coyly tap-dancing around."

"It's not because you think something bad's going to happen with this invasion and you won't have to follow through?" He was teasing; I could tell by the tone of his voice.

"I'll run out and get the license now, if that's what you want." I shook my head. "And I thought Wesley asking Lainey to marry him in an elevator moments before a possible world-ending battle was weird. I think this is probably the weirdest proposal in the history of proposals. But what can you expect from us, right?"

"How about if I phrase it better after we stop the invading aliens? Now, how about a distraction from the craziness of today?" He held out a hand.

I took it. "That sounds fabulous."

CHAPTER THIRTY-TWO

"Are you sure you can do this?"

I frowned as we went over the plan again. Logistics might have changed a bit, but we were still solid. "Yes, Paul. I'm fine." I glanced over at Fantazia. "Are *you* sure you can do this?"

She shrugged. "I'm sure it'll work out fine."

I looked at Wesley. "Now I'm not so sure."

"She's just being . . ." Wesley gave Fantazia a dark look. "She's just being herself. She can do this without any trouble."

Fantazia snorted. "It's so easy? You try working a tele-portation spell to an alien ship miles above the Earth's atmosphere, then the subjects mucking around a bit up there and then turning around and transporting back. Oh, wait! You don't have the power to do that any-more." She gave him an equally dark look. "So it looks like you should be quiet."

I looked at my foster brother. "Assuming she can even transport us up there, what guarantee do we have that he won't just blow us away?"

"None," interrupted Paul. "Which is why I've been working on this all night." He tossed me a small device that looked like a garage door opener. "It's a personal shield. I can't factor in for all of the alien weapons they might throw at you, but it is calibrated to deflect every-thing I know."

"And when exactly did you make this?" I turned the device over in my hand, admiring the workmanship.

"After you fell asleep."

"You didn't sleep?"

"Sleep is for people that don't have access to intravenous caffeine drips," Paul said.

"Thanks, babe," I replied, leaning in and giving him a kiss.

Toby groaned and looked away. "No making out in the war room."

"What about the people risking their lives but not sleeping with you?" Fantazia grumbled.

"As long as you're standing close, the shield should protect you," Paul said.

Fantazia snorted. "I love how you say *should*."

"You can cast a shield on yourself," Paul pointed out. "I've seen Lainey and Wesley cast them."

Fantazia threw up her hands. "Do you people think I have an unlimited supply of magic? Because I don't!"

"Can you take some of mine?" Lainey asked. "Since I'm staying here with Emily, I don't need much."

"You need some," Wesley pointed out. "No way am I leaving you in the midst of a possible invasion powerless."

"Not exactly powerless," Lainey retorted. "And I'm in a pretty heavily guarded fortress."

"Which the Dragon tore through last time," Wesley said.

"We're fighting aliens this time, not magic users."

Fantazia actually gave Lainey a small smile. "Thanks for offering, Lainey, but I'll be okay, I'm sure. I'll just take a very long vacation afterward."

"Okay. How's the decoding, Cyrus?" Wesley asked.

"Won't be able to tell until they get here," the Virus replied, not looking up from his computer. "But so long as the information our alien friends have provided is remotely correct, with a few minor tweaks I should be able to upload this program to disable their defense systems in a short amount of time."

"Time that we'll spend fighting them," Paul said.

"Better hope it takes effect pretty quick," Cyrus muttered. "Just like in the movies."

"Like anything works like it does in the movies," Luke said.

"That's why the military is on standby to nuke their alien butts," Toby said.

"And that's why we had better hope our plan works," Paul added. "I don't know about anyone else, but I get worried anytime anyone mentions the words nuclear and government in the same sentence."

"I must go prepare my people," Dyvinsher said. "We are getting reports that the Vyqang are nearing."

"I'll relay that to the military," Wesley said. "They'll be the next line of defense should the Vyqang punch their way through yours and into the atmosphere."

"If they do, ready your ground troops," Dyvinsher said. "They waste no time in transporting down."

Paul nodded. "Wesley and I will be leading the forces below."

I hugged Dyvinsher. "Good luck."

He hugged me back. "To you as well, Man-dei."

I wrapped my arms around myself as he took a few steps backward and transported himself away. Now we would have to watch as the Kalybri attempted to keep the Vyqang from reaching us. I had a feeling that it would only be a matter of time before a few of the enemy's ships slipped through and they made their way forward. Once the battle started on the ground, we only had a limited amount of time for our plan to work: Cyrus taking out their defense systems and Fantazia and

I trying to take out their leader . . . or convince him to go away peacefully before the military stepped in.

Paul stepped up behind and wrapped his arms around me.

I sighed. "There's nothing we can do now, is there?"

"Not yet," he agreed. "We don't have spaceships equipped with the appropriate weapons yet."

"Maybe we should invent some."

"I'll get right on that." He noticed how tense my body was. "What about you? Is he talking to you?"

"All's very silent," I reported. "I get the sense that he's here, and if I push I can almost make out some words, but I'm afraid. Because if I can hear him, he can likely hear me, and I don't want him getting an inkling of our thoughts."

"Good idea," Paul said. "And probably similar to what he's thinking."

Wesley waved his hand from the side of the room, where he was monitoring the communications from the Kalybri ships. "It's starting."

Selena burst into the war room with Simon trailing after her. "I'm sorry, but I couldn't stall him anymore."

"What are you doing here, Simon?" Paul growled.

"Look, I know things are a little tense between our two teams . . ." Simon held up his hands as if to ward off blows.

" 'A little tense'?" Paul shook his head. "That's like saying we might have a little problem if the Vyqang make their way through the Kalybri defenses."

"Exactly," Simon said. "My people and I, we just want to help."

"Your *remaining* people, you mean—and 'try to save face' is more like it," Kate spat. "You helped start this mess."

"Well, maybe I want to try to help clean it up," Simon blasted. "But you won't let me."

"You made the government believe we were practically villains while you were inadvertently working with the real villains. Again," Wesley said. "Pardon us for not trusting you with our plan. But if you want to help, we'll put you on the front line should the time come."

"I'm going to head down there," Paul spoke up. "Gather the teams already assembling down there and start coming up with a plan of attack. You're welcome to join me," he said to Simon.

"I'll head down as well," Kate said.

"Everyone make sure you keep a communicator on at all times," Wesley ordered, tossing one to each of us. The devices were some of the inventions that had survived the fire sale. "We need to maintain contact."

"I'm here on babysitting duty and manning home base," Lainey said. "I'll be helping coordinate everyone once Wesley heads down."

"When I show up, it pretty much means things have gone south with the Kalybri," Wesley pointed out. "I'd like for each of us to head up an assault team of the other heroes who have volunteered, so Lainey knows where each of those teams is at all times."

"Does that include me?" Simon asked. "Do I get to lead one?"

"Don't push it," Paul said.

"I used to be a member of this team," Simon sniffed.

"'Used to' being the operative words."

"Bicker later," Wesley said. "Get down there."

Paul stepped over and took me by the shoulders. "Be careful up there," he said.

"You be careful down there." My heart was pounding. Neither of our courses was safe. It was likely that one or both of us could die. I suddenly felt the urge to grab hold of him and never let go.

He must have been feeling the same, for he pulled me close, hugging me tight and burying his face in my hair. "I love you so much," he whispered.

"I love you too." I kissed him hard, pouring everything I had in that one kiss—in case it was our last. How unfair that we had found each other so late. "Please come back to me."

"I'll try my best. You do the same." He kissed my lips and then turned away quickly, changing from my Paul to our hardened leader. "Let's go, people." He strode off, at the head of Simon, Kate, Selena and Toby. They were going into battle.

I shivered, hoping that wasn't the last sight I'd ever have of him. And then I noticed the light seemed to dim outside, like the day had gotten suddenly cloudy. And I had an uncomfortable flashback to my last day back on Kalybri.

"They're here," I whispered. "It's one of their ships. One of them must have gotten through the Kalybri's defenses. They've hit atmosphere."

Just as the alarms screamed to life and everybody jumped to action, the almost whispering voice in the back of my mind turned into a bone-jarring shriek. I could vaguely hear Lainey calling out orders to the teams as Wesley scrambled to help others. Cyrus's fingers flew across the keyboard of his laptop . . . and someone pushed against my brain.

Mindy, the voice roared in my head. The voice of the Vyqang leader, my son. *Come out and watch the destruction of your planet.*

Why don't you be a man and face me yourself, you big coward? I thought back at him. *This is between us, not the rest of the people on Earth.*

No, but it will hurt you to see them destroyed.

Don't you want to see that pain yourself? You'll have to face me to do that.

So you can try to destroy me? I don't think so.

Don't you want to see me? Your own mother?

We are the Vyqang. We spring from the loins of our battleships, not from feeble female bodies. He sounded affronted.

Fantazia had walked over to me, sensed my interaction. "Concentrate, Mindy," she said, placing her hands on either side of my head. "Show me where he is."

I tried to zero in on him, my son, on a ship hovering over our planet, overseeing this battle, his dark blue eyes glittering in the darkness.

What are you doing? he hissed. *I can feel you pressing against my mind. What are you doing?*

"Got it!" Fantazia crowed, and she threw powder into the air and began the teleportation spell.

Luke stepped up and handed me my weapons belt. "Let's do this," he said.

I could hear Fantazia's chanted Italian and my nerves felt raw with fear and adrenaline.

I'm coming to visit, Dunvyn, I said, his name suddenly coming to mind. Why had it not come earlier?

Fantazia's hand clamped down on my arm and Luke's. The familiar surroundings of the Elite Hands of Justice headquarters disappeared.

CHAPTER THIRTY-THREE

We appeared in shiny steel corridors similar to the memories-slash-nightmares of my past. Strange Klaxons blared, and the air felt strange, cool and clammy. Almost thick.

"Should we be breathing this in?" Luke asked.

"I did before, so you should be fine," I said. I prayed I was right.

The ship shuddered under our feet and we all swayed; it had clearly taken a hit from a Kalybri craft. We heard the Vyqang ship return fire. Growling language sounded over the intercom, and though I couldn't translate, my link with my child told me what it meant. More of our enemy were transporting down to the Earth's surface.

My mind was buzzing like a beehive. He was here. He was close by. Dunvyn.

Apparently, he was experiencing similar thoughts, because the door opened and four large Vyqang armed with some sort of blasters came barreling forward.

Fantazia immediately sprang into action, snapping something in Italian and pointing a finger at the guards. Their guns became useless, and they looked nonplussed as they pulled the triggers to no effect. Luke took advantage of the momentary confusion to attack, screaming and charging forward. The Vyqang stumbled back, horror crossing their faces as Fantazia followed her previous spell with lightning bolts.

"I hope Cyrus is doing his job," she snapped, ducking as a guard swung at her. "Go, Mindy!"

"Let's show them how Earth defends itself," Luke was snarling, attacking the disarmed guards, who were now going for the blades attached to their sides and backs. Before they could reach them, Luke snatched them away in a blur of agility.

I shocked the closest guard with the small disk in my palm, but gasped as more foes appeared from the far door. "Fantazia!" I focused my emotions and energy into a small concussive telekinetic blast. It worked! Two went flying into the wall, hard, and I thought I could hear the sounds of their necks breaking. The remaining guard swiveled his gun. I had no time to react except for Paul's shield.

The blast hit the shield, and it held, but there was some feedback in the form of heat. It felt like getting a burn from the door of hot oven. I winced but knew it was better than the alternative. I didn't particularly want to be in the oven itself.

"I see them!" Fantazia quick-fired some Italian, and these guards too lost their guns.

But not before one of them got a shot off. The laser caught Luke in the back. I screamed in horror.

"Just . . . go . . ." he grunted, ripping a dagger off the belt of a Vyqang and immediately stabbing the blade up into the alien's stomach.

"Take out the leader one way or another, Mindy," Fantazia ordered, before hissing some Italian. The guards blocking the door were instantly thrown backward and into the wall.

I ran at full speed at the door and punched the

button with my mind. The doors swung open and then closed just after I dove through, leaving my friends to battle alone behind me. And . . . I was face-to-face with my son.

The guards sitting around the captain's chair immediately pointed their guns at me. I stood immobile, arms up, trying to act like I meant no harm.

"Drop your weapons," a familiar voice said in English. I fumbled to drop my belt to the floor. "Kick them over this way." I did so. Dunvyn growled something to his men and they stood down, going back to watching the battles outside and on Earth on the myriad screens around the room.

I was struck by how human he seemed. Dark hair, those dark blue eyes, and weirdly enough, he looked a bit like my father, which hit me like a knife to my gut. That similarity made everything all the more real. But there were also alien features when you looked hard enough. His eyes were just a little too blue, his fingers were too long, and the way he moved was just a little too fast, almost like his joints weren't proper.

"So, you're her," he said in heavily accented English, surveying me. "So weak. So frail. So . . . human."

"You're a bit human yourself," I retorted.

He frowned. "We all have our problems. I have paid for the weakness in my bloodline for years. I have fought and struggled to get to where I am today." He spread his arms wide. "And now I am a leader among my people. I could take a seat of power amongst our kind. But first I must make a display of power, show that I am willing to eradicate my past forever."

"And that means destroying the Earth," I said.

"Not even the Kalybri and your people can stop us," he agreed.

"The Kalybri stopped your people before," I mentioned.

"The Kalybri never faced me," he replied. "Now . . . *Mother*." He spat the last word. "Should I make you watch your world's destruction before you face your own?"

"Dunvyn, I'm here to give you a chance, and I suggest you take it," I said. "The humans have great weapons that they have pointed at your ships. They will destroy you, there's no question about it. Unless you turn around and leave. Never return."

Dunvyn looked at the rest of the Vyqang and laughed. He growled something to them in their language and then turned to me. "Do you know what I just said? Did our mind link translate for you?"

I nodded. "You said for them to prepare to launch the spear, but I don't know what that means."

The ship vibrated so violently I thought it was going to blow up. I wasn't sure if that wasn't a good thing.

"The spear will drill down to your planet's core. It will rip through your world and knock it out of its proper orbit. The Earth will smash into neighboring planets and eventually your sun, destroying everything. Of course, we will first have taken what we need—probably not much of anything."

"Dunvyn, you don't have to do this," I said. "Take your people and just go peacefully."

He laughed. "No. We are Vyqang. We never 'go peacefully.'"

A sudden turmoil sounded. "Sir, our defense systems have just crashed!" one of the Vyqang said in his language.

"Go Cyrus," I breathed.

Dunvyn whirled. "What have you done?" he snarled.

"Spear is launched, but its guidance systems are off as well," another Vyqang spoke up.

"Weapons systems are down to fifty percent," added another. "And the Kalybri are still out there!"

"And human attack satellites as well."

"It doesn't have to be this way," I said. "You've only known the Vyqang way of life, all destruction and chaos. I know that, but you . . ." My stomach roiled, but I continued. "You're part of me too. Part human. And humans create and explore. You're more than just a Vyqang."

He glared at me. "There is nothing more than Vyqang. You are lesser. And we will win no matter what."

"No," I said softly. "No, you won't. And if only you'd—"

Any other words were cut off by what felt like an electric sword stabbing through my brain. Dunvyn glared at me. "I'm going to melt your brain inside your skull, bitch!"

I fought back with my telekinesis, as hard as I could, trying to push him away even as I could feel him dig deeper, almost like with razor-sharp nails. I pushed with everything I had in me; every thought, every emotion, every feeling inside I channeled into one thought directed at him.

Stop this.

It wasn't enough. He was stronger than me. I could tell, even as I struggled against him. He had more power than me. He was genetically modified to be the perfect soldier, to be stronger than anyone. As much as I struggled, I was going to weaken. And then, he would win.

"Sir, kill her quickly. We need to get off this ship," one of the other Vyqang said. "We're losing stability."

"So go," Dunvyn snarled. "Take the transport over to the *Draken*." His men took him at his word and hurried off, heading out another door at the back. Dunvyn looked down at me, where I was kneeling on the floor in agony. "You see, Mindy, the Kalybri might blow up this ship eventually, with you still on it, your brains fried," he growled. "But you seriously don't think we build our ships without escape pods, do you? I'll escape, and I'll bring back more men and more weapons and your planet will be incinerated. It will never end until I succeed!"

"You . . . talk . . . too . . . much," I managed.

The door to the chamber opened. Fantazia stood there, a hand at her side, blood running down her black dress to drip on the floor. It was making a puddle at her feet. "Mindy, *aumento la tua potenza di mille volte.*"

Power hummed through me. Fantazia had worked her magic, my brain was no longer going to liquefy in my skull and it now burned with power. It leaked off of me and into the nearby machinery, short-circuiting everything and setting it on fire. Dunvyn actually jumped.

Once again, I focused all of my thoughts; every emotion, every feeling inside I channeled into one blast directed at him.

I'll do to you what you threatened to do to me.

Dunvyn grabbed his head and started screaming. It was a bloodcurdling scream and it went on what seemed like forever. It seemed like it would never stop until I went insane.

I reached out, then, feeling not only his mind but every Vyqang in the attack force, and maybe even others. I poured his pain and anguish into every one of them. It felt like my mind would split apart from the strain of it all, and their screams were terrifying. But I reminded myself that they had come to do far worse.

Dunvyn staggered and fell. I looked down at the shell he had become, limply writhing in agony. "It didn't have to be like this. You could have just left," I whispered.

Fantazia stumbled up to me, looking weak and in pain. "You need to finish it."

I looked down into Dunvyn's eyes, eyes that were eerily like mine. I saw a man who looked like a twisted version of my father. Dunvyn was a creature who had come to destroy the Earth and everything on it. He was the leader of an evil people, sprung from my DNA. But there was one crucial difference between us. I wasn't a cold-blooded murderer.

"He's not going to hurt anyone anymore," I said. "He'll probably not even be able to feed himself after this." The ship rocked again. "And I don't think this ship will take many more hits from the Kalybri. Let's go."

Fantazia sighed. "As much as I appreciate your youthful optimism . . ." She picked up a nearby Vyqang dagger and without so much as an eyeblink plunged it into Dunvyn's chest. He shuddered, his breathing went shallow and then stopped. The light died in his eyes.

I stared at the Reincarnist's daughter in horror. "What the hell did you do that for?"

"When you live as long as I have, you learn that sometimes you've got to get your hands dirty to make sure they won't come back for you," she said. "This is one of those moments."

I stood and stared for a moment, caught by inexplicable grief. He had been evil, but I couldn't deny that he had been a part of me.

Fantazia grabbed my arm. "Come on."

I regained control of myself. "Wait. Along a similar vein . . ." I reached out with my mind as far as I could, far into the deepest reaches of space. I felt other Vyqang waiting. If I pushed just hard enough, I could reach them, I could tell them:

Your . . . leader . . . is . . . dead.

Each word was torn out of me. I felt blood start running out my nose and knew I was using too much power after a fight that had already taken too much out of me. But thinking of Luke and Paul, Lainey and Wesley and their baby and the EHJ and my parents, and all the rest of the people I loved or had vowed to protect: *The Earth . . . is protected. We will not take any attacks lightly. Do . . . not . . . bother . . . us . . . again.*

"You're burning out," Fantazia shrieked, shaking me. "You're going to kill yourself. Stop!"

My head felt strange. I sank back in Fantazia's arms, knowing all of my energy was drained.

"We've got to get out of here," she said, dragging me back the way we came. I lunged for my belt of gadgets that lay forgotten on the floor and didn't think I'd be able to right myself; my head was really that messed up. I was beginning to wonder if I had some permanent brain damage from that fight. From the way Fantazia was breathing, I could tell she was in distress, too.

"W-where's Luke?" I managed. "Is he dead?"

"I patched him up as best as I could, but we've got to get back now before this ship gets blown up by either the Kalybri or the Earth military." She helped me past the bodies of the dead guards and collapsed next to one of them. No, not one of them; Luke. I was relieved to see he was still breathing.

"I used up too much power boosting yours," Fantazia admitted. "I don't think I can transport all three of us to the ground."

I reached into one of my pouches and fished out three small patch devices. I slapped one onto each of our bodies, pushed tiny buttons on them to set coordinates. "These are transporters. Boost the power to them and we should make it," I said.

"I'm not a techno mage."

She was right, but it was our only chance. I wanted to get back to Paul and the world. "Just do it, Fantazia!"

"All right!"

As she spoke words in Italian, I took one of her hands and then Luke's. "Pray to God this works," I muttered.

"If it works, I'll start praying to him again," Fantazia replied.

I clicked the button. My world was torn apart.

CHAPTER THIRTY-FOUR

I woke to the noise of machines beeping and my head pounding, which is not exactly the way anyone wants to wake up. I tried to raise my head and look around, but felt like a sledgehammer had struck me between the eyes. I groaned and raised a hand to my forehead.

"You're awake!"

"I'm kind of wishing I weren't," I said, trying to rise up to see Paul, who reached over and took my hand. "How long was I out?"

"A few days. Your parents have been here almost constantly, worried sick. I just convinced them to go home and get some sleep."

My parents? That was a fence I was going to have to work on mending. They had never forgiven themselves for what had happened to me, I realized, and had done what they could at the time to help. All those feelings of rebellion I'd aimed at them . . . Well, I'd now seen firsthand how much pain could be caused by a child seeking to destroy everything you believe in. My parents and I needed to sit down and work through the problems of the past. It wouldn't be easy, but we could do it. I had faith.

"They're going to be thrilled I hooked up with a scientist," I laughed, sitting up in bed. But I could now see him sitting next to me, in a chair drawn up to one of the beds in the EHJ infirmary. And that wasn't the only thing I noticed. "Oh my God, what happened to you?"

Paul wasn't sitting in a chair; he was in a wheelchair. He had one arm and one leg in multiple bandages and slings. That whole side was pretty much bandages.

"Everyone got pretty banged up. I'm one of the lucky ones. Simon and the rest of his team . . . not so much."

I blanched. "They're dead?"

He nodded. "Led an assault team against a group of the Vyqang. They may have died, but they died taking those Vyqang with them. They died brave heroes. A lot of people did. We succeeded. We saved the world."

"But at a pretty high price."

He nodded again. "But the Vyqang are gone, Mindy. We haven't seen a trace of them even several solar systems away, and the Kalybri are checking even further. They're going to stay in touch, they said. To keep us informed. You are to be their official contact."

"Good. Is . . ." I cleared my throat, feeling unshed tears stick in my throat at the fate of our comrades in arms. "Is the rest of our team okay?"

"Kate pulled out some scary goddess powers no one even knew she had. Sent a bunch of the Vyqang screaming in terror." He glanced pointedly at me. "I could have told you she could do that. Anyway, she wished us luck and said she's really happy for us. I think she was being genuine. She's gone to visit her 'brothers and sisters'—the other gods and goddesses—to regroup."

"I think the fact that we became serious took her a bit unawares."

"Yeah, I think so too." He squeezed my hand but looked unconcerned.

"Luke?"

"We patched him up. He's still recovering in the hospital. He's also talking about taking some time off—to recenter himself, he said."

Poor Luke. I actually did feel bad for how emotionally messed up he was. "What about Fantazia?"

"She ran home to her pocket universe as soon as this was over. Wesley doesn't seem too concerned, so I guess neither are the rest of us. But she's an official reserve member of the Elite Hands of Justice now." He frowned. "So is Cyrus, actually. We can't get rid of him. He's taken to hanging out at headquarters. Wesley doesn't seem upset by it. Wesley came through relatively unscathed, and so did Selena."

I studied Paul. "So, what happened with you?"

"The Vyqang shot off some sort of missile. The Kalybri called it a spear."

I nodded and then winced. "I was on the ship that was getting ready to detonate it."

"I think Cyrus's program interfered with the trajectory, but it was still going crash into the Earth. Wesley was going to let the military blow it up, but I didn't want to chance fallout radiation from their weapons. I led a team to fly up to the outer atmosphere to dismantle it just in time. It exploded, and we got hit with the shrapnel. My whole left side."

"Babe, are you going to be okay?" I asked.

"Yeah, they dug out most of it." Seeing the look on my face, he hurried on. "Don't worry about me, Mindy. The doctors are saying there will be some scarring, but I'll pull through. I'm indestructible!"

"Not unless you gained a new power while I was out," I growled.

"Yeah, um, speaking of powers." He looked worried. "I don't know if you've noticed yet, but your telekinetic powers are gone. Fantazia told us what happened with Dunvyn and the telepathic message you sent to the rest of the Vyqang. I don't want to scare you, but you did suffer a bit of brain damage in that fight. Sending that message further cemented it: You've burnt out all access to those powers."

I tested. He was right. There was no power to tap. There was also nothing in there anymore, no more voice. No more Dunvyn. I couldn't say I was sorry. How many of our heroes had died stopping his people from tearing apart our world?

"So, will I be okay?" I asked.

"We'll run some tests now that you're awake again, but we think it was just the section of your brain that had controlled those new powers. The section the aliens tinkered with."

"So I'm probably just your average superintelligent girl now."

"We'll test to make sure . . . but probably."

I sat up in bed. "So, Paul. We did it. We survived, not completely uninjured, but we survived! Now what are we going to do?"

"The team will rebuild. Yes, we're short a few members, but we've also gained some reservists. We'll try to get back out there as soon as possible, to reassure the people that we're still around, making things safer. The government has apologized profusely, and Forrest has been named the new Presidential Secretary of Heroes, so he'll be there to make sure things run smoothly on that end. Life will go on."

"And what about us?" I pushed.

He smiled. "Well, I was thinking about that. There was some discussion before all of this about what we'd do after. Licenses were involved."

"I'm still up for it if you are," I said. My heart was pounding.

He leaned over to kiss me. "You bet I am."

As I kissed him back, I realized he was right: Life did go on. We would mourn our fallen heroes and then we would get back to business, which was saving the world. It was all in a day's work, and before we were healed up or prepared there would be another day's work, another threat we'd have to face. That's who we were: heroes. We saved people not for fame and fortune, but because it's who we are. And if you can do it with the man you love at your side—as I now can—well, that's a bonus.

And it's as happy an ending as anyone can write.

PHENOMENAL GIRL 5

Lainey Livingston has just been made a member of the Elite Hands of Justice, the world's premiere cadre of superheroes. All her senses are extraordinary, and her great strength and ability to fly are equally remarkable. But no one gets a free pass to active duty, and Lainey's next test is going to be her hardest. She's to train with Robert Elliot, the Reincarnist. A magician who has lived multiple lifetimes, he's the smartest man in the world—and Lainey's last obstacle.

Lesson #1: Romantic entanglements among crime fighters are super exploitable, and falling in love with a man who "can't die" is like waving a red flag at a bull. Especially when the most fiendish plot ever is about to break over Megolopolis like a wave of fire.

A. J. MENDEN

ISBN 13: 978-0-505-52786-8

Tammy Kane

BREATH OF FIRE

"A fantastic new world of dragons!"
—Jade Lee, *USA Today* Bestselling Author of *Dragonbound*

When the dragon came to claim him, Karl knew his great plan had gone horribly wrong. If he had known the creature was real, he wouldn't have scoffed at the villagers…and he *certainly* wouldn't have been so quick to let them chain him to a rock. Mattaen Initiates trained as warriors, but no man could defeat a dragon.

"My name is Elera daughter of Shane. And you, Initiate, are my virgin prize."

She had vanquished the beast and named her price: one night with the virgin sacrifice she'd saved. He'd taken a vow of chastity, but Karl still had a man's needs—and Elera's sultry curves made him ache to taste his first woman. With a scorching kiss she shattered his defenses…and led him into a world of deception and seduction, where he'd be forced to choose between the brotherhood that had raised him and the woman whose courage set his heart on fire.

ISBN 13: 978-0-505-52816-2

Autumn Dawn

WHEN SPARKS FLY

Polaris just got a little hotter.

"Dawn injects a fresh new energy into the futuristic romance genre... Brava!"   —*RT BOOKreviews*

WHERE FIRES RISE

Perhaps it was his wild black hair and indigo eyes, or maybe it was his enigmatic aura, but there was something about Hyna Blue that drew Gem. The man had clearly done hard labor, his cybernetic implants gave him increased strength, but he was no longer whole...and now he was getting drunk in her tavern. Yes, Hyna Blue aroused instincts both carnal and nurturing. Gem's blood had been fiery to start with. Blue heated it even more.

Of course, since the planet of Polaris discovered its trainum mine, things were hot all over. Prosperity had blown in on a solar wind, along with many disreputable types, the least deceptive of which were some shape-shifting aliens. The ruined beauty of one patron and his drunken proposals were the least of Gem's worries—and perhaps her one solace. Like her father had named it long ago, this inn was The Spark. Gem had to survive the blaze.

ISBN 13: 978-0-505-52802-5

Tracy Madison

A Stroke of Magic

You know how freaky it is, to expect one taste and get another? Imagine picking up a can of tepid ginger ale and taking a swig of delicious, icy cold peppermint tea. Alice Raymond did just that. And though the tea is exactly what she wants, she bought herself a soda.

ONE STROKE OF MAGIC, AND EVERYTHING HAS CHANGED

No, Alice's life isn't exactly paint-by-numbers. After breaking things off with her lying, stealing, bum of an ex, she discovered she's pregnant. Motherhood was definitely on her "someday" wish list, but a baby means less time for her art and no time for recent hallucinations that include this switcharoo with the tea. She has to impress her new boss, the ridiculously long-lashed, smoky-eyed Ethan Gallagher, and she has to deal with her family, who have started rambling about gypsy curses. Only a soul-deep bond with the right man can save her and her child? As if being single wasn't pressure enough!

Available July 2009!   ISBN 13: 978-0-505-52811-7

ELISABETH NAUGHTON

Antiquities dealer Peter Kauffman walked a fine line between clean and corrupt for years. And then he met the woman who changed his life—Egyptologist Katherine Meyer. Their love affair burned white-hot in Egypt, until the day Pete's lies and half-truths caught up with him. After that, their relationship imploded, Kat walked out, and before Pete could find her to make things right, he heard she'd died in a car bomb.

Six years later, the woman Pete thought he'd lost for good is suddenly back. The lies this time aren't just his, though. The only way he and Kat will find the truth and evade a killer out for revenge is to work together—as long as they don't find themselves burned by the heat each thought was stolen long ago . . .

STOLEN HEAT

ISBN 13: 978-0-505-52794-3

✂

☐ **YES!**

Sign me up for the Love Spell Book Club and send my
FREE BOOKS! If I choose to stay in the club, I will pay
only $8.50* each month, a savings of $6.48!

NAME: _____

ADDRESS: _____

TELEPHONE: _____

EMAIL: _____

☐ I want to pay by credit card.

☐ **VISA**   ☐ **MasterCard.**   ☐ **DISCOVER**

ACCOUNT #: _____

EXPIRATION DATE: _____

SIGNATURE: _____

Mail this page along with $2.00 shipping and handling to:
Love Spell Book Club
PO Box 6640
Wayne, PA 19087
Or fax (must include credit card information) to:
610-995-9274
You can also sign up online at **www.dorchesterpub.com**.
*Plus $2.00 for shipping. Offer open to residents of the U.S. and Canada only.
Canadian residents please call 1-800-481-9191 for pricing information.
If under 18, a parent or guardian must sign. Terms, prices and conditions subject to
change. Subscription subject to acceptance. Dorchester Publishing reserves the right
to reject any order or cancel any subscription.